FUR

KATHERINE BLACK

Katherine Black Books
TWISTED MYSTERIES

Best Book Editions

Best Book Editions

1 3 5 7 9 10 8 6 4 2

Paperback ISBN 9798867241964

Cover by Best Book Editors

A CIP catalogue record of this book is available from the British Library

CONTENTS

Trigger Warnings:
 May Disturb Some Readers

Chapter 1

Coco was in agony. Fear twisted her gut, and she struggled to control her bladder. She'd been beaten every day of her miserable life, but she'd never had pain like this. She snuck up the stairs and checked every few steps. They weren't watching her. But terror made her furtive. Coco was in trouble. She didn't know what she'd done wrong, but knew there was never enough food. She would be hit.

Carla's bedroom door was open, and the bare walls were shrouded in murky greyness. Coco snuck inside with a glance and a reflexive flinch in case they were behind her. It was freezing, but she had to find somewhere to be alone. She took comfort from the smell of the squalor. It was all she'd ever known, and it brought its own brand of familiarity because the odours were there when she wasn't being beaten as well as when she was. The room smelled of the damp towels thrown in a corner, dust and grease, stale female underwear and rancid men's socks. But she was alone here. No blaring music or noise from the TV hurt her sensitive ears. Downstairs, they were yelling at each other again.

The baby—the one they called Tammy—was crying. It was

1

always screaming. Coco had never been safe, but it was quieter here. She looked around the room for a place to hide. The wardrobe had been open forever, clothes spilling out of it. The bottom of the laundry pile hadn't been touched in months, and more was added as garments were discarded from hangers. Only the top items were ever taken for washing. Coco could squeeze behind the dressing table or under any dirty laundry piles. She wanted to be invisible and disappear somewhere she couldn't be harmed, but that place didn't exist. She loved her family. She'd lay down her life for them. Her agony was complete, and hiding was futile.

The pain came harder. If she didn't lie down, she'd collapse. After jumping on the bed, Coco had to scratch herself. She clawed at the bedding and then tore at her side. With the pain, there was always the itching. Her body was a mass of open, infected sores that, like her, wept and bled.

She tried to curl and make herself small, but the pain made it difficult. She whimpered, and her brown eyes looked at the open door. She longed to feel a gentle hand against her back. All she'd ever wanted was a soothing voice to be kind to her and a tender hand. She craved a loving touch.

Coco's mistress and the boy burst into the room.

'The dog's giving birth on my bed. Don't just stand there. Bloody, do something,' Carla screamed at the top of her voice, even though her son, Kyle, was standing beside her. The dog, lying on the filthy bed, watched her mistress pointing at her as she screamed. Coco flattened her ears against her head. Her eyes were soft pools of misery, and she looked terrified from the pain, suffering, and being shouted at. She looked at Carla. Her eyes were more white than brown, and she trembled. She knew a beating would follow. Carla was yelling at her. 'Get down.' The dog tried to obey, but she couldn't move. She tried to get up, and Carla pulled a face as Coco's sides contracted and her labour neared the birthing stage.

Kyle ran to the stairs.

'Where the hell do you think you're going?'

'To boil a kettle.'

'Is this the time to be sitting down to a cup of tea, for Christ's sake?'

'I'm going to get some towels and boiling water. That's what you do when someone's having a baby.'

'This isn't someone. You stupid moron, it's the damn dog. When I said do something, I meant to get it off my bloody bed.'

Kyle sulked but lifted Coco. She cried in pain, and as he pulled her up, supported only under her forelegs, a puppy hanging from her backend dropped onto the floor. It was still. Kyle screamed and dropped Coco. She lay where she fell without moving. Her eyes lifted to Carla, expecting to be kicked, and she whimpered. She'd landed on a comfortable pile of filthy washing, and only stopped squinting when the foot didn't boot her in the side.

In a rare moment of tenderness, Carla bent and picked up the puppy, still encased in its embryonic sac and put it in front of its mum.

'Is that your baby? Aren't you a clever girl?'

She patted the dog on the head, and Coco licked her palm once. Carla turned her nose at the pink, wet patch on the bed, a spreading mixture of diluted blood and amniotic fluid. Lifting the quilt, she shook it, making Coco cower, and she turned it over so the bloodstain was on the underside.

'Get that light bulb out of its fitting so your dad doesn't notice the stain when he pulls the quilt back. I haven't got time to change bedding today.'

Kyle did as he was told and watched the dog giving birth.

'Get out, then. Coco doesn't need an audience.'

Carla pushed her fifteen-year-old son in the back and grumbled down the stairs.

'Like we need any more animals in the house. And where will the money come from to feed the little bastards? That's what I want to know.'

Coco felt her insides contract. She held her breath and pushed hard, and as the contraction ebbed and a second puppy was delivered, she bent her head and licked the sac containing the dead firstborn.

Chapter 2

'John. I've found one. Come here.'

Shelly was excited.

'I've found an advert.' She read from Facebook as her husband looked at the screen over her shoulder.

For Sale: 4 eight-week-old, German Shepherd X puppies. Dogs and bitches, both parents can be seen. £550.00. No offers.

'Look at them. Aren't they gorgeous?'

She enlarged a photo of the pups to fill the screen. 'Look at that little black one. He'd be perfect. Please. Let's ring up and see if there's any left.'

'Hell. Five hundred and fifty's a lot for a mongrel, isn't it?'

'I'd pay ten times that if it makes Sammy smile.'

'And I wouldn't?'

'I didn't mean that. And it's not all about Sammy. It would be good for us to have a dog, too. Before we were married, we said we'd have two children, one of each flavour—and a puppy.'

John laughed, but the sound had a bitter ring.

'And along came Sammy, and all our dreams changed overnight. Now I'd give everything we own to see him smile for the first time.'

'Doctor Watkins thinks it's a good idea, and I'm ready to go along with anything he suggests.'

'But, honey, do we have to go for a German shepherd? What's wrong with a little dog that will be less bother? Puppies are a nightmare. It makes sense that the less puppy you have, the less trouble it can be.'

'Stop grumbling. I'm going to make the call. You know you want this as much as I do, and we're only using Sammy as an excuse.'

As she picked up the phone, she saw John had his fingers crossed.

'It's ringing.'

'Phones tend to do that, Shelly. It's a miracle of modern science.'

When she ended her conversation, she told John that the advert was listed that morning, and half the puppies were still available. The woman said that if they came with the money, they could have the pick of what was left, and she wouldn't go a penny less than the stated price and to not bother trying. Shelly established that they hadn't been wormed or had a flea treatment, microchip, or vaccinations.

'She sounded a bit rough, love.' Shelly had her doubts, too, and wondered if this was the right dog for them.

'Well, it's a good job we're buying the puppy and not the owner then, isn't it?'

John had his coat on and was putting his wallet in his pocket.

'Come on. What are you waiting for? Let's go and get our boy before Sammy gets in from school.'

'Girl.'

'Boy. Definitely a boy.'

When they got to the address Shelly had written down, John pulled a face. Shelly was too horrified to do anything. The gate was hanging open by a creaking hinge. The garden was filled with cigarette butts, dog dirt and rubbish. An old motorbike lay in the garden with its front end smashed in and no back wheel. The weeds grew high and pushed between the mossy paving stones thrown over what had once been a lawn.

'Nice,' John said.

'Don't be a snob. We're here to buy a dog, remember? We're not here to judge their lifestyle. Be nice.'

'Are we sure that Sammy's ready for this? It's a big step.'

'John, we've been preparing him for months. He knows a puppy's coming.'

'Yes, but he doesn't know when. Are we sure? That's all I'm asking.'

'Only one way to find out.'

Shelly spoke with conviction, but her expression was anything but sure. The place was awful, and if there was an omen that it wasn't a great idea, this was it.

Before they got to the door, they heard furious barking from at least two dogs. A skinny ginger cat jumped from the bay window to investigate the visitors. John knocked.

CHAPTER 3

'That'll be them,' yelled a voice from inside. 'Go on, then, open the door. And don't you say nothing to embarrass me. They sounded posh. No swearing, you hear?'

Shelly's heart sank, but it was too late to run. The door opened, and a belligerent teenager stood on the doorstep. His nose was streaming, and he wiped it with the back of his sleeve.

'You come about the dog?' he asked before John introduced himself.

'Yes, that's us, son. We rang a little while ago.'

'Come in then—Dad.'

Shelly hid a smile, and the boy opened the door wider, kicking a black and white cat out of the way. He walked ahead of them, leaving Shelly to close the door. The boy went into a front room and threw himself full length on a dirty leather sofa. An enormous flat-screen TV was blaring, and he went back to watching his show.

Shelly gagged on the smell of cat pee and covered her mouth before the hag in front of her noticed.

The woman stood in the middle of the room with a tabby cat

in her arms. The ginger cat they'd seen from the window was under the dining room table by the far wall, scratching the floor. Another was lying along the back of an armchair. There were no dogs to be seen—but they could be heard. The barking from the rear of the house was cacophonous. The living room smelled of cat pee, but it wasn't as bad as the hall, or Shelly had grown accustomed to it in the time it took her lungs to expand since she'd held her breath. John and Shelly smiled and tried not to let their disgust show. From the moment they walked through the door, neither of them had any intention of buying one of the puppies. Shelly's only thought was getting the hell out of there before they were contaminated.

They weren't posh, as the woman had suggested. They considered themselves average, but neither of them had been in a home like this in their lives. A child, naked except from a full nappy that was heavy enough to hang to its knees, tottered in from the kitchen. It held a filthy blanket to its face. The cover had *Property of Furness General Hospital* stamped along the edge. The child—Shelly couldn't determine whether it was male or female—stared at them and raised its arms to Shelly. It wanted to be picked up. It was filthy and probably crawling with lice and scabies. She didn't want to pick it up and turned her face to John in a silent plea to rescue her, and when he looked helpless, she saw the squalling mass of puppies writhing in a matted and filthy playpen. She ignored the infant asking to be picked up, and she felt horrible for snubbing the child. But she couldn't touch the dirty human thing. Or stroke the mangey cat rubbing itself around her legs. She thought the child might be female, and, unperturbed by the snub, it wandered off, clutching the dirty blanket to its chest.

The woman lifted pups out of the playpen and threw them onto the floor in front of John and Shelly. The dogs, bleary with sleep, took a moment to wake. A couple shook themselves. One sat on its haunches and scratched. Two more instigated a game of two-headed puppy ball and rolled around the room. One sat on John's shoe and looked at him.

Despite himself, John picked the animal up. Shelly nudged him in the ribs to say, 'Put that filthy animal down, or you're never setting foot in our house again. And as for sex, you can forget it, mate.' They had internal conversations down to a tee.

John ignored her and stroked the fawn and grey puppy. Shelly watched as he fell in love. In that second, she knew the flea-ridden monstrosity was coming home with them, and there wasn't a damned thing she could do to stop it.

They went through the motions. John asked to see the puppy's parents, and Shelly wished, with all her heart, that he hadn't. They were taken from the living room, where the cat under the table finished doing its business on the floor. The stench was overpowering. Because her eyes were drawn in that direction, Shelly noticed dried patties of faeces. One of them had grown a white furry jacket.

The kitchen was like nothing she'd ever seen. The floor was littered with faeces, canine, feline, and human in origin. The animals were allowed to do their business anywhere they chose. The kitchen bin was overturned, and the rubbish—nappies and takeaway debris—was scattered over the filthy floor. Some of the nappies were ripped open and their contents flung across the room. A festering pile of clutter, with a sleeping cat on top of it, spread from one corner. It went up the wall and into the centre of the room. It had over-spilt a broom cupboard and carried on growing. The sink and worktops were stacked with disgusting crockery. A cat lapped from the dishwater while another ate the remains of old pizza from a plate.

John had the puppy in his arms. He hadn't given the others a second glance, and nothing on this earth could have persuaded him to put the pup back on the floor. They navigated through the landmines of mess into the backyard. When the door was opened, it was clear why the two neglected dogs and a bevy of cats used the house as a toilet. The yard was full of excrement, and the dogs walked among it, squishing it between their toes. One of the animals had Alsatian somewhere in his heritage. The other was smaller and part collie. They were thin, with their long coats matted and dirty. The bitch had trails of hardened rheum in the corners of her eyes that seeped over her eyeline and made her look as though she was crying. When the door was opened, the dogs stopped mooching and flung themselves at the people coming out.

The woman, who was first through the door, kicked the big dog. He yelped in pain and retreated to the far end of the yard, where he sat in a corner and watched.

'He's a big strapping lad, isn't he? And Coco's Mummy's little princess, aren't you, baby? The pups will make show dogs. They could win Crufts, they could.' The woman pushed the bitch away with her foot.

'I'm sure she must scrub up well,' John said.

The bitch launched at Shelly and put its filthy front paws on her new jeans. She pushed the dog down. But, undaunted, it leapt back up, begging for attention. The dog wagged her tail in delight at the prospect of being stroked.

Shelly felt sorry for it and held it down with a hand on its head. She stroked it with the tips of her fingers. The dog was in rapture. Shelly looked towards the back door and relative safety. She couldn't stand to see the neglect and abuse. All these animals wanted was to be loved.

'I think we've seen enough to make a decision. Haven't we, John?'

Her words begged him to get her away before she burst into tears and took them all, including Stinky and Stinkier, from the yard. And she'd take all the cats and the poor androgenous child—though they could keep the belligerent teenager. He was beyond repair.

Getting back into the house was harder than getting out. They had to fight the dogs and push them back. On seeing the door open, the male flew across the yard, not even trying to avoid the excrement on the ground. He wrestled his way into the kitchen. The woman blocked him with her leg, and while she held him back, the bitch slipped through on her other side.

John and Shelly had to squeeze around the large woman's sweaty body. When they saw their mother, the five pups not in John's arms ran to her, attaching themselves to her low-hanging teats. The bitch was emaciated and had no milk to give. She tried to shake them off, but they stuck to her as she walked, bow-legged, to the corner.

She was the epitome of abject misery, slumping to the floor as she resigned herself to the mauling. The woman yelled at the dog as she flopped onto a sofa and lit a cigarette.

'Give us one, then,' the boy said. He hadn't moved from the other sofa. She threw him a cigarette.

'That's three you owe me now, and I'd better get them back before you go to school tomorrow. And you need to change Tammy's nappy while I deal with the grownups.'

A girl then, Shelly thought. The kid would probably be a mother herself in a little over a decade. She hated herself for being judgemental.

Tammy grabbed the ginger cat by its tail and dragged it from behind an armchair. Her mother sniffed. 'That one in your arms is the pick of the litter. It'll be six hundred if you're keeping it.'

'John, have a look at the other ones,' Shelly said.

'The ad said five-fifty,' John said.

'Take it or leave it, sweetheart. I don't care. Prime dogs, they are, and I've had people ringing all morning.'

'Okay, then, I'll give you five eighty. It's all I've got on me.'

'There's a cashpoint down the road.' She eyed his wallet, chancing her arm, but accepted the thirty-pound bonus when she'd pushed it as far as she could.

John and Shelly paid five-fifty for the puppy and another thirty for its fleas. They couldn't get out of the house fast enough. John clutched the dog in his arms and demanded that Shelly drive.

When they got home, Shelly wouldn't let him into the house

until the dog had been bathed. Either the pup was thoroughly cleaned from a bucket in the garage, or it didn't come into the house—ever. John said it would be too traumatic to bathe him straight away, and Shelly argued that John would be traumatised if he didn't. She brooked no argument.

His choice.

The puppy whimpered and trembled its way through his first-ever bath. They'd prepared in advance for the arrival of their dog with a bed and blankets, toys, lead, collar, food, and puppy training pads.

What they hadn't thought to buy was worming and flea products. The dog hadn't received either treatment and Shelly wasn't prepared to wait until they took him to the vets for his vaccinations. She went to the pet shop while John dried the pathetic bundle of misery. Before coming into the house, he needed to be wormed and treated for fleas. Then, and only then, did she deign to have her first cuddle with him.

He was soft and fluffy. His clean fur was electrified with static and stuck out from his body. He was dusted in baby powder, making him even softer. He had sweet puppy breath, and as she held him close, he nuzzled into her chin and took comfort from her warmth and kindness. It took Shelly an hour and a half longer than her husband to fall in love with the dog, but once that bond formed on the first embrace, it was fixed and true. She vowed that he would never experience another second of squalor and neglect for the rest of his life.

But she was worried about Sammy.

This could go either way.

The clock ticked in the stillness of the lounge. Another hour and he'd be home. They waited and alternated between watching the clock and the puppy sleeping in Shelly's arms, heralding what could be Armageddon.

They'd discussed the ramification of getting the puppy for him. At one point, they were going to take Sammy with them when they found one. But it was decided it would be too stressful for him. Sammy's autism would never have coped with that.

He couldn't manage anything new. Shelly was glad they hadn't taken him. He wouldn't have handled that place—and God knows what he would have said. She imagined him pointing out the faecal matter on the walls.

As she held the pup, she cried. The tears came, and she couldn't stop them. Her heart broke, and she couldn't get her feelings under control.

'What's wrong with you?' John asked. 'Christ, I've just spent a ton of money on a dog for you.'

'I can't stop thinking about all those poor creatures we left behind. And the toddler. Oh my God, that poor little girl.'

'Are you sure it was a girl? I don't think even its mother knew.'

Chapter 4

The school bus pulled up. Sammy was in the third seat from the front—his seat—staring through the window. He showed no recognition of his house and didn't move to get off the bus. Sandra, the care assistant, got out, opened the side door of the minibus and guided Sammy onto the pavement. He was as unpredictable as the weather, and his mood changed from one day to the next. Sometimes, he let people touch him, sometimes not. He might allow contact when he'd had a bad day and you could expect him to be at his most unreachable. Likewise, on a good day, he might not. There was no way of telling what he could tolerate.

Shelly saw that he was withdrawn and that always signified a bad day. There was no margin for change. She knew her son's moods like the tides on the local shore and forced a smile before greeting him.

Today was an awful day.

'Hi, Sammy.'

No response.

She pulled on her maternal strength. Today she needed a good mood, but it wasn't going to happen. Sammy refused to make eye contact with her and stared at his shoes as she took his hand from Sandra. He gave no indication that he knew his care had changed hands. Shelly prayed that the puppy was a good idea, hoping it would open the door to her son's locked-down emotions.

'Thanks, Sandra. How's he been?'

'No problems at school. They said he was fine, but we had an incident on the way home.'

'New route?'

'No. Worse. The traffic light sequence was wrong. They worked on them over the weekend. The first one was green, which was fine. However, when we came to the second set, they should have been green, too, but because they'd been changed, they were on red, which knocked the rest out of kilter. He's not happy, and he's been counting seconds for the last ten minutes. He's hit out a couple of times, so watch your face. And he tried to bite Gracie, so while you're watching your face, you might want to keep an eye on his teeth, too.'

Shelly laughed. Gotta love that boy. 'Traffic light sequencing, that's a new one. We'll suffer for that when he replays it. Batten down the hatches. Come on, Sammy, let's get you inside.' Shelly squeezed his hand and felt him tense.

'Red.'

Sammy lifted his head and rolled his eyes from one corner to the other. The eye-rolling was the first thing that set him apart. Sometimes he did a decent job of being normal—it was only when his eyeballs danced that strangers got their first inkling that he was different.

17

'Red.'

'Here we go. Sooner than expected, but we might as well get it over with.'

'Green, green, green, green, red, amber, green, green.'

His voice had no inflexion, but to express the depth of emotion behind his flat words, he punched Shelly on the arm. It was hard enough to bruise purple and then turn yellow after a few days.

'Should have been green.'

'I know, honey. I know it should. Just goes to show you can never trust a traffic light.'

'Samuel May must write to the highway authorities. This cannot be allowed to happen in this country in Europe called Great Britain. Samuel May knows it is not right. On eight sets of lights, it is green, green, green, green, red, amber, green, green. Samuel May must write and tell them that green, red, red, red, green, amber, red, red, is bad.'

His echolalia kicked in, and he recited the traffic legislation appertaining to the history of traffic lights.

'Traffic lights, which may also be known as stop lights, traffic lamps, traffic signals, signal lights, robots, or semaphores, are signalling devices positioned at road intersections, pedestrian crossings and other locations to control competing flows of traffic. Traffic lights were first installed in 1868 in London and today are installed in most cities around the world. Traffic lights alternate the right of way of road users by displaying lights of a standard colour and using a universal colour code and a precise sequence to enable comprehension by those who are colour blind.'

As quick as he came, the erudite fifteen-year-old was gone. His default expression was back, and the light went out. He dropped his head and counted seconds with the intensity of a mathematician. It could have been a breakthrough equation—but he was only counting seconds, from one until he reset. It gave him comfort. Shelly was careful not to overwhelm him with contact and walked him into the house with the lightest touch a mother could provide.

Dad rose from his seat as though welcoming a visitor. His voice was as bright as artificial lighting and raised a semi-tone too loud. 'Hey, Sammy. How are you doing, fella? How was school?'

He spread his arms as though to fold Sammy into an embrace and was careful not to touch any part of his son. Sammy stiffened his core and withdrew from the faux hug. John called it an air cuddle and said it was the future. Sammy didn't respond to his dad's question about school, and John looked at Shelly. She shook her head.

They couldn't decide which mood was worse. When John asked about school on a good day, Sammy would give him an itemised account of his itinerary. When it didn't happen, John knew his son was upset. It didn't bode well for introducing him to the dog. Shelly watched John stifle his excitement. She wished he could let it loose in a big fat holler and share it with their son, but his joy over the puppy was wrapped in an outer patina of tension.

John was great with dogs, but the father-son new-puppy sharing experience could go either way, and it wasn't looking good. Sammy understood algorithms, but people were aliens to him.

He absorbed anxiety and made it his own.

Shelly made Sammy a snack. The milk touched the half-pint level mark, and the glass was spotless. She laid out four biscuits, keeping the Jaffa cake and the pink wafer separated. Only plain biscuits were allowed to meet. Before taking it to him, she waited until Sammy was at the downstairs computer desk. He'd hung up his coat and took his homework from his satchel. He put his books and a pencil, pen, and eraser on his homework desk. The books were positioned an inch from the edge of the desk. The pen and pencil were laid next to each other, a quarter of an inch apart, along the top of the books. The eraser was horizontal to the end of the writing tools. He'd been to the upstairs bathroom, washed his hands, urinated, and washed and dried his hands a second time. He told her every day, 'You do not touch your penis with dirty hands. This is how infection spreads.'

Shelly handed the snacks to him so he could position them. She wanted to smooth his hair but didn't. It was easier that way.

Sammy couldn't tolerate surprises. Bombshells were, by the nature of the beast, unpredictable. And predictability was what made Sammy's sun rise in the east and set in the west. Anything contrary to order and routine was a disaster. John and Shelly united in combat and broached the subject of the puppy.

Chapter 5

'Sammy, we talked about getting a puppy, didn't we? You and Mum talk about that every day when you get home from school. You've been reading about it, haven't you?' John said.

'When you get your pug puppy, it will require four small meals a day. Every part of your pug puppy's body is growing and developing at this stage, so it's important to feed him little and often. Feed your pug puppy one ounce of food for every pound he weighs. For example, give him three ounces of food if your pug puppy weighs three pounds.'

It was a long speech, and John knew better than to cut in, so he let him recite his website information until he got to the end. It could have been worse. Sammy might have read a fifty-page book about pugs rather than a five-page website.

'That's right, son. But, mate, we didn't get you a pug. Puppies don't have to be pugs, do they, mate?' The tinge of desperation spiked over John's words.

'All puppies are pug puppies.'

'No, Sammy, you have collie puppies, spaniel puppies, and terrier puppies. There are lots of different puppies in the world.

You know that, mate. Remember watching *Marley and Me*?'

Shelly said, 'We got you a German shepherd. Well, technically, it's a German Shepherd crossed with something else. I know you like to be precise about these things.'

'Crossed with what?'

'Crossed with another type of dog,' John said.

Shelly gave him a warning look, and John shut up to let Sammy process the information. An overload of data would cause his circuitry to blow—and that was never pretty.

John had put the pup in the garage until proper introductions took place. It was crucial to go at Sammy's pace. However, the pup had his own timetable and didn't like being left alone. He'd had time to mooch about and sniff the different smells. He'd peed to mark his territory and establish himself in this new place and had whined for attention. When attention didn't come, he'd sniffed at sealed paint tins and knocked over a stack of plant pots. He was hungry and scratched at the garage door, yelping in earnest.

Shelly, John and Sammy heard him. The adults held their breath, waiting to gauge Sammy's reaction. He rolled his eyes, processing complicated code from an invisible computer screen in his head, and then scowled.

'John May got a dog.'

'Yes, we did, Sammy. But only a little puppy dog. We got him especially for you.'

Shelly moved things around on the coffee table so that Sammy wouldn't pick up on her nervousness. She shifted a coaster, dropped it on the floor, picked it up and put it back in its rightful place. She didn't dare look at him.

'I'll go and see to him, Shelly. He's probably frightened,' John said.

'What do you think, honey? Do you want to meet the new member of the family?'

Shelly didn't think Sammy was going to answer. His silence stretched out in a cavern of expectancy. He was twining his hands in his lap and giving his fingers his full attention. It wasn't a good sign.

'Is it a human being? No. Does it share any lineage with Samuel May's ancestors? No. Does any part of its DNA string match any part of Samuel May's DNA string? No. Is it a member of Samuel May's family? No. So it is a pet belonging to Samuel May. It is not a member of Samuel May's family.'

Sammy's hands stopped twining. He was calmer after processing the information. Despite the negative questioning, Sammy speaking was a good thing. Silence in the face of new situations was ominous.

When he was younger, Sammy read a sentence in his father's newspaper. It said, 'People are identified by names—not by their titles.' He had always addressed people by their full names. Shelly and John tried to get him to call them Mummy and Daddy and later, Mum and Dad, but those two words made no sense to Sammy. As well as titles, he found adjectives hard to grasp because he couldn't picture them. Words like *please* and *thank you* had no concrete meaning to him. He understood names because they were a means of identification. His teachers were resigned to being called by their full names. If Sammy couldn't see something as a picture in his head, he didn't acknowledge it.

'He's going to be your dog, sweetheart. You need to think of a name for him,' said Shelly.

Without hesitation or time to blink, Sammy said, 'His name is Carthenage. That is his name.'

Shelly waited for Sammy to recite facts that he'd read about the name.

He didn't.

They heard the back door open and the sound of claws trying to get purchase on the laminate floor in the kitchen.

'No, you don't. Come here, buddy. Oh, shit.'

'John May made a bad word.'

'Yes, he did, Sammy.'

'Wash John May's mouth out with soap and water.'

John grunted, and they heard the excited dog panting. Sammy's eyelashes fluttered—a sign that he wasn't comfortable with this variable.

John came in with the squirming puppy in his arms. He knelt in front of Sammy. His son turned his head and looked at the far corner of the ceiling. He didn't acknowledge the dog. His fingers twined and moved fast in his lap. He was processing. It was okay—so far.

'You can stroke him, Sammy,' Shelly said. Sammy didn't move his gaze from the farthest corner of the room. 'You should have put him on a lead,' she said

'I tried. It's impossible. Have you seen how much this thing can wriggle?'

The puppy squirmed free and jumped from John's hands. He

leapt at Sammy's legs, scratching and scrambling to climb onto his knee. Sammy's eyes rolled, and John made a grab for the pup. Before he could get him out of Sammy's way, the boy's hand came up in a fist and lashed out. He did it without looking. He wasn't trying to hurt the animal, it had invaded his space, and when that happened, Sammy hit out.

The dog was half on Sammy's knee, and John reached out to him as Sammy belted the dog off his lap and across the room.

The puppy yelped. Shelly's hands covered her mouth. 'Oh, my God. Is he all right?'

John picked the whimpering puppy up, scratching him behind the ear and making soothing noises. He checked him over to see that he hadn't been hurt.

'Yeah, he's fine. He's just frightened. It's okay. It's all okay, isn't it, buddy?'

He talked into the dog's ear as it calmed. Shelly stooped in front of her son. She didn't try to touch him. It would have sent him over the edge. She told him that everything was okay.

Sammy looked at his hands in his lap, twisting and turning. His fingers wiggled, and he brought them up to his face, where they floated and flittered in front of his eyes, intertwining like butterflies.

'Carthenage is his name. That is his name. Carthenage is his name. That is a good name. Carthenage is his name. That is a good name. That is his name.'

He was on a loop and coming to terms with the change. Shelly was glad to hear him repeating the dog's name. After the fright of the pup scratching to get on his knee, Sammy wasn't denouncing the dog as a bad thing. By saying his name, Sammy was claiming ownership. It could have gone better, and the puppy needed to learn that Sammy couldn't be jumped all over, but it wasn't a disaster. She was optimistic.

'You know, honey, he's so small that we must be very careful and try hard not to hurt him. You should have put him on a lead,' she shot at her husband.

'Carthenage needs his lead. Carthenage needs to learn some manners. That's what Carthenage needs.' Sammy lurched into pages of text that he'd read in a book on dog behaviour.

CHAPTER 6

Shelly was in bed. She heard Sammy downstairs. When he opened the kitchen door, Carthenage's claws scratched the floor as he bounded forward. Sammy was going into the living room, but Carthenage got there first, and Sammy slammed the door behind him. Shelly listened for the possibility of trouble and smiled. When her son was up, she had to be, too. It wouldn't be long before he'd be shouting for her. John was at work. He used the office as a shield of invisibility, his armour against home comforts. Shelly did the mornings. And the evenings. And the weekends.

Standing caused her bladder to squeeze like a lemon. She needed to pee, but Sammy came first.

She tied her dressing gown on the way downstairs. She ran her fingers through her tangled hair, yawning herself into another day of Sammy's life. He spread his hands as she walked into the kitchen, looking at the mess. The waste bin was overturned, and everything that had been in it was spread all over the place. A blue and white checked tea towel lay on the floor, chewed into strips of tattered fabric. But that wasn't the worst thing.

'Shelly May. Shelly May. Shelly May,' Sammy shouted at the top of his voice. He kept calling his mother's name until she ran in the room

'What is it? What's the matter?'

Sammy raised his voice louder. She heard the horror he felt splutter in every syllable. 'It's done a shit.'

He stared at the poo, shaped like piped cupcake icing by the back door. His hands butterflied in front of his face.

'Samuel May didn't kick Carthenage when he jumped up and scratched Samuel May's leg. Samuel May's leg moved by itself, but Samuel May made it go down before it kicked Carthenage. Samuel May was very good.'

'That is very good, Sammy.'

Shit. Sammy said shit. Shelly didn't know whether to laugh or be outraged. In his fifteen years, she'd never heard her son swear.

'Sammy. You don't use language like that. You know better.'

'Oops.'

She cleaned the mess while Sammy played with his fingers.

'Wash hands, Shelly May. Wash hands. Now, Shelly May.' Sammy recited a textbook passage about how many bacteria were in dog faeces. He named them and sorted them into alphabetical order as fast as a computer.

'Of course, I'm going to wash my hands.'

She squirted handwash into her palms and rubbed them together before rinsing them under the tap and drying them.

'There. Is that okay?'

'Again. Wash your hands again. Scrub your hands, Shelly May.'

She picked up the antibacterial cleanser from the windowsill beside the handwash.

'I'll put some of this on. We'll be fine if we use it after we've stroked Carthenage. It kills all known germs, diseases, and bacteria, so you'll never have to worry that you're not safe to pet him. This will protect you like a superhero's cape.'

Sammy obsessed about hygiene, and Shelly thought it was a good idea to implant the sanitising suggestion into his brain before stroking Carthenage became an issue.

It was going to be a difficult day. Sammy had an epileptic fit through the night, but he'd woken in a better mood than expected. The puppy had howled when they left him to go to bed, and the decision to make him sleep in the kitchen lasted for a couple of hours before they caved, and John brought him into their room.

Sammy needed at least eight hours of sleep because his brain worked harder than most people's. If he didn't get it, he was difficult. He couldn't tolerate noise. The disruption of the howling puppy caused Sammy to have a fit. The fit caused Shelly and John to argue—and the argument caused Shelly to be sleep-deprived and irritable when the pup peed on the carpet at five in the morning. She resented that John didn't wake up and suspected his snoring was a ruse as she got up to let the dog out. She felt as though she'd been up and down stairs all night and locked Carthenage in the kitchen with his bed and some toys at seven. The first night was bound to be difficult, she reasoned. It could only get better.

'Sammy,' she said, getting his attention. 'Should we go into the living room and see him? If you wait there, I'll put his lead on and then he won't be able to jump up. I'll call you when we're ready. Okay, Sammy?' He didn't answer. 'Is that okay, love?'

He grunted, so she left him to think about it and squeezed through the crack in the living room door before the puppy shimmied through her legs to get into the hallway.

Carthenage was chewing one of John's slippers. He growled at it, wagging his tail. When he saw Shelly, he left the slipper and ran to her. He was so excited that he shook in delight and his bum and face nearly connected. Shelly got the lead on him, but when she tried to walk him to the farthest chair from Sammy's, Carthenage dug his hind legs into the carpet, refusing to move. He shook his head, trying to dislodge the binding around his neck. Shelly had to drag him across the room and lift him onto her knee.

'Come in when you're ready, Sammy.'

Sammy didn't come in. She reassured him that it was okay.

'Come in when you're ready, Sammy,' he shouted back from the kitchen. Sammy often repeated the last thing that was said to him, mimicking the voice that said it.

'I'm ready, sweetheart. I've got the puppy on my knee. He can't come near you. It's okay for you to come in and sit in your chair. We're right across the room in Dad's seat.'

'Come in when you're ready, Sammy,' he said again.

Shelly sighed and ruffled the dog's ears. She tried a different tack. This could take some time.

'Sammy, I need your help, love. I have the puppy on my knee, right over at the far side of the room. I'm sitting a long way from your chair, and I've got the puppy on my knee. I can't reach the curtains to open them, and it's dark in here, and the puppy's all the way across the room on my knee. Will you come in and open the curtains for me, please?'

'Come in when you're ready, Sammy,' he said.

Sammy came in, moving with caution. He looked at the pup to make sure Carthenage couldn't get to him, and Shelly was glad he'd made eye contact. On seeing a new person, Carthenage yelped and wriggled to get out of Shelly's arms and go to Sammy. Sammy switched his concentration from the puppy and only looked at him when he walked across the room to get to the second set of curtains. He pulled them back and ensured that every pleat was symmetrical and perfect. Gauging the distance of the opening between the curtains to check they were even, he made adjustments. When Sammy was satisfied, he went to his chair and sat down. He dropped his gaze to his hands, raised them in front of his face and played butterflies with his fingers.

'Oops.'

'Oops, what, Sammy?'

'Oops. John May's slipper.'

Shelly laughed. 'Yes. Carthenage found it and brought it in for him.'

'Bad Carthenage.'

'No, honey. He's not bad. He's just a puppy. We've got to expect him to pick up lots of things and chew them. He's only a baby, and he doesn't know any better. I'll tell you what, if you see him with something he shouldn't have, you call me, and I'll come and take it off him. How's that?'

Sammy thought about it. He looked at his hands but darted lightning peeks at the dog. Shelly talked to the puppy and Sammy until he got used to being in the room with Carthenage. She kept her voice calm.

'Carthenage is an unusual name for a dog, Sammy. Your dad and I were wondering why you chose it. It's the name of a place, isn't it?'

'The ancient city of Carthage was situated on the North Coast of Africa in what is now modern-day Tunisia. Carthage was built on a promontory with inlets to the sea on the north and south.' He spelled out the word.

'Ah, so, he's called Carthage, not Carthenage. Did I get it wrong?'

'Shelly May did not get Carthenage wrong. Shelly May got Carthage wrong.'

Sammy was still looking at his hands, but his fingers were moving less. He was relaxing.

'Carthenage is called Carthenage. That is his name. That is a good name.'

'What does it mean?'

'Carthenage is a none sense word. It is not nonsense. It is a word of no meaning. It is non-sense. Samuel May made it up.'

'Why Carthenage, though? Why not Ben or Rover?'

Sammy let his hands fall to his sides. He looked at the dog before lowering his gaze to its normal position. Sammy had a big problem with eye contact.

'Carthenage means greatness.'

'Look, Sammy. Carthenage has curled up on my knee and is

asleep. I thought you said you made his name up.'

'Samuel May did make the name up. Samuel May made the meaning up as well.'

'I think that makes it a great name.'

Sammy risked a glance that encompassed both his mother and the dog.

'Carthenage is his name. It is a good name. John May said Carthenage is a German shepherd crossbreed. Samuel May knows what a German shepherd crossbreed looks like, and Carthenage is the name for a German shepherd crossbreed. Carthenage is his name. That's a good name.' Shelly loved these conversations with her son. She couldn't give her love to him with cuddles, and sometimes words were all they had. She envied other mothers. She wanted her son to hug her—all she could hope for was a word-hug.

'Should I bring him over so that you can stroke him? I promise I won't let him jump on you.'

Sammy didn't answer, but his hands flew to his face. His gaze went to the far corner of the ceiling.

'Don't worry, sweetheart. There's no rush. I'll put him in the kitchen, and you can see him again later.'

'Shelly May can sit on this chair,' he said, indicating the seat beside him.

She lifted the pup without waking him and sat next to Sammy. He examined the ceiling on the other side of the room, but his hands were still. Shelly sat for a few minutes stroking the sleeping dog and talking to her son.

'His fur is so soft, Sammy. It's the nicest feeling ever.'

Shelly's head pounded, she needed the bathroom, and she longed for her first cup of coffee of the day. Sammy was a full-time job, and the thought resurfaced that throwing a puppy into the mix might not have been her best idea. He raised his hand and moved it towards the dog before losing confidence and putting it back into his lap.

They sat for another five minutes until Sammy reached out again. He touched the puppy without stiffening or screaming. He made no attempt to bite or headbutt her or the dog. He tensed but dropped his fingertips onto the puppy. Resting his palm on the back of the dog's neck, Sammy buried his fingers deep in his fur, stroking him from his neck to his back. Carthenage didn't wake up. Sammy's eyelids fluttered and the blank canvas of his empty face filled with expression.

The left corner of his lip creased, and Shelly couldn't be sure, but she felt that Sammy was learning to smile.

CHAPTER 7

'Shelly May. Shelly May. Shelly May.'

As much as she loved him, Shelly wished her son would stop parroting her name for just one hour. Fifty times a day, he yelled for her at the top of his voice. The yell was the same, and the volume was a default. If she was in a different room, he wouldn't come to find her, and it made no difference if she was standing within touching distance. Brenda and Jack next door were great neighbours and loved Sammy, but they never doubted what was happening in the May house.

'Shelly May. Shelly May.'

'Yes, yes. I'm coming. What's the dog done now?'

'Shelly May.'

She went into the kitchen. Carthenage had a pair of John's underpants and was dragging them around in ecstasy.

'Oops, Shelly May. Oops, Shelly May.'

'It's all right, Sammy. I've got them. No, Carthenage, give them back.'

'Shelly May is a fibber. Shelly May has not got her hands in John May's underpants.'

Damn. Technically, it was true. She'd made a grab for the boxers, but Carthenage pre-empted her takeover, and, as she lunged, he'd whirled around and ran off with them, but she'd have the brute in a minute. Sammy's shouting was more bearable as the day went on, but it was like nails on a chalkboard first thing in the morning.

Shelly looked at the stubborn tuft of hair, rising like a scarecrow's straw on the side of his head. It refused to lie flat, and any amount of hair products only tamed it until her back was turned, when it would spring to prominence. Sammy had one sock on, and his jog pants were back-to-front. Her heart melted.

'I've got hold of one-half of them.' Shelly was victorious as she pulled the boxers with the puppy hanging onto the other end.

She retrieved the pants and put on a wash. She came back to Sammy holding out a doggie treat and lecturing Carthenage. The pup jumped at his master, salivating and whimpering. Shelly guessed Sammy had been holding the treat the whole time she'd been in the laundry room—and Carthenage wanted it.

'Carthenage, if you do not sit down in front of me, I can't give you your treat. You only get the treat if you sit down. Then Samuel May can put your lead on. Then Shelly May and John May and Sammy May can take you to the dog park where you can run and play with other dogs comprising many breeds and sizes. And when we get to the dog park, you can poop at the side of the doggie play area, and Shelly May can pick it up and put it in the poop bins that say 'Dog' on them, and John May can say, 'God, that stinks.' And Sammy May can say, 'Good boy, Carthenage,' while holding his nose. And Carthenage can wag his tail.'

'Sammy, honey, it's lovely that you talk to Carthenage a lot. He likes that, but you have to give him short commands when you want him to do something. You know when you get too much noise in your head at once, and you find it hard to make out the voice talking to you? That's what it's like for Carthenage, too. You need to just say the one word, Sit, and give him the hand signal.'

'Is Shelly May training Carthenage?'

'No, Sammy.'

'Is John May training Carthenage?'

'No.'

'Is Wanda Jackson training Carthenage?' Sammy had gone from their immediate family to his teacher. If Shelly didn't break the loop before he settled into it, he'd be reeling off names for hours. He'd begin with every person he knew, and when he'd run out, he'd start on authors, scientists, actors, directors, pop stars, and, if the idea occurred to him, he'd begin at A in the phone book. He had it stored in his brain and could load it from his databank to his voice box.

'All I'm saying, love, is that maybe, you should look at some more dog-training books. I think they'd help you.'

It was Saturday, and Sammy was up at six. He was like most fifteen-year-old boys in that he had formed a deep attachment to his bed—that was before he was excited about having a pup. Pre-Carthenage, they luxuriated in lie-ins while Sammy slept late.

They tried to get him to knock on their bedroom door before barging in for years, and they'd cracked it— until Carthenage came along. That morning, he'd burst into their room shouting

Shelly May at a top decibel and demanding that they all get up to go to the park. They persuaded him to wait until after breakfast.

When Shelly put the idea of downloading books into his head, all thoughts of going to the park were forgotten. He went to the laptop with Carthenage's biscuit still in his hand. The dog whined, sighed, and flopped in a heap on the carpet. Shelly got him another biscuit. Carthenage was learning *Sammy*.

Sammy had an eidetic memory. It took him ten seconds to scan a page of text. He uploaded every book he could find on dog training to his brain and scoured internet sites. He watched dog-training TV shows. They had to drag him away from his obsession to take Carthenage out, and when they got back, he rushed his dinner to binge-watch another show.

The next day was Sunday, and the library was closed. He didn't cope with the inconvenience well. Sammy had the patience of a machine when he was working on a task, but if he was prevented from doing it due to circumstances out of his control, it was the herald for trouble. He wrote to his MP. Sammy felt that this person belonged to him alone and was his to keep. Writing to him was a pastime he was fond of.

Because of the possessive pronoun, he took ownership—of the MP as his property. In his letter, he demanded that the library be opened on a Sunday so that he, Samuel May, could search for books on dog training. Shelly took the letter from his outgoing mail rack—Sammy hand-wrote a lot of letters— before going to the mailbox with the rest of his day's post. They'd had a bad day that Sunday, beginning with general unease, leading to widespread unrest and culminating in three grand-mal seizures in rapid succession.

Sammy was exhausted. Shelly would keep him at home the next day if he was an average boy, but the upheaval that a change to his routine would bring about was worse than letting him go to school tired. She felt sorry for his teachers. He'd be moody and violent all day. Sandra would let the school know what they were in for. They'd be pre-warned and could keep an eye on him, especially around other kids.

The fact that the library was shut that Sunday gave Carthenage a couple of days' grace. The content puppy had no idea what was in store for him. Sammy's poor mind was a computer. It worked like a computer. He was methodical no matter what he did.

He'd wanted to read everything he could find at the library and then undertake Carthenage's training regime after lunch. That was his plan, and plans, once laid, should never be upset. He'd written Sunday and the date. He'd made spreadsheets to chart their progress. Anybody else would have moved it one digit forward on the calendar and dated it from Monday. Sammy couldn't. He spent hours making the spreadsheets and had to delete his work and make new ones. But that didn't appease him. The original sheets were deleted, but they had been in existence. They were stored on the computer's hard drive— and his own. He saw them as coloured Tetris blocks of fragmented programme scattered across his brain's database. It offended him and worried him beyond anything an average person could comprehend. As the day wore on, it drove him to illness.

Anybody else would take what information they'd found and work with it until they could access the library. He could have opened the training as planned and wouldn't need to spend the afternoon re-doing his charts and graphs, spreadsheets and working timeline because the date was a day out.

Shelly tried to tell him that he'd already downloaded every book the library carried. She doubted he'd find anything new. But there might be one that he didn't have.

The minute Sammy came in from school on Monday, Shelly's peaceful world evaporated. It was time to hang up his coat, wash his hands, urinate, and wash his hands again. It was time for Shelly to make him a snack. It was time to sit at his desk and do his homework. But it was also time to go to the library to read dog training books.

As well as information on training, he wanted to scour their encyclopaedia. He needed to know everything published about canine disease and illness, diagnoses, treatment, and re-covery times. He had to have every word that he could glean about canine genetics. He needed a list of dog breeds—all of them—because he was going to work out what breeds comprised Carthenage's ancestry.

When there was a break to an established routine, it was a disaster equal to the sinking of the Titanic.

When he was very little, Shelly devised a tool to help. They moved heaven and earth to keep Sammy's routine organised, but there were times when breaking it was unavoidable. A routine could be established quickly but breaking it was something Sam-my couldn't deal with.

When he was five, a home visit was organised as part of his six-monthly assessments. Sammy attended consultations at the hospital, but he never did well. His stress levels would be high, and his behaviour erratic. Because he was a savant autistic with total recall and echolalia, his progress was monitored and documented.

All the experiments that could be were done at home to record accurate results. Peter Heller was employed by the Medical Sciences Division of Oxford University to conduct his tests. The first time he'd come, Peter had offered Sammy a mint to gain his trust. It was a simple gesture of friendship aimed at breaking down barriers.

Sammy had so much information in his brain that he was late talking and didn't utter his first words until he was seven years old. But from age three, he'd displayed savant abilities and drew the scientific world's attention. Autistic savants, while well documented, are rare, and Sammy's abilities were monitored.

Peter visited six months later. Sammy sat for the first part of his interview but displayed agitation symptoms during their chat. He rolled his eyes and sighed in frustration. It was clear that he was waiting for something. When that something wasn't delivered, he huffed like a petulant teenager and stood in front of Peter with his mouth open.

'What's the matter, Sammy? What do you want?'

Peter looked to Shelly and John for answers.

'Search me. That's a new one,' Shelly replied with a shrug. They tried to complete the tests, but Sammy was distracted and went back to Peter and pointed to his open mouth. Shelly thought he associated Peter with a doctor and was trying to tell him he was in pain. That led to the assumption that he had a toothache. Shelly worried. Sammy didn't tolerate any form of pain. He didn't understand it. She said she'd ring the dentist to make him an appointment when Peter left. It wasn't the same as with average children—in, out, and a bribe for good behaviour. A dentist's appointment involved hospital time because Sammy had to be put to sleep to have his mouth examined.

He had been polite for long enough. The third time he went to Peter, he took matters into his own hands. He thrust his fingers into Peter's pocket, grunting in satisfaction when he came up with a packet of mints. He took one and put it in his mouth, handing the rest of the pack back to Peter. In one visit six months earlier, a routine had been made. Every time Peter visited, he made sure he had a mint for Sammy.

Sammy was fifteen now and more dependent on routine and stability than ever. When he was little, Shelly had devised a structure to help Sammy cope with change. It needed to be tweaked over the years, but it worked well enough. Any change was stressful but posting helped. Like everything relating to Sammy, what was a good idea morphed into a complicated and evolving regime. John said she pandered to Sammy, but he didn't have to cope with the fallout when it wasn't in place.

Sammy went to his desk and got his Basildon Bond watermarked writing pad and a matching envelope. Writing down his usual home-time routine in a bullet-pointed list meant it had to be sealed in the envelope. He addressed it to himself and added a first-class stamp. Going into the hallway, where he had a letter holder for his outgoing mail, he put the envelope in the appropriate slot. Shelly would post it next time she went out.

They'd been doing this since Sammy was five. At first, Shelly only had to put the letter in an envelope and pretend to post it, no matter where it went.

Sammy grew and insisted on watching it being posted. Shelly felt guilty about the hundreds of unaddressed envelopes with rubbish scribbled on them, first in Shelly's hand and later in Sammy's. She knew that wasting police time was an offence, but what about wasting the postal sorting office time? She wrote an explanation to the postal manager and then put Sammy's name on the envelopes so they could be disposed of.

Soon, that wasn't enough. Sammy wanted to know what happened to his broken routine once the list was sent.

Shelly devised the idea of sending it back to him. It was a godsend and a financial cross to bear. She got away with second-class postage for a time, but when Sammy learned about the different pricing systems according to the time the letter took, he wanted the best. Shelly bartered with him and agreed on first class postage in return for not having to go out to post the letter the minute Sammy had finished writing it. That made a huge difference in their lives. They averaged a letter a day and, sometimes, they did as well as a couple a week, but the record number of letters that Shelly had to post in one day was thirty-eight. It was costly and debilitating, especially in the early days, when Sammy insisted they had to be dispatched immediately.

When they'd moved to a new house, while other buyers looked at the proximity of schools and shops, Shelly and John only cared about the nearest post box. They had one on the corner of the street.

Sammy kept every letter that came back to him. He had suit-cases full of them. It was enough for him to know that when he altered his routine, the routine didn't die. It was still there, alive, well, and shooting along conveyor belts in the postal system. When the letter was returned, he could pick up his routine and resume it as normal. If the post was late or, on the rare occasion, a letter was lost, there was hell to pay. It caused a new set of problems. Sammy had to write a letter to accommodate the extra time it took for the first one to arrive. He would write a routine letter about his missing routine letter. It was a system that worked and kept Sammy level. For Shelly, any extreme was not extreme if it worked. Parents did what they had to do.

She took Sammy to the library and posted his letter on the way, along with two others that had come about due to Carthenage messing with Sammy's routine that morning. There weren't any books Sammy didn't already have—and that was okay. He wasn't disappointed or distressed because he'd expected it, so it fell into the normal category. It was what came to pass—no surprises there. After what might seem like a wasted journey to some, Sammy was happy. He was ready.

Carthenage was going to be trained.

Chapter 8

Sammy's condition made him single-minded. Taking on sole duty for the dog training was a grave responsibility and one he flung himself into. He learned to talk to Carthenage in simple terms. But sometimes, he forgot and gave the puppy commands that would have confused Einstein. Carthenage took it in good humour. He'd cock his head and wag his tail. Being seated in autism wasn't always a negative condition. Sammy's ability to use his brain differently to others meant he didn't suffer from impatience. When Carthenage didn't respond to a command, he would put him back into the 'sit' or 'down' position and ask him to do it again.

Shelly watched the training sessions. The dog was young and tired easily. His attention span was nowhere near as great as Sammy's, and she'd intervene to give the dog some downtime. For the most part, training was one big game. Carthenage loved it. Even so, at the weekend, Shelly would separate dog and boy—for the dog's sake. She'd put Carthenage in the garage, where he had toys and a comfortable bed that let him be a dog for a couple of hours. Carthenage was bright, Sammy was patient, and the training went well. He was obedient and did what he was told. It didn't stop him from being a terror when he was separated from Sammy, and he would howl for hours. Boy and dog were one being. Where one went, the other was at his heels.

Carthenage unlocked Ponocchio's prison and turned him into a real boy. Carthenage could jump all over him. For fifteen years, the boy had never tolerated physical contact. The dog was his world, but Sammy still couldn't handle being licked. He was worried about germs and contamination to the point that he'd have a seizure during extreme moods. Carthenage learned this without physical reproach. Shelly bought mouthwash for the times when Carthenage caught Sammy off guard. Over time, the dog learned not to lick his master at all.

Shelly charted Sammy's seizures, which decreased after they got the puppy. He still had them, but they didn't happen as often. Carthenage learned to be Sammy's assistance dog without specialised resources or training from healthcare organisations. He'd fuss and get in the way when Sammy had a seizure. The puppy fretted and cried until the boy could speak to him again.

Shelly was vacuuming and stopped to let Carthenage out because he was being a nuisance. 'Go on, get outside and stop mithering me, daft dog.' He did it again the following week, and Shelly put him in the garden to do his business. The dog scratched to come back in. It often happened that Carthenage would jump up at her, whining and agitated.

She was changing the beds when she heard Carthenage barking downstairs. He'd been driving her mad for the last ten minutes and she'd had to lock him in the living room with Sammy to get anything done.

The dog was still going mad when she went downstairs to shut him up. 'Oh my god, Carthenage, it sounds like Timmy's fallen down the well.' She ran, realising that the dog might have been telling her that Sammy was in trouble. She threw the door open. Sammy had fallen on the floor and was jerking through a grand-mal seizure. The dog ran between her and Sammy and nudged her with his nose as she knelt beside her son.

Carthenage had been a pest for fifteen minutes before Sammy's fit. She laughed at her imagination but put a mark on the seizure chart anyway. It wasn't a coincidence. Fifteen minutes before Sammy's next seizure, the dog was fussy. He was clever enough to come to Shelly rather than show his concern to Sammy. Carthenage trained Shelly and John while Sammy was training the dog to fetch.

And then he trained Sammy to laugh.

She thought he was choking the first time she heard it. They were playing in the garden, and the pup was trying to take a ball from him—and Sammy laughed. It was an odd sound, robotic and stilted—but that was okay. He was an odd boy. To Shelly, Sammy's laugh was sweeter than the sound of rainfall on a parched desert.

Sammy and Carthenage had normal human-to-dog contact, but Sammy couldn't relax his phobia about being touched by anybody else. Watching them play, he seemed like every other fifteen-year-old. She envied the dog for having his affection. She was jealous of the animal. It was ridiculous.

Sammy taught his puppy elaborate tricks, and it took to each new game with delight. The boy never tired of teaching him.

They walked together because Sammy couldn't go out alone. He was competent enough to learn a route and stick to it. The problem wasn't with Sammy but the cruelty of the town's young people. For the first time in his life, it was an issue. He'd always been happy at home, and he had no friends. He wasn't sociable, and attempts to integrate him into groups or activities had never gone well.

When Carthenage had to be walked in the evening, and at weekends, Sammy stuck to what he'd learned from the training books. Shelly and John cursed the writer who said a dog could walk fifteen miles a day. By combining the words of several books, they managed to talk Sammy down to three, split between two walks, morning and night. A mile and a half, and more at the weekend, was doable.

Shelly didn't feel guilty when she promised she'd walk the puppy every day while Sammy was at school. Mostly, she didn't keep her word and put him in their garden. Taking turns with John to walk him in the evening was bad enough. They dreaded the onset of winter. John lost a stone and Shelly nine pounds in the first three months.

Her new slimline husband found a ramblers club, and they took to weekend rambling. They were mostly all active pensioners who loved Sammy. Some took longer than others to get used to his ways, but they were patient, and he was safe with them.

But Shelly worried about him. She worried about him every day and every night. He encompassed her every action of every day. However, she had built a morbid fascination with her death, and John's too. It started as a small thing and grew to phobic proportions. She turned herself inside out, worrying what would happen to Sammy when they died. He would outlive them unless he had an accident or an incurable disease. Then he'd be alone in the world. Shelly wasn't afraid of spiders, or snakes, or ghosts. She was scared of dying before her son.

When he was five, and they had a good idea of what to expect for the rest of his life, Shelly and John hit a rough patch. She was devoted to Sammy, but John found him hard to cope with. His love for their son was never questioned, but dealing with his demands was difficult for both of them. Shelly managed, but John couldn't.

She wanted another baby. She thought about Sammy being left alone, and she wanted a child so that it could grow up to take her place when they were gone. They were chronically tired. Being exhausted went with having a Sammy. Shelly took the brunt of the childcare, managed her exhaustion and worked with it—and sometimes, against it. John didn't. He resented the care Sammy needed.

He refused to give her another child, and they almost divorced. He didn't leave home, and neither of them had affairs. They suffered counselling, and their marriage, though chipped, was salvageable. What didn't kill them made them suffer.

Over the years, Shelly often asked for a baby. Her reason hadn't changed, and each time she pleaded, John refused. He told her that their marriage would be dead if she went behind his back and trapped him into fathering a child. Shelly had to sign a stupid contract to that effect. Contracts were one of their condescending counsellor's tools for a solid marriage. They were so stupid that, in retaliation, Shelly said she'd make John sign one before she'd ever have sex with him again.

'Okay, big man. If we're playing the contracts game, I've got a few of my own for you to sign. I'll give you a blow job if you promise never to ejaculate in my hair again. Agreed? And when your mother comes, you don't get to go to the pub, leaving me with her—understood? Good. Sign here.'

They hit an even keel, and Shelly learned to manage her fear which had escalated to the point of obsession. But, just as the moon orbits the sun, Shelly would often bring up the age-old argument.

They talked about the relationship between Sammy and his dog and what would happen when the dog died. This was a new worry for Shelly. It played on her mind when she wasn't worrying about Sammy after their death. John's answer was simple, they'd get another dog. Great, in theory, but Shelly wasn't convinced that putting it into practice would be easy. John said they'd worry about it when the time came. All well and good for him to say, but Shelly was worried about it now.

'John, I want another baby.'

'Why?'

'Because I'm thirty-five, my biological clock's ticking, and I like Farley's Rusks.'

'Bullshit.'

'It's not bullshit.'

'Shelly, we've been through this a hundred times. Sammy takes all our attention. It wouldn't be fair to the child or you. Come on, love, how would you cope?'

'We'd cope fine—we, John. For God's sake, lots of people with autistic kids have other children. It's not the end of life as we know it.'

'It feels like it sometimes,' John said with a bitter laugh.

'And what do you mean by that?'

She used the tone. Neither of them wanted it, but they were settling in for an argument. Shelly knew it from the moment she said the word baby.

'Shelly, every minute of every day is concerned with Sammy. We have nothing, and do nothing that isn't about him. Our conversation revolves around him. It's all you ever talk about. Where did our lives go in the last fifteen years? And God help us—what about the next fifteen?'

'He's your son. You make him sound like a life sentence.'

'And whether you like to admit it or not, that's exactly what he is.'

'John, please don't talk about him like that. You know it's only going to cause an argument. If that's how you feel, surely you can see the sense of having another child. By the time they've grown up, they could help us take care of Sammy. It would give us our lives back until we could hand Sammy over to our child who loves him at the end of our days.'

It was the same old argument, going down the old train tracks it always had. 'You disgust me, Shelly. You don't want another child. You want a grow-your-own-carer. What if our second child had the audacity to have a character of its own? Imagine that. What if it had dreams and ambitions that don't include being a genetic arse-wiper? God forbid, what if they wanted to have their own family, and rejected the idea of taking on our damaged firstborn? I can't believe you've turned into such a selfish bitch.' He was screaming at her, and spittle flew from between his lips.

Shelly slapped his face. She didn't mean to do it, but her hand came up, and she put all her frustration into the slap, leaving John with angry finger marks rising across his cheek. She realised that she'd hit out the way Sammy did without thinking. It was reactionary and instinctive. The thought proved John's point that she brought every incident back to Sammy.

'How dare you speak about your son like that. How dare you.'

'I know what we can do with him,' John said, his eyes wide, his face mocking, with the eureka moment. He wouldn't slap back, but he could hurt Shelly with cruelty. 'We can bequeath him to a travelling circus, and they can keep him in a cage like they did in Victorian times. The fairgoers can poke him with their walking canes until he tells them the weather on the day they were born. The owners will have to feed him to protect their investment. There you go—problem solved.'

'You cruel bastard.'

'When was the last time we made love?' He spoke to her back. She turned with tears tracking down her cheeks, but she didn't answer.

'When was the last time we succeeded in having full-on, penetrative, go-until-the-end sex? I don't mean the last time we attempted anything resembling a love life. Do you remember that? It was nearly two months ago, so you might have forgotten. Last week, we got romantic and settled down to business, and there he was, standing outside the locked door shouting, "Shelly bastard May," at the top of his bastard voice. Couldn't ignore him, could you? Couldn't block it out, for five damned minutes, to pretend to be a proper wife. No. The first time, last time, every damn time, Sammy comes first. What about me, Shelly? What about me?'

She glared at him and left the room.

CHAPTER 9

On Saturday morning, Sammy packed his rucksack and then unpacked it, and packed it and unpacked it. Shelly came in to help him break the loop. She was tired. They'd fallen out again. She'd argued with John until late the night before because he didn't want to go to the rambling club that day. Who could blame him? He was a hardworking man. For the last five mornings, he'd been up at five and here they were, at the weekend, up at six for a seven o'clock start. Like every other nine-to-fiver, he was entitled to a lie-in at the weekend, but they had Sammy, and they had Ramblers, and they had a gruelling day ahead of them.

John tried every trick in the book to get out of it. Sometimes it wasn't as bad as this, they'd have a healthy eleven o'clock start and be back by four. Sometimes he even enjoyed those days. This wasn't one of them, and Shelly felt the same trepidation he did. It was a hard climb by anybody's standards and John was convinced that at least one of the old biddies would need coronary care by the time they reached the summit. Shelly laughed and told him that those pensioners were inhuman and would outlast John any day of the week. On this day of the week, Saturday—precious

Saturday—John felt old.

'Come on Shell, let's give it a miss. We'll take Sammy and that damned dog to the beach instead, this afternoon, after a lie-in, a long, lie-in and a soak in a hot bath. Are any of these adjectives making a difference? We can go back to bed, snuggle under the duvet, pretend that we've gone deaf when he stands outside screaming your name, and we can let the world jog on for another couple of hours. What do you say?' He'd grabbed her around the waist, but Shelly twisted out of his grip with an impatient sigh.

Taking the hint, his mood dropped. 'For God's sake. You go, then, if you have to. Be a martyr to him, as usual. Don't you think that it would do him good to be told no now and again? Maybe, Shelly May—and here's a radical idea for you to mull over while you're huffing your arse up a sodding great mountain—just maybe, Sammy wouldn't be half as bad as he is if his mother didn't pander to him. A bit of hard discipline might do the kid good.'

Shelly ignored him and packed her contribution to the communal picnic. She'd heard it all before, the blame, the recriminations. Before long, he'd be blaming her genes for Sammy being the way he was.

'You told him you'd go. Look at last week, we had all this before we set off and then, when we got back, you were raving to the neighbours about how good you felt.'

'It's raining.'

'It's drizzling.'

'I'm tired.'

'We're all tired.'

'I'll mow the garden.'

'You'll climb a damn mountain.'

'It's barbaric. Let me be.'

'You know what the book said.' Sammy had quoted the same paragraph repeatedly, for days, '"At the weekend, it is a wonderful activity for the whole family to explore the countryside with your dog. In this day and age, families are often too busy to put time aside for togetherness. There is nothing quite like having a dog, to bind a family together."'

'Or blow it wide apart,' John had said more than once. 'That's the best argument you can come up with? The gospel according to Caesar Salad.'

'Milan.'

'Whatever.'

John grudgingly struggled into his hiking boots. He knew when he was beaten. Shelly rewarded him with a hearty breakfast of bacon and egg to keep his strength up. They were going to need it.

They were ten minutes late because Sammy went into meltdown in the car as he'd convinced himself that he'd forgotten his compass. It didn't matter that John May also had a compass. Samuel May was convinced that Samuel May didn't, and that worried him. They had to pull the car into a lay-by while Shelly unpacked his bag to show him it was there. He put it around his neck, as Shelly had suggested he do an hour earlier. But Sammy was frightened that the cord would snap, and it might get lost. Or worse, it might tighten around his neck and strangle him. Sammy liked to think of every consequence for every action.

The group were assembled in the car park behind the Skiddaw Hotel in Keswick. Everybody welcomed them and made a fuss of Sammy, while Shelly muttered their apologies. There were no recriminations. The group understood what it was like. In the general melee, Carthenage was straining at his lead to greet everybody. A good walk was coming, and he was full of energy and almost bent himself double in excitement. After greeting the humans, he made a beeline for Ballad, a well-behaved gun dog belonging to Ian Spencer, one of the youngest men in the group. Carthenage yapped at Ballad and bowed to the floor with his head between his front legs and his bum up in the air. He was ready to pounce. The older dog gave him a look, as though to say, 'Behave yourself pup,' and looked up at his master with devotion. Later, Ballad would forget his manners when both dogs were let off their leads to run in the heather. They would chase each other for hours until they came back to the group, tongues lolling and exhausted until the next chase five minutes later.

They left the car park and walked a couple of miles along the lakeside to the assent of Ashness Bridge. Shelly was knackered, and they hadn't even got to the climb yet. From the roadside, the mountain drew away sharply and within seconds they'd stepped from flatland to a steep gradient. After the initial stage of the climb, they stopped at Ashness Bridge, shared coffee from flasks and had Kendal Mint Cake. Shelly loved Ashness, one of the most painted and photographed bridges in Britain. Underwhelming in its design, being a small bridge made from Lakeland stone, it was picturesque and a favourite spot for hikers and ramblers in the Lakes.

Two minutes from the bridge they saw the first viewpoint. The mountain fell away in a sheer drop to the lakeside and from a gap in the woods, directly above the eves of the Lisdoonie Hotel, Shelly stood on the edge of the rock and gazed down to Derwent Water. The view was stunning, and one of her favourite places, though preferably by car. Beyond the lake, rising like gatekeepers watching over Keswick, were the big boys of the Lake District. She could see Dodd Wood, nestling in the skirts of Skiddaw, the third largest of the Lakeland Mountains, at the far end of the lake. In the middle ground was Saddleback and from there one mountain led into the next to Hellvellin and Scawfell Pike, the daddy of them all. She'd made love with John right here in this very gap in the woods in the days before Sammy. They were young, reckless—in love. Having sex in the open air was daring and exciting—these days, romance of any kind was a rare occurrence, over and done with quickly, leaving only a leaking mess to be cleaned up, and a vague feeling of dissatisfaction. She smiled, remembering the happy times and pulled herself away from memories to warn John to keep Sammy away from the edge.

The next four miles were merciless, but the reward was sublime. Sheep grazed the land and despite both Carthenage and Ballad being well trained, they were put on leads to obey the countryside law. Tinky-boo, the old miniature poodle, belonging to the equally old Esther Faye, was carried half of the time by one of the younger members and posed no problems. When they first met, Carthenage tried to play with Tinky-boo but the canine old lady, pulled her lip back to expose rotten teeth and gnarled gums. Carthenage decided she was no fun. He'd taunt her every so often, just for the sport of seeing her snarl, but other than that, he respected her age and left her alone.

They trekked through the fells to the café that felt as though it was at the very top of the world. Sammy told everybody the story of Watendleth and the urban myth about how it was named. They already knew but let him tell them anyway. The story went that William Wordsworth had walked this very trail. Like Shelly—May, not Shelly the poet—and millions of others, Wordsworth was blown away by the beauty of the scenery. The great Lakeland poet had a lisp and, while having tea in the café, Wordsworth said to the proprietor, 'What endleth blith to live in a plath like thith.' From that day forward, the name stuck and the tiny outcrop of dwellings, built for only two families, has been called Whatendleth, ever since.

Sammy went on to tell them that since the sixteen hundreds, the smallholdings and farmlands had been owned by the Tysons and the Richardsons. Shelly went to school with one boy from each family. There was no public transport, or taxis five miles up a mountain, and, summer and winter, the boys either had one of their older family members bring them up and down on the tractor, or they had to walk to the main road. Shelly remembered them being snowed in for weeks on end, and, even on good days, they'd often wander into lessons at ten or half past. They were simple people, who farmed their land and tended their animals. Nothing had changed in over five hundred years. Shelly envied them for their simplicity.

They had tea at the café, solely to give the owners their custom. Birds flew down and fed at their tables. Pigs, ducks, chickens, sheep, and geese roamed freely and flirted with the visitors for morsels of cake. Carthenage yapped at them, but they barely stopped long enough to give him a baleful look. They'd come up against bigger and better dogs in their time. This mongrel was no threat to them. One of the geese hissed and spread his wings and the dog went into a frenzy of delighted barking.

After tea at the café, they walked around the tarn behind the property to restore their appetites. It was on the far side that they laid out their fine spread. Everybody had contributed something delicious to the picnic. The rain had long since been beaten down by a forceful sun and the scents of early summer blew over them on a light breeze. The old ladies and gentlemen of the group refused the offer of the picnic table bench, and gamely lowered themselves to the blanket on the grass, along with everybody else.

Few people progressed further than Whatendleth Point. They would make the trek up that far, have tea and retrace their steps back. One road in, one road out. From here on, the land was inaccessible to cars, but walkers could continue through hard countryside to drop into Borrowdale seven miles further on. It was John who suggested that some of them continue to the bitter end. It wasn't twelve o'clock yet. They still had nine hours of daylight. He wanted to see the slate caves, one of which, Mulligan's Cave, was rumoured to be haunted by a giant dog that roamed the quarries at night looking for humans to feast on. Shelly saw that, despite his surly manner that morning, John was enjoying himself. He liked being with the men. He had formed friendships with them over the weeks they'd been rambling, both physically and verbally. Shelly was pleased for him and smiled about his tantrum that morning. She knew when they got home, John would be buzzing about his day almost as much as Sammy. The women tended to group together, talking about gardening and recipes, while the men philosophised and put right the wrongs of the world. That's what happened with older people. They talked about cars and football and politics. They were a sexually divided group, with the genders comfortable with their stereotypical roles.

The old ladies didn't continue and opted to go back the way that they'd come. Henry Grayson, the elderly club secretary, used the excuse of escorting the ladies to safety to take the easy way down. Shelly suspected that he'd had enough, too. She wished she could join the leavers, but she didn't want to abandon Sammy. He wanted to go on with his father and the fitter members of the group, so she had little choice but to trudge along. It would kill her, her thighs were already screaming for mercy and she wanted a long bath.

Martha Coulton, a brisk lady in her fifties, said she had nothing better to do and as it was a glorious day, she'd keep Shelly company. The men going forward with them included Martin Bott, a young English teacher from the same school that Shelly attended years before. They'd filled up on sandwiches and pork pie with egg in the middle, sausage rolls and Victoria sponge. The group were well-fed and in excellent spirits. Shelly was glad to see Sammy so happy, there would be time enough to worry about blisters and aching limbs when she got home. The walk may finish her, but the scales would make it worthwhile.

She was trailing behind with Martha. They walked at their own pace, leaving the men and dogs to race ahead. She would have seen Sammy's distress building had she been at the front with him. She might have avoided the calamity, but she was deep in conversation with Martha about clematis and wisteria.

She heard somebody shouting his name. It wasn't John who was still talking to Martin.

Sammy had wandered off and was missing in the middle of the Lakeland mountains.

Chapter 10

Sammy had to pee. John told him to use the bathroom at the café, and Sammy went with every intention of using it. But when he got to the bathroom, somebody was already in the tiny cubicle. The person grunted, and Sammy heard a splash and smelled a smell. He washed his hands and left without using the facilities.

Now he needed to pee really bad. His bladder was full, and he had a pain in his stomach from holding it in. He knew they were hours from home, and he couldn't hold it for much longer. It was hurting him. The men would often veer off from the group and disappear behind bushes or rocks. He knew what they were doing. It was disgusting. He was glad that none of them ever tried to touch him after handling their penis and not washing their hands afterwards.

He needed a toilet, a sink, and antibacterial liquid soap. He was agitated, and his eyes flickered in their sockets. His dad was talking to Martin about discipline in the classroom and didn't notice. They were at the front of the group, and John had Carthenage on his lead because there were sheep around.

Mr Athersmith was talking to Sammy about the war at the

back of the men's group. Gordon Athersmith was telling him about being in the army, and Sammy was enjoying the talk until his bladder was full, and it was too distracting to listen. Sometimes Sammy got overloaded with stimuli and needed to be left alone. Gordon said he was going to catch up with Ian because he wanted to ask him about his photography group. They were all within forty feet and in sight of each other, so he went ahead.

All the men were in front of him. He looked behind, and his mum and Martha were still around the last corner, a long way down the path. They hadn't come into sight yet. Sammy knew he was going to pee his pants soon. He remembered that he could use the wipes in his rucksack, but he still needed to pee. He left the path and disappeared into the slate quarry, searching for a rock pool or a small waterfall so that he could relieve himself. If he was quick, he could rejoin the group before they noticed he was missing. He knew he should have told somebody, but he wasn't going far. 'Samuel May stepping off the path,' he muttered. 'Samual May moving now.'

He heard them shouting, but he didn't want to be found. He'd be embarrassed to say he needed to relieve himself. It was a shameful thing to have to tell somebody. Ian and the others might not mind, even his dad and the old ladies had done it sometimes, but Samuel May couldn't bring himself to tell anybody that he needed to pee behind a bush. Touching himself with unwashed hands was unthinkable, but he didn't have a choice. Bathrooming should be done exclusively in a bathroom.

He climbed high, and soon the voices were less audible. He wasn't worried. He could catch them up. He was going to wet his pants. There wasn't a soul in sight, but he couldn't do it there in the open. He made for a gorse bush halfway down a shingled scree. And then he fell. He lost his footing in the loose stones and slipped onto his side. He was rolling down the steep mountainside, and he was wet down his leg. He felt himself peeing in his pants, but he couldn't stop. He stood up and wasn't hurt. He felt the urine inside his hiking boot, and it squelched when he walked. He looked at his trousers, and they were light blue—and they were partly dark blue. Samuel May was ashamed.

Shelly and Martha came into view as Ian turned around to check on the progress of the rest of the group. Sammy was missing. Ian shouted to the men ahead, and John ran down to him, asking where he was. 'I don't know, mate, he was here five minutes ago.' They called him, and Shelly and Martha broke into a run up the mountain.

'Where's Sammy?' Shelly screamed at John as she drew level with the group. She was huffing and gasping for breath but had rising panic in her voice.

'Don't fret, lass,' Gordon tried to calm her. 'We'll find him. He won't have gone far.'

They shouted for him, but their calls reached the distant mountains and came back to them as echoes on the wind. They scanned the area. Far in the distance, two people wearing cagoules were specs on the horizon. 'That's not him,' Martin said. Despite the grazing sheep, John let Carthenage off his lead and told him to find Sammy. It was a new game and he leapt at John, barking and grabbing the lead in his hands. Ian said that his dog was a working dog and therefore had superior intelligence. He let Ballad off and gave him the same command. Off their leads, both dogs chased each other across the countryside, glad to be free to run again.

They knew Sammy hadn't doubled back towards Shelly and Martha, and he hadn't managed to get ahead of the men in the front. He must have left the path. The men split into two groups, leaving Martha and Shelly on the track in case Sammy came back. The men went in different directions with one dog in each group.

Sammy was tired, wet and ashamed. He couldn't go back to the ramblers with pee on his trousers. He didn't think about the worry he'd bring his parents. His mind didn't work that way. His only concern was not being seen in his shameful state. He would go home. He remembered the way into Keswick, and then it was only another forty miles to Barrow. Every year they had a Keswick to Barrow run, and people did it in one day. It couldn't be that hard, and once his pants had dried, he could get out his maps and his compass and navigate his way home.

But with falling down the scree, and then having a big shame and walking while he worried about it, he'd strayed a long way from the path. He came to some thick bushes that went a long way in the direction he wanted to go but were blocking his way. They had thorns and prickles, and he had to walk around them. It took him further into the wilderness of the lonely fell. His legs were aching, and he missed his dog. He wished Carthenage was with him.

He walked over a mile and came to a deep gully. He carried on in the dip of the gorge with high mud banks on either side. It was all uphill. At the end of the ravine, he came to a face of sheer rock. He couldn't climb it. He'd have to retrace his steps and go back to the start of the prickly bushes. He looked around. Samuel May was lost. He didn't know which way to go to get down the mountain to Keswick. Above him was only the fellside and below a deep incline covered in gorse.

There was an overhanging ledge sticking out of the rock. Underneath it was a carpet of tall grass. It was shaded under the ledge. He climbed beneath it and sat far back into the shade. He was covered from view, and it was like being in a cave. He took his bottle of water out of his rucksack and had a drink, and then he closed his eyes and thought about being a caveman. He could be a caveman, and Carthenage could be a cave dog, and they'd hunt dinosaurs and drag cave girls around by their hair. But in real life, he knew that cavemen and cave dogs didn't overlap with dinosaurs.

It was cool, and it was nice. Sammy was wet and tired, his feet ached, and the top of his legs were sore from walking in wet trousers. He fell asleep.

They met on the path after an hour. Shelly was weeping, and Martha did her best to comfort her. Several walkers had passed them, and they'd all promised to keep their eyes open for Sammy. Shelly stopped crying long enough to shout at John. They argued in front of everybody, and she was upset that John was seething. Shelly blamed him for this when he said it wasn't his fault.

Ian searched for the number and called Keswick Mountain Rescue on his mobile. The lady in the control room kept them on the line while she mobilised a unit. Shelly took the phone and gave as many details about Sammy as she thought would help. But she didn't mention the big one. It was defensive. He was a child, lost and alone. It didn't make a difference that he was autistic. She didn't need to label him. She was thorough in her description and told the woman what he was wearing. She was doing something constructive to get her son back.

A helicopter circled overhead, spreading in widening circles from their point of reference in search of Sammy.

Ten men with mountain rescue dogs arrived at the café in Range Rovers, and more were going to get there as they could. They separated into groups and spread over the mountain, sending their dogs to search. One man, William Bates, followed the path to the family and reassured them that everything possible was being done to find their son and that he was confident that he'd be located before it was dark. He assured them that men were already searching further down the mountain. He stayed, talking to the teams of rescuers on his walkie-talkie.

Damien Peat and his dog, Valour, were searching scrubland on the north-western face of the fell. They'd been out an hour and a half when the dog found a scent and kept his nose close to the ground as he followed it up the scree bank. He entered a gully, and Damien followed. The bushes on either side had been disturbed since the last rainfall. The dog whined and looked at his master for confirmation that he should continue on the new path.

'Good boy, Valour. Go on, lad. Find.'

The dog put his nose to the ground and set off. His pace was rapid, and his nose was sure. Damien knew the scent was strong.

Sammy woke and heard a dog barking. He smelled pee and re-membered his shame. He was dry, but the top of his legs burned and felt sore where they'd chafed with all the walking in wet trousers. He felt a warm snout and hot breath on his face.

'Get down, Carthenage.'

The dog barked, and Sammy opened his eyes and saw that it wasn't Carthenage. He didn't think he'd turned into Rip Van Winkle, but a much older German shepherd was looking at him. This wasn't his dog.

CHAPTER 11

Damien broke into a sprint on the rough ground. He was already thumbing his walkie-talkie.

'Delta Charlie Three. Over.'

Static noise filled his ear, and a calm voice replied, 'Delta Control. Receiving you, Delta Charlie Three. Go ahead. Over.'

'Code Green. Found something. Going to investigate. Over.'

Valour was a seasoned dog. He didn't make mistakes. But there was no movement coming from under the shelf of rock the dog indicated. Damien looked up. There was a sheer rock wall above him. If the kid had fallen from that height, it didn't look good. He wasn't dead on contact because he'd managed to scramble under the shelter of the rock, but he could be seriously injured. Damien guessed the lost boy was unconscious. A terrified kid would be yelling the place down. It wasn't good at all. He made this initial assessment as he ran. Hoping he was in time.

He got to the overhanging coverage—covering what? He didn't know what to expect. A body?—and he hunkered down. He patted the dog and told him he was a good boy before commanding him to move back. The dog, his work done, wagged his tail and moved out of the niche.

A pair of solemn brown eyes, wide and curious, stared at Damien. The kid didn't look hurt, but he didn't say anything. Although curious, his eyes had a vacant expression. Damien reassessed the situation. He came to the conclusion that the boy was in shock.

'Hey there, son. My name's Damo, and I'm a first aider. I've come to help you. It looks to me as though you've got yourself in a bit of a pickle. It's okay. Don't be scared. Are you hurt?'

The boy didn't speak.

Oh, Jesus. He must have had a knock to the head. It could be blunt trauma. A bad trauma. His eyes were doing a rapid St Vitus dance from one side of the socket to the other. The kid looked as though he was suffering a heavy concussion. Although conscious, he could be having a fit. It might be brain damage. Damien swallowed. His adrenaline was on overdrive, and it roared through his body. He calmed himself, and the boy, who was pressed against the wall of the overhang, mirrored him.

'We need to get you out of there, son. It's going to be all right. I'm here to look after you. Your parents are worried. But we can tell them I've found you and you're safe. Can you give me your hand, son, and I'll help you out? It looks pretty cramped in there for a tall lad like you. Can you do that for me?'

Damien wasn't bothered about getting the lad out. That could wait. He was trying to assess his medical status and wanted to know if the boy could speak or follow basic instructions. He kept his voice low and soft while maintaining a steady stream of words.

'Can you tell me your name, son?'

The eye-flitting stopped as suddenly as it started. He was looking at a rock above him and there was something weird about his eyes. It didn't look natural.

'What is your last name, sir?' asked the boy in an odd, polite voice. He made no attempt to look at Damo as he talked, and his eyes didn't move an inch. He spoke in a dull monotone.

'Peat. My name's Damien Peat, son. But you can call me Damo. What's your name?'

'You are very confused, Damien Peat. Samuel May is not Damien Peat's son. Samuel May is John May's son. Samuel May realises that Damien Peat may be confused on the matter. But Samuel May comes from a long lineage of Mays due to the heritage of John May. In seventeen ninety-six, Benjamin Alfred May married Agnes Bertha Coulthard. They bore nine children, six boys and three girls, with Emily being the eldest. Followed by Alfred Henry.'

The boy continued reeling off names and dates. He gave Damien a run-down of what each person died from, their dates of birth and death, and their respective ages at the time. Sammy only stopped reciting facts about his family tree when Damien touched him on the forearm.

Sammy stopped in the middle of the word parentage, and, without making any attempt to move or even change his expression, he let out a run of high-pitched screams so loud that the echo rang along the valley and came back to him many times. In the confines of the rock covering, the sound was ear-splitting. Sammy stopped screaming the second Damien removed his hand, and he finished the word parentage as if it hadn't broken off. He continued his string of facts.

'Well, I'll be dammed.' Damien thumbed his walkie-talkie. He'd been about to call an ambulance. Now he was angry.

'Control,' he said into the receiver. He didn't give the correct call signs. 'I've found the boy. He's all right—I think. Dammit, Gaynor. Why weren't we told that this kid has problems?'

The boy stopped reeling off names and dates. He was only up to eighteen sixty-four.

'Samuel May has indeed got problems. Oops. Samuel May has got big problems. Damien Peat would not believe Samuel May's big problems. And in eighteen-sixty-four, Emily Geldart married Howard Johnson May, and they had seven children. The firstborn—'

'It's okay, Samuel May. We're going to get you out of here and back to your parents. Okay?'

Sammy's eyes dropped from the roof of the cave and met Damien's before darting back.

'Samuel May has indeed got problems. Samuel May is a dirty, dirty bad boy.'

'Why don't you come out here into the nice sunshine and tell me all about it, Samuel?'

'Samuel May cannot come out of this hole. Samuel May lives in this hole forever now. Samuel May is a dirty bad person and must live in the hole. Samuel May is fifteen years, five months, and sixteen days old, and Samuel May has peed his pants.'

Chapter 12

Shelly had never wanted to slap Sammy before—but she'd never felt fear or relief like this, either. When her son was brought down from the mountain she shook him and screamed in his face. 'What the hell do you think you're doing?'

Martin Bott moved Shelly's hands from Sammy's forearms where she held him so tight that the skin was indented. 'It's all right, Shelly. He's safe. That's all that matters.'

'Piss off.' Shelley turned her rage on John. 'I'll never forgive you for this.'

Sammy suffered no ill effects from his hours alone on the fell and said he may write a book on survival after his experience. Shelly didn't speak to John for four days and she was damned cold for a few more, but she thawed over time in the following weeks.

John was in the shower when his mobile rang. She heard him whistling, and a fresh, cedarwood fragrance of masculine shower gel seeped under the door. She felt her lower belly contract. Warming to him again, she thought about sex and then dismissed it. Sammy was in the garden with his dog. John wasn't the only one who missed having an active love life. They needed time together, and she must make some this week, sometime, maybe.

His phone was still ringing. She thought about taking it to him, but if he tried to drag her into the shower with him and she had to say no again, it would only cause an argument. By the time she got to him, it would have stopped ringing anyway. It was his office. Leaning over to his bedside table, she grabbed it before swiping the green button and saying hello.

'Hello,' she repeated louder. There was no answer, but she could hear somebody breathing on the other end of the line. She was impatient. 'This is Shelly, John's wife. Did you want to speak to him? Hello?' The person hung up without speaking.

It was Easter break and the start of the holidays. They had intense, concentrated, undiluted, wall-to-wall Sammy, in high definition for the next two weeks. John was off work for four days, but Shelly knew he'd rather be there.

They'd had Ramblers the day before and had walked around Bassenthwaite Lake, before dropping into Portinscale and sitting in a beer garden until sunset.

Everybody had taken care to keep their eyes on Sammy. The scare three weeks before had made the local news and still played on their minds.

'Can't we just put him in a set of toddler reins and bring him a bucket to pee in?' John had whispered to Shelly.

'Why don't we put him back in a pram and be done with it?'

There was another meeting arranged for Monday, and they were going to Grassmere to take on The Lion and The Lamb, a mountain rising above the village with a rock formation that looked like a hunkered lion and a tiny lamb cuddled beside him. John called it Crouching Lion, Hidden Lamb.

Today was Easter Sunday, and there was no rest for Shelley. They were going to the garden centre that morning, and they'd spend the afternoon tidying up the patio before having friends over for a late afternoon barbeque. They always ran late into the night, straying into the house as the weather cooled. They were lucky. Although early in the year, it was a glorious day, and the weather report was good.

She made Sammy breakfast. As she made a cup of tea, she thought about sex. What was wrong with her? John's mobile rang again. She answered and when the caller didn't speak, she called out to John. He came from the bathroom with a towel around his waist. There'd be toenail clippings left on the unit beside the toilet again. John had a guarded expression on his face as the phone disconnected. She looked at the screen and passed it to him.

'Probably a wrong number,' he said. He turned his back on her and put the phone face down on his bedside table as he rubbed his body dry, then slipped into boxers and his jeans. The caller ID said Accounts again.

'How bloody rude,' Shelly complained. 'They could have the decency to speak to me.'

He pocketed the phone and left the room. Shelly sighed and went into the bathroom to shower. The water felt good on her skin. As she turned the shower off and stepped onto the bathmat, she heard John's muffled voice. He was talking to somebody on the phone. She went into the bedroom to dress and worried about Sammy. If John was on the phone, he wasn't keeping an eye on their son while she was showering. Anything could have happened to him. Even as she was drying herself, she'd had the window open and her ears peeled, listening to his dull monotone as he talked to Carthenage. She was alert for any sign of distress in his voice—or for it to cease. She went to the window. Sammy was at the end of the garden, throwing a ball for Carthenage just as he had been before she'd used the bathroom. He would throw it relentlessly, never getting bored or distracted. They could play ball for an hour, and the dog always gave up first.

John burst into the bedroom, making her jump. He sprayed himself with deodorant and squirted some aftershave on his neck before opening his wardrobe and grabbing the first shirt he saw. He buttoned it quickly. Shelly was towelling her hair dry.

'They got through, then?'

John didn't answer. He was sitting on the bed with his shoes on, doing up his laces. He grabbed his jacket from the back of the chair.

'I've got to go out. I won't be long.'

He pushed his fingers through his hair the way he did when they were on the point of arguing.

'What? Where? What about the garden centre? What about Sammy's Easter eggs?'

'Sorry love. No can do. There's been an emergency at work. I've got to dash.'

He kissed her on the forehead and left. She heard him taking the stairs two at a time. The front door slammed. He hadn't said goodbye to Sammy. He'd looked worried. She heard his car reversing out of the drive and listened to it receding into the distance. He'd driven in the opposite direction to his office.

He worked in upper management for an electrical components manufacturer, assembling parts for computer motherboards. The money was good and gave them a secure lifestyle. It meant Shelly didn't have to work, and for that, she was grateful. He wasn't quite a shareholder and wasn't welcomed into the boardroom golfing fraternity, but he was as far up the ladder as he could climb in his current position. Most of the running and day-to-day organisation of the plant was down to him. His name had been put forward to the board, and the next time they floated a portion of shares, it was understood that John would be given them. When that happened, it would make him a rich man and give him decision-making power.

Had he lied to her? Shelly and John didn't tell lies. If he said he was going to work, that's where he was going. He must have detoured into town to pick something up first. She accepted it as fact and moved on with her day, a busy one with plenty to do. She was irritated that he'd bailed on her when Easter was supposed to be a joint effort. The lawns might not get mowed, and they had guests coming. She doubted she'd have time to cut them. It wasn't good enough when this had been planned for weeks. He'd better not be away long.

'Sammy? We're going out.'

'Can Carthenage come?'

'Not this time.'

'Why?'

'Because. It's not a good idea.'

'Why?'

'Come on, Sammy, get a move on.'

'Why can't Carthenage come?'

'Because I said so.'

'Carthenage needs to go in Shelly May's blue car to get used to being in blue cars, and then he won't be car sick.'

'He can't come this time, Sammy, because we're going to the garden centre, and he's not allowed.'

'Carthenage can sit in Shelly May's blue car with the windows down ten centimetres.'

'No, Sammy, it's too warm today. Leave him and come on.'

'It is twenty-three degrees. That is not too hot for Carthenage to sit in shelly May's blue car with the windows down ten centimetres.'

'If it's twenty-three in here, imagine what it would be like inside a little car.'

Sammy looked at the barometer and digital thermometer on the kitchen wall. 'Twenty-three point one degrees.'

They had to be so precise about every detail and it was exhausting. 'If it's twenty-three point one degree in our cool kitchen, think how hot it will be in the car with the sun pouring in. Somebody will break my windows to get him out.'

This was logical. Sammy coped well with logic. He'd read in his books about not leaving dogs in hot cars. He'd read horror stories in the newspapers saying that some dogs could cook in minutes. Sammy didn't believe they actually cooked, like sausages or tonight's roast chicken. But he did believe that they actually died because he'd seen some actual pictures. He didn't want

Carthenage to die in Shelly May's blue car with the windows down ten centimetres.

At the garden centre, Shelly bought some new planters. The gardenia needed repotting, as did two of her mini roses, which had proven to be not mini after all. She made some mundane purchases of plant food and bamboo canes while Sammy tried to get her to go to the herb and vegetable section. She told him she'd buy him three new herbs for his own garden instead of one if he waited until she'd finished getting the things she needed. On a whim, she decided to treat herself. Having guests over for a party in the garden demanded two things. It governed that a new outfit be bought—that was boxed off and sorted through the week while Sammy was at school—and it required at least one new plant to make the garden pretty—alcohol was a given.

They went into a poly-tunnel housing the trees. Sammy was calm in there. The foliage affected him. It quietened him and appealed to his senses rather than assaulting them. Shelly watched him sniffing and smiled. He reached out and touched, feeling the different textures of bark and leaves. He wasn't allowed to touch things in shops, but here it gave him so much sensory pleasure that she never told him off. Apart from when he was in somebody's way, Shelly didn't speak at all. She didn't want to intrude.

After a few minutes, they had the tunnel to themselves. A water feature in the corner trickled from a small waterfall into the koi carp pond, and Sammy touched, smelled, listened, and enjoyed the noise of the falling water and the serene quiet. Shelly wished that time would stop and this could be Sammy's world forever. He would be happy here.

She bought two Japanese maple trees. One with generous red leaves that spread like umbrellas and caught the sun like molten metal. The other one was different. It was amazing that two trees of the same genus could be so far removed from each other. This one was called *Heart Strings,* with feathered fronds that were delicate and soft enough to be reminiscent of gossamer. She couldn't choose between them, so she bought both.

Sammy, who was so eager to get to the herb section earlier, had lapsed into a waking trance. Shelly had to coax him back to the present. He was reluctant to leave the coolness and quiet of the tunnel where only trees and the water talked to him.

'Samuel May needs beetroot seeds and curly kale seeds and carrots.' Outside, the magic spell was broken, and Sammy reeled off the names of vegetables that would be enough to feed a nation.

'Hey, Buster. I said I'd buy you three new herbs. I never said anything about seeds, as well.'

'*Goodblood* or *Heart Strings*? Which one? *Goodblood* or *Heart Strings*? I can't afford both, but how to choose between them? Oh, to hell with it, we'll have both.' Sammy recounted, verbatim, her inner turmoil, using his echolalia to mimic Shelly's voice as though she'd spoken herself.

'Shelly May did not need either *Goodblood* or *Heart Strings*,' Sammy said. 'Yet Shelly May bought both hybrid trees. Samuel May does not need three packets of seeds to go with his three new herbs. But Samuel May would like to have three packets of seeds.'

'All right. Good point, you win. Three herbs, three seeds and, unless he specifically asks, we don't need to mention what this lot costs to your dad, do we?'

'Three new herbs, three packets of seeds, a hot chilli plant, and a MacDonald's double cheeseburger, hold the gherkins.' He said 'Hold the gherkins' in the voice of an American actor who had used the same line in a film. 'With large fries, a McApple Pie, A Crunchie McFlurry and two sour cream dips, Shelly May.'

'Three herbs, three seeds and a don't-push-your-luck, Al Capone.'

'Not three seeds.'

'No, Sammy,' Shelly sighed. This kid was so concise, and every word was taken literally. 'I meant, three packets of seeds.'

He related every fact that he'd ever read or heard on television appertaining to Al Capone, going in and out of voices as he narrated.

And Shelly switched off.

CHAPTER 13

Shelly pulled into the drive to see that John's car wasn't back and the lawns hadn't been mowed. They'd been done the week before, so they looked okay, but they didn't look perfect. Shelly wanted them to be buzz cut, and number one grade stunning for that night.

Sammy let Carthenage out and five minutes of bedlam ensued while the dog did fifty laps around the house and garden. After letting him out and attempting to stroke the whizzing ball of movement, Sammy went to the computer and looked up the planting and care of his seeds.

Shelly had to do some gardening, prep the food, clean the house—and make herself presentable. And John had been gone for over three hours. She rang his mobile, but he didn't answer. That was normal, so she rang his work phone.

'Hey, Dave. Can I speak to John, please?'

'Hi, Shelly. Looking forward to later on. John's got a lot to live up to, he reckons his barbies are better than mine. He's not here today. Isn't he with you, marinating that fine beef? He's off all weekend.'

'He got called in this morning. He left ages ago.' There was a long pause.

'You must be mistaken. I'm sure there's a simple explanation, he's probably gone to buy you some flowers, soft sod. He hasn't been here.' She thanked him and ended the call.

She rang his mobile again, but it was engaged. Dave must have got in first. She sent him a text using capital letters, shouting.

Where the hell are you?

He called her a few minutes later and she didn't give him the chance to speak.

'You lied to me. Where are you? People are coming in less than three hours. What the hell are you playing at? I suppose Dave warned you that I know you lied to me. Can you imagine how I felt ringing him, to be told you aren't even there?'

'Well, if you'll let me get a word in edgeways. I didn't lie to you. I'm not in the office but I am at work. It's business-related stuff.'

'On Easter Sunday?'

'Shelly May. Shelly May.'

'A client's computer system went down and the dickhead was about to pull the plug on the entire contract. I had to come down here to smooth things over.'

'Shelly May. Shelly May.'

'I've got to go. Just get home.'

Shelly was distracted and Sammy was demanding. The barbecue was upsetting him for the fact that people were going to invade his life and his routine. Shelly told him that he could do everything that he normally did and that nothing would change.

'Carthenage has to go for a walk now, Shelly May.' She was

mixing diced pork in a bowl of sticky marinade.

Now? You're freaking joking, right? She calmed herself before replying.

'Not now, Sammy. He might not get his walk today. He's fine playing in the garden. One day doesn't matter. Honestly, it doesn't. I promise you. We're going to have lots of fun and so is Carthenage.'

She held her breath and waited for the fallout.

It came.

She tried to reason with him, cajole him, and talk him down. Sammy bit her and tried to headbutt her. Shelly got his writing paper and an envelope and told him to write the routine change. He calmed down and wrote his letter, then he put it in his out-going mail rack before using his special mouthwash—envelopes carried germs. He was still agitated and wouldn't shut up. Shelly gave in and walked the damned dog.

At least afterwards he was less anxious. However, if he didn't come down from his mood soon it would bring on a seizure.

Where the hell was John?

Later, germs became an issue again. Shelly was making various salads when Sammy stood behind her, his eyes flitting around in their sockets. Couldn't he just leave her alone for five minutes?'

'Shelly May will cook Samuel May's meal in the oven. Samuel May will not eat outside. Samuel May will eat food cooked in the oven, sitting at the pine dining table in the dining room.'

Shelly drew on her reserves of patience and counted to ten while her son continued talking at her. 'Samuel May will have two pork sausages, one burger made with one hundred percent beef, one kebab that must not be on a skewer, one tablespoon of Shelly May's homemade potato salad— just like mother used to make—three lettuce leaves, four slices of tomato.' He continued to list exactly what he wanted to eat.

They'd long since given up trying to get Sammy to use only Christian names, but they persevered with manners. It was a slow road with limited success.

'Get me a drink, Shelly May.'

'Get me a drink what, Sammy?'

'Get me a drink, Shelly May.'

'Get me a drink, please, Sammy.'

'Get me a drink, Shelly May.'

'Sammy, you know how to say please.'

'Please has no meaning. It is a nonsense word.'

'No Sammy, you're wrong. Please and thank you are important in our culture. They show humility and gratitude. These are appealing character traits that make people like us. It's a social norm.'

'Our culture is stupid and isn't compiled on logic. It takes an average of 0.8 seconds to say thank you. Times that by the population of 7.888 billion people. If people didn't use manners, it would save seventy-three thousand and thirty-seven days. That's 200.1 years. Get me a drink, Shelly May.'

'Can you save me a few seconds and get your own drink please, Sammy? I'm busy.'

Why wasn't John here yet? Their guests were arriving in an hour. He'd been away all day. She hadn't planted the new trees and they stood at the back of the patio in their ugly plastic pots.

Her planting had to wait, but Sammy's couldn't.

He'd insisted that she watch him plant his purchases. He'd bought three exotic varieties of mint. Pineapple mint, chocolate peppermint, and tangerine mint. He measured precisely, planted them, and fed them. The seeds were a nightmare. Shelly wanted to rip them out of his hands and throw them into the earth. She had so much to do, and John still hadn't come home. Sammy used a ruler to measure where each tiny seed would go. There were hundreds of them, and Shelly looked at her watch and saw the day slipping away. But if Sammy was going to get through it, he had to be kept calm which required appeasement. She sat on the bench with a coffee and was resigned to watching her son plant his bloody seeds. He looked so ordinary—until you took note of his precision and the kneeling cushion that he had to have to stop his knees from coming into contact with the dirty ground. And he wore gardening gloves. Most boys would be up to their armpits in muck. She smiled and relaxed. People understood. What the hell did it matter if everything wasn't perfect? The guests were her family and close friends. Everybody would be happy to help when they got here. She looked at her watch again.

Brenda from next door knocked on the back door and let herself in. Shelly was in the kitchen trying to wrestle the oven glove away from Carthenage. Sammy was yelling her name two inches behind her and she felt her body tense. He wanted her to do his washing. It was Saturday afternoon. She always did his laundry after their walk on Saturdays. He was standing in the middle of the kitchen with his washing basket in front of him.

Shelly's face was red, and tears brimmed in her eyes.

John's phone was off. She'd rung him repeatedly and sent unpleasant texts, escalating in venom as the afternoon progressed.

'It's a good job I came over early,' Brenda said, putting a large apple pie on the counter. 'It looks as though I got here just in time.' She chuckled. 'I thought this would happen. I wouldn't like to lay bets on which of you is going to meltdown first.'

Brenda shooed Shelly out of the way and took Sammy's washing from him. Three minutes later, the satisfying sound of water filling the machine allowed Sammy to relax, while Shelly took stock of what had to be done. She sat with a coffee at the kitchen table and told Sammy to give her a break.

'It's okay, Pet. I'm here to help you now. Give your poor mum five minutes.'

'Brenda Robinson, Carthenage pooped in the garden.' She was putting two quiches in the oven.

'Okay, pumpkin, I'll be there in a second.'

'Now, Brenda Robinson.'

More cavalry arrived an hour later and Shelly was pushed out of the kitchen to get ready. It was John's parents, and while Pauline helped in the kitchen, Brian was despatched to deal with the offending dog mess.

From then on, people arrived every few minutes. It was comfortable chaos, and the barbecue was a success, despite the other host missing in action. Everybody was fed and Brian, who stepped in as the replacement chef, was relieved of his duties at the barbeque, though some charred sausages loitered on the griddle for anybody brave enough to attempt them. The drinking had begun in earnest and the karaoke machine had come onto the patio. A terrible rendition of *The Climb,* sung by two of the mothers from Sammy's school, rang over the garden.

Shelly had played lone host, saw to it that everybody was happy and sank into sod-it mode, with her third vodka and coke taking the place of her absent husband.

Sammy had coped with the party well. There were enough people to see to his needs.

Shelly May, Shelly May, Shelly May, was having a night off.

John got home after eight-thirty. He appeared at the back door and smiled a tense hello to his guests. His mother flapped around, asking where he'd been and telling him how worried she was. He kissed her on the cheek and told her not to fuss.

Shelly sat in her garden chair, in a rosy glow of vodka haze and ignored him. He bent down and kissed her on the forehead. His body was charged with a tension that echoed in his expression. She felt it through his chest. He looked sheepish but unrepentant.

'Where've you been?' she hissed through clenched teeth. She fantasised about what would happen if she threw her drink in his face. She stopped herself from doing it.

'Oops, John May is late. John May is in trouble.'

If Sammy was aware of the tension it must have been palpable.

'Not now,' John rasped back at her. 'Leave it. We'll talk later.'

She smiled at him, realising that she couldn't care less where he'd been. Raising her head, she brushed her lips across his cheek.

'Drop dead,' she whispered into his hair.

CHAPTER 14

She was at the sink using the crash-dishes-together-angrily method of washing up. She was drunk, but not falling over. He'd had more than her. Since getting home he'd swerved the food and had gone straight for the whiskey. He wasn't a big drinker, neither of them were. Coping with Sammy was hard. Doing it with a hangover would be impossible. They'd learned this early on in their parenthood. They rarely had the opportunity to socialise.

Shelly swayed. John should have been on his back, but he was upright. His words, when he'd bothered to use any, were only faintly slurred. He seemed unaffected by the drink. The tension that John brought in with him behaved like a yobbish uninvited gate-crasher. The icing on the shitty party cake was when Shelly was called upstairs because Sammy was having a seizure.

John kicked the bathroom door in to get to him. Her lovely party was unravelled and had gone tits up. She knew it was going to from the moment she'd put her two trees in the corner of the patio and didn't have time to plant them. That was his fault, too. It was the herald of disaster. To carry off the act of being the perfect party host you had to pay attention to detail.

Shelly had let the details get away from her. The party disbanded, and the guests left amid awkward air kisses and uncomfortable platitudes.

Samuel May tried very hard to maintain his evening routine. He'd gone upstairs at nine as he always did. But he'd had to wait for the bathroom—as he usually didn't. People were using both the upstairs and downstairs toilets. This upset him. The one downstairs was for guests and the upstairs bathroom was just for Samuel May, John May, and Shelly May.

David Moss was John May's workmate and he came out and left the door open behind him. It was one indignity too much.

And he hadn't heard water running. David Moss hadn't washed his hands. Samuel May didn't like open doors, they were untidy. Doors should be kept closed apart from when you walked through them, which was the way that it should be. David Moss passed him on the landing. Sammy chanted a list of germs and bacteria and plaited his fingers together in perpetual motion.

'Hey, Sammy. Great party, eh, bud?'

He didn't answer as Dave went by. He didn't even lift his head, but as the man spoke to him, his hand came up all by itself and hit Dave hard on the top of his arm.

Samuel May went into the bathroom without touching any handles and locked the door behind him by pulling his sleeve over his hand. He left David Moss with his mouth open in shock as he rubbed his shoulder.

He took off his shirt, careful not to let the contaminated sleeve come into contact with his body as he threw it on the floor. He filled the sink to wash before bed. He was uncomfortable and felt vulnerable. He didn't like being half-naked when there were so many people in the house. He'd put soap on his sponge and was rubbing his armpit when he heard footsteps pounding up the stairs. He panicked. Somebody tried the bathroom door and found it locked. They continued to rattle and a woman's voice shouted.

'Come on, dude. Piss or get off the pot. There's a dam about to burst out here.'

It was Marlene Taylor. Robert Taylor, her son, went to Samuel May's school. She'd left him at home. Samuel May wished that she'd stayed at home with him and wasn't rattling the bathroom door and shouting bad words while he had his shirt off and frothy soap on his body.

He tried to wash the soap off quickly, but quickly wasn't his way. He had to do it right. He washed with his sponge, washed it and put it in a fresh tub. Then he rinsed himself with a clean flannel that he took from a pile of zip-lock bags under the sink.

'Sponge on, flannel off,' he chanted his mantra. He had to be careful that his things were clean otherwise bits of soap got stuck in the middle of the sponge and made a horrible slimy blob. He still had to brush his teeth. The door rattled again.

'Come on. What are you doing in there, playing with yourself? Is that you, Dave?'

Sammy had stopped moving. He stood with the flannel in his hands. His eyes were erratic, his knees buckled, and the world fell away from him.

Sammy hit his head on the edge of the sink and had the makings of a black eye. It was touch and go whether Shelly should take him to the hospital. Pauline, who was a nurse before she retired, checked him for a concussion before letting him go to bed. Sammy was fine, but the mood of the party wasn't. The goodbyes were tense as everybody left. Shelly was mortified that Sammy had lashed out at one of their guests.

John came into the kitchen and had his back against the counter on the other side of the room. He watched Shelly crash and bang. The silence drew out between them in a battle of wills. Neither wanted to be the first to speak. John gave in. 'I don't know what to say.'

She saw him reflected in the darkness of the window. He ran his hand through his hair. He needed a haircut. She'd book him an appointment the next day. He clutched the unit behind him as though it was holding him up.

'Shelly, I'm leaving you.'

'Oh.'

'I'm sorry.'

His hand twitched back to his hair, the limb was full of nervous energy, but his body resembled a limp rag.

Just like that.

They were over.

It was one small sentence. There was no preamble or lead-up. He didn't ease her into it. Just wham. She was washing a wine glass. There'd been no bubbly, only supermarket wine. She had the nylon brush inside the glass, twisting it, wishing it was bigger and made of barbed wire, wanting to ram it up John's arse. She'd twist it and hurt him the way she was hurting.

Everything was still. John's hand stopped in mid-hair rub. Shelly's hand stopped mid-glass scrub. The only indication that a switch hadn't been thrown to end the world was the traitorous tick of the kitchen clock. It was loud in the silence. The steady motion of the second hand, moving around its mechanised central pivot was an indicator that, even with an emotional bombshell, life goes on.

'What about Sammy?'

He smiled. It was the saddest expression.

'And that's why I'm leaving you. Never mind Sammy, what about you? How do you feel about it?'

'You weren't at work today?'

'No.'

'You lied to me. I can't believe you did that and then went on after I asked you for the truth. We don't tell lies. I trusted you. Is there somebody else?'

'No. Of course not. Don't be stupid.'

Her husband was walking out on them. Wasn't it natural to assume that she had been replaced? He couldn't operate the washing machine—or at least, he'd never had to try. And yet he called her stupid. Stupid little housewife, Shelly May.

'Why are you leaving?'

'I can't do it, Shelly. I can't live like this. He's suffocating me. Killing me.' He banged his fist on the counter. She finished washing the glass and put it on the draining board. She had no excuse to keep her back towards him like a shield. She turned, hating this—hating him.

'Sammy hasn't changed. He's still the same.'

'I've changed. I want more. His voice—that damned voice, it's in my head every minute of every day. Even when I'm at work I can't escape it. It's there, pecking at me. I dread coming home. I hate walking through that door at night. I'd stay at work if I could.'

'Poor John. Poor, poor you. What a terrible life you have.' Her voice dropped an octave. 'He can't help it. You blame him for everything. You turn what Sammy is into feeling sorry for yourself. You're pathetic. You're a weak, pathetic wanker.'

'If you could see the contempt on your face, you'd know why I've got to leave. There's nothing left for us here. You know it as well as I do. One of us has to do something before we destroy each other. I need to be brave enough.'

'My hero. I was wrong. You aren't weak, after all. You're a goddamn sodding saint. You're doing this for us. Only you could put a spin on this to make you the sodding Messiah. You weak bastard. Leave if you want to, but don't blame us for this. You're leaving because you're an emotional coward. Yellow to the core.'

'I expected that reaction. You're a nasty drunk.'

She opened her mouth to throw more abuse at him but he held up his hand to stop her.

'Let me finish. I need to do this now, or I never will.'

She swallowed her next attack.

'I don't blame Sammy. I blame myself. I can't cope with him. It's the same old words. The repeated argument that we had last month, and the one before. We could record it and play it back—this and the baby argument. I'm not a good man. I can't do it like you can.'

He picked up his glass. There was still a drop of whiskey at the bottom, but the ice had melted. He slugged it back and grimaced.

'Want to hear something new? I'll tell you something I've never said before.'

'Tell me more about poor old John. Life is so hard for you, darling. Give me all your self-pity. Make me feel sorry for you. I dare you.'

He ignored the taunts. 'It's got harder. All these thoughts come into my head. I don't want them there. I try not to think bad things, but it's impossible to tell your mind what to do. They're ugly, nasty thoughts, and I can't stop them.'

He took a breath, looked at his empty glass as though it might have refilled, and carried on talking. 'He starts, and I want to take my fist and smash it in his face. I want to hit him and keep on hitting him until he just shuts up.'

He was screaming at her with his fists balled.

'Then it's best that you do leave. We don't need you.'

He was ranting, but she'd calmed. She was quiet, her voice dull. It was a little voice in an expansive room.

'I know.'

His eyes welled with tears while she was dry-eyed and empty.

'That's just it, you've never needed me.'

'You are seeing somebody else, aren't you? I know you, John. You can't manage on your own. You won't leave as long as I'm here doing your washing, making your meals, ironing your shirts. You wouldn't leave unless you already had somebody to do all of those things for you. Who is she?'

'There isn't anybody.'

'Who is she?'

'This is about us. You, me and Sammy. It doesn't concern anybody else. There isn't anybody.'

'Liar. Who is she?'

He shrank. Right in front of her eyes, he caved in on himself and was smaller. He stooped and looked tired. 'Somebody from work. She's called Marian. You don't know her.'

Shelly cancelled the mental hair appointment.

'Marian.' She tested the word out for the first time to see how it fit in her mouth. She was surprised that it worked just like any other word. 'I hope you waited long enough to ask her if she had any disabled children before you screwed her.'

'She's pregnant.' With a single sentence, he destroyed her.

She knew what he meant about taking his fist and smashing it into somebody's face—she hadn't understood it before. He could stop talking now. She'd heard enough. She just wanted him to shut up.

'That's why I had to go out today. Marian had a scare. She was bleeding and thought she was losing the baby.'

His hand swept through his hair and dropped to his side. The movement was faster. There had to be some movement in the stillness to prove the world hadn't ended. He raised his palms and spread them in front of her in a calming gesture.

'It's okay, though. They're all right.' He let his breath out in a whoosh.

As if she cared. What planet was he on? Why would she have one ounce of sympathy for the woman who was stealing her husband? Did he honestly believe that she cared about his unborn bastard? She wished the little twat had died. Leaving them was one thing. But replacing his damaged child with a normal one and wiping the slate clean as though he could start again from scratch was too much for her to take. She didn't care if Marian and Baby Perfect were dead.

It was coming. She felt it rise and couldn't do anything to stop it. It might have been the drink. Or the news that her husband was leaving her for another woman, a pregnant one. She clamped her hand over her mouth and ran from the room slamming the door to the downstairs bathroom behind her.

With a gag and a heave, she emptied sixteen years of marriage into the toilet.

Chapter 15

In the months that followed, new routines were established. Shelly was amazed by how easily Sammy adapted to John not being around. She wondered if she would be so easily forgotten. Maybe all the years of morbid worry about Sammy's care after her death had been unnecessary. He could take his handkerchief on a stick and walk into a home for people like him without any problems. The thought horrified her.

She was shocked by how little she missed John. She'd expected to fall apart and find it impossible to manage without him. But nothing much changed. The worst thing was that she had to walk the dog with Sammy every night instead of three or four nights a week. Even financially, although things were tight, she managed. Throughout their marriage, they'd been overpaying on their mortgage to get it cleared faster. It only had a couple of years left to run, and John said he should be able to continue with the payments until then.

Marian was very understanding, apparently. Well, three bloody cheers for Saint Marian the Marvellous. Shelly got a job selling cleaning products from home, and she had a lot of help from various benefits. She was amazed at how much they gave her for having a disabled child. Instead of career dole scroungers churning out fifteen kids to rake in the child benefit, they should just have one child with problems. They'd be as well off. Financially, Shelly had barely been hit, and she had the bonus of not having to wash her husband's pants.

Social Services offered to give her a carer for two hours to look after Sammy, twice a week. If she preferred, the person would help around the house to give her some respite. Shelly baulked at the idea of a stranger coming into their house and taking control of her child. She told them she didn't need any help. She felt they were denigrating her and attacking her abilities as a mother. She was concerned about how Sammy would take to a carer even for a few hours a week. She refused their offer. It was only later when she was talking to Pauline about it, that her mother-in-law pointed out the positives. It would be good for Sammy to interact with somebody new.

'What if he doesn't take to her?'

'Then she goes away. What have you lost? Give it a go, Shelly. You can't take everything on your shoulders all the time. John should do more.'

Shelly laughed—but it was a sarcastic sound that caught in her throat.

'He brought her round to our house the other night,' Pauline said.

Shelly sat up straighter, keeping up with the sudden change of topic. She was dying to know what the other woman was like. Pauline pursed her lips. Before even asking, she knew her mother-in-law wasn't impressed, but she was still jealous. The interloper had taken her husband, and now she was trying to get her claws into the rest of his family.

'No way. How did it go?'

'She said she can't cook. They eat out three times a week, and the rest of the time John has to get home after work and prepare a meal while Lady Muck lies on the sofa watching soaps. She drives a fancy car with no roof. I didn't like her, and I told John what I thought. Her skirt was too short, indecent. And dressing like that while she's pregnant. There's a name for women like that.'

'Has she got a good figure?'

'If you like that sort of thing. Too skinny, apart from the baby that sticks right out as though she's flaunting it, and him a married man. They're living in sin, and that tight top—indecent.'

Shelly felt tears stinging her eyes. After all the arguments they'd had about having another baby, this woman was pregnant, proud, and carrying his child. And, according to Pauline, the bitch was still slim. How was that fair? Shelly ballooned like Pavarotti by the third trimester.

'Is she pretty?' She was torturing herself, but couldn't help it.

'She thinks she is, that's for sure. Looks like a cheap barmaid in a business suit. A very short business suit. I wouldn't wear stilettos when I was pregnant. It's not good for the baby. It was sensible shoes and maternity dresses in my day. You couldn't wait to have enough of a bump to warrant your smock. It was a rite of passage, and the day you declared your happy condition to the world. And then, by the end, you never wanted to see a maternity smock again as long as you lived. I don't think she's in a happy condition. John says she's puking, fit to burst. "That's what you get for taking another woman's husband, dear," I said to her.'

'You didn't?'

'Well, no, I didn't. But that's what I wanted to say.'

They talked about Marian until Pauline had exhausted every bit of gossip, leaving Shelly feeling frumpy and inadequate. Then they went back to the carer and talked around the houses until Pauline persuaded Shelly to give it a go.

They sent the Health Care Worker for her first shift three weeks later. Joan had a dog, too, and used her experiences with her puppy to break through the barriers and connect with Sammy. After a few weeks of integrating her at the house, Joan would bring her terrier, Toby, and they'd go off with the two dogs for long walks, often exceeding her two-hour time allocation. To show her gratitude, Shelly would prepare a meal for them coming in. Sitting around the table, a friendship had grown between them, and sometimes they'd look at the clock to find it was Sammy's bedtime and they'd chatted the hours away.

Shelly was isolated even before John left. It was difficult to form friendships because of Sammy. They had friends but Shelly didn't have anybody close enough to confide in. Most of them were John's workmates or neighbours. Joan was ten years older than Shelly, but the bond between them grew to the point where she could tell Joan anything, and vice versa.

Joan had divorced two years earlier and was single. She said she liked it that way and was in no rush to find another man. She was devoted to Sammy and formed a bond with him. Sammy liked her. It couldn't have worked out better and was a huge help.

Shelly said she'd swapped a John for a Joan and the latter was a damned sight handier to have around.

John made his obligatory visits at the weekend. Sometimes he still joined them for Ramblers but it was awkward. Shelly was sad to see him disconnecting with Sammy. He forgot how to talk to him. His ready smile had too many teeth and no sincerity. He talked about the weight of guilt he carried, while Shelly bore the weight of looking after their son. He'd had his teeth whitened and he'd taken to wearing contact lenses.

Sammy wasn't daft. He knew his dad came out of a sense of duty. He was a stranger in their home. John regretted his terrible words about his son and swore he'd die rather than hurt him, but Shelly still used the legality of it against him when it came to solicitors and paperwork. He loved Sammy. She hated seeing the rift between them grow wider every week. They were strangers.

John made vague threats about taking Sammy out for a day. He said it nicely, but all Shelly heard were stupid words that suggested her husband might take her son away. Like hell. Even if it was only for a few hours, she'd run him through with a pitchfork first. While he was talking, she drifted, wondering if that was the best implement to kill your husband with. The day out was with the intention of introducing him to Marian. 'Then we can work towards having him for weekends and school holidays,' he said. Was he soft in the head?

Shelly fought him hard the first couple of times it was mentioned, but as time moved into October, she saw it was more of his empty words. She decided to burn that bridge down with John and Marian on it when they came to it. There was no point in making unnecessary waves.

Pauline said she may have no choice. As much as neither of them liked it, John had rights. 'After all,' she said, 'you introduced Joan into your lives. Maybe, for Sammy's sake, you could do the same with Marian.'

'Over my dead body.'

It came sooner than expected. John rang to tell her he wasn't fulfilling his duty as a father. His guilt had tweaked his conscience when the girls at work kept asking about his time with Sammy. 'I miss him. I'm suffering, too.'

'What on earth makes you think we're suffering?'

'I want more access.'

'You can go to hell. It's not happening.'

'Marian is my family now, and part of Sammy's. He's going to have a half-sister any day now, and we want to integrate Sammy into our lives before she comes.'

'Like you introduce roughage into your diet to make you shit, you mean?'

Shelly put up barriers. She responded to his threats by barring him from the house. Then she stopped him from seeing Sammy altogether. They argued on the phone almost every night.

'If only you were this attentive when you were here,' she said. John talked about solicitors and court cases. Shelly heard a woman's voice in the background. Damn her, she sounded placating. How dare she?

Shelly imagined Marian putting her hand on his shoulder and telling him to calm down. Maybe she gave him advice and told him to reason with his wife. The thought enraged her. It was none of Marian's business, the whore. Sammy had nothing to do with her. John had played his cards.

'You need to do what's best for our son and be reasonable,' he said.

A letter from his solicitor suggested mediation to reach an amicable compromise—or they'd be going to court.

'You think you're the perfect mother. But Sammy should be taken away from you. You're not fit. It's worse than cruel keeping him from me,' John said.

She told Pauline.

'You know I'm on your side, but it isn't fair punishing Sammy to score points with John.'

Shelly felt as though she'd been slapped.

That night, after bullying her on the phone, she agreed to let Sammy meet Marian. She hated the idea.

'I need to meet the homewrecker first.'

'How can that happen with an attitude like that?'

'It's the only way she's getting within ten miles of my son.'

'You're being unreasonable.'

'Okay, I need to meet my son's sweet and beautiful future stepmother. We'll have tea and cakes, and it will be perfectly splendid. Better?'

'Give her a chance, Shell.'

'You don't get to call me that anymore.'

'In other circumstances, you'd like her.'

'I've just thrown up in my mouth.'

She'd seen a solicitor, too. What a waste of money. John was right. She was wrong. John had the law on his side. He could see his son. And he could introduce Sammy to anybody he liked. Eat that shit for dessert, Shelly May.

She justified that if this was happening it was important. She should meet the enemy. She talked herself out of killing them slowly every day.

She didn't justify herself to John, only to herself.

Later, in front of her dressing table mirror, she examined her hair for grey and checked on the downward slant of her breasts. She was still a good-looking woman. On a good day. One when Sammy had a good day, too, she could hold her own. But Marian was prettier, Pauline had said as much, slimmer, prettier, richer, younger—better.

They'd agreed to meet on neutral territory in a pub midway between the two of them.

'There won't be a scene, will there? We don't want anything unpleasant. Marian's nervous about it.'

'Good. In tactical warfare, you should always have the upper hand over your enemy. No scenes, as long as you keep your bitch to heel.'

'You know what? I'm done. I don't give a shit what you say anymore. He's my son, too.'

Shelly smiled. Result. John relented.

'There's no need for any of this.'

She hung up on him.

But it didn't stop the meeting. She had two choices—meet Marian or let Sammy go for the day out without Shelly meeting her. She'd torture herself if that happened. The chat with her husband's girlfriend couldn't be avoided.

Joan agreed to sit with Sammy and said she was doing the right thing and she should act with dignity. She intended to try. She'd never had a catfight in her life. Joan said she'd help her choose an outfit and turned up two hours early on her day off so Shelly could get ready in peace.

Shelly asked Sammy if he even wanted to go to Alton Towers with his dad. She'd told John not to take him there. It would be a disaster. She point-blank refused. But John mentioned his solicitor's letter and told her she was controlling. Taking your weekend kid to Alton Towers was what dads did.

If Sammy didn't want to go she wasn't going to make him. She explained about John's new girlfriend and told him only as much as he needed to know so that he could process it in advance. She interspersed the talk with, 'But you don't have to go if you don't want to. It's entirely up to you.' Sammy played with Carthenage and wasn't paying attention.

'So what do you think, Sammy? Do you want to go?'

'Okay,' Sammy said, as though she'd asked him if he wanted a biscuit. He wandered off with Carthenage and Shelly felt betrayed. But that was that. Sammy was going to play happy families with his dad and Cruella de Knickerless and she had to pretend she was okay with it.

CHAPTER 16

Shelly was worried sick. She hadn't slept and didn't want to go ahead with this awful plan for John and his girlfriend to take Sammy without her. She was powerless and had no control. The solicitors had talked and it felt as though they were all ganging up on her. If neglect or abuse couldn't be proven, then John had to be allowed to see his child. It was this way—the nice way—or a long court battle for access that she'd been told she couldn't win.

She'd dressed with care, wearing a blue gipsy skirt and a white blouse. She wore her pretty sandals that had rhinestones set into the leather. Her hair was taken away from her face at the sides and clipped in place with a wooden barrette. Her make-up was fresh and simple.

She looked good when she walked into the bar and saw her husband. He was having a drink at the bar, hand in hand with a dark-haired woman while they waited for her. Her self-perception changed in that moment. She was a middle-aged frump who might as well have worn her gardening clothes.

Marian was even younger than Shelly imagined. She couldn't have been more than twenty-six. She had thick chestnut hair that fell in curls to her mid-back and a face that wouldn't look out of place in a L'Oréal advert—because she's worth it.

Perhaps the worst insult was that John had gone for a woman who wore the perfect ten. Shelly's size fourteen wasn't elephantine, but it was no good. She felt old, used up, and thrown out.

She forced her mouth to mimic a smile as she walked over to them. John moved closer to welcome her. He was about to embrace her but she took a step backwards. He'd lost the right to ever touch her.

'Hello,' she said in greeting.

He was awkward and then recovered as though remembering his prize exhibit. He put his arm around Marian's shoulder to move her nearer to Shelly. And he grinned like a boy in a toy shop. 'Shelly, this is Marian.' He might as well have said, 'Look what I've got.'

Marian held her hand out to shake and Shelly took it. Each of them sized up the other's jugular. Marian was very pregnant. Pauline had told her she was big, but she hadn't expected it to impact her own gut so much. She felt as though she'd been punched. She'd wanted another child with John for so long.

'Michelle, how nice to meet you,' the woman oozed insincerity. Pauline told her Marian was used to breaking balls in the boardroom and schmoozing new clients at business dinners. Marian might speak Japanese, but Shelly spoke fluent Sammy and that was the hardest language in the world to break down.

'Hello,' she said. 'Call me, Shelly, everybody does. I'm glad the baby's okay.'

'Oh, thank you.' She said. 'They're due next week and it can't come too soon for me.'

'They? You're having twins?'

Marian laughed, and it was the sound of a twinkling bell in a choir of angels. She had the perfect laugh. Why couldn't she snort like a pig? God could have given her that one.

'No. Just the one, thank God. They-them until they're born. John and I didn't want to know beforehand so it would be even more special.' She smiled up at him and he dropped a non-kiss onto the top of her head. It was as though he wanted to kiss her but didn't want to hurt Shelly's feelings. So he stopped short with only his chin touching. It made it more intimate. And who gives an unborn child pronouns? Shelly realised she'd missed the point and laughed at the ridiculous notion of labelling a foetus.

'Our special surprise,' John beamed. 'I'm glad you're okay with this, Shelly. It makes everything so much easier all around. Thank you.' And then he did it. The worst thing he could have done. He put his hand down and touched Marian's stomach.

Shelly had tried her best. She'd wanted to be good for Sammy, but she couldn't take anymore. Like a boiling volcano, it had to come out somehow.

'I'd like to say I forgive you,' she said, 'but that would be so—what is it they say on television?—Fake. I'm here for my son, if you're taking him out next weekend, you need to know what you're letting yourself in for. He bites. Did John tell you?'

Before Marian could answer, John cut in with a forced laugh. 'I told you she has a sense of humour. Shall we get a table?'

They found a quiet four-seater in the corner and John brought over their drinks. Shelly wanted vodka but had to settle for cola because she was driving. There was an uncomfortable silence. 'He told you I've got a sense of humour? How magnanimous of him. He hasn't. Dry as a nun's crotch.' She couldn't stop herself and felt guilty for jabbing again. She laughed to try and take the sting out of it. The point of coming here wasn't to fight and she'd promise herself that she wouldn't let her jealousy get the better of her. She failed in the first five minutes.

Marian took her time to answer. She raised the glass to her lips and drank delicately before putting it back on the beermat. She left no lipstick mark on the rim—expensive. 'He was lying. He didn't say anything complimentary about you. In fact, he's said remarkably little. But I knew we'd have nothing in common, so I haven't asked.'

The cat had claws and this was descending into an undignified word-brawl. 'I'm sorry. Can we start again, please? Shelly said.

'Sure, but don't try to take me on. I eat older women like you for breakfast, sweetheart.'

Sweetheart? Shelly willed her mouth to behave. She thought about Sammy, aged two, sleeping in his cot and holding his favourite digger. It was her favourite memory of him. She tried to keep in mind why she was there. It didn't work.

'Actually, we do have something in common. My husband. I don't get what you see in him, but there's no accounting for taste. When I got him, I took him from new. He was unattached. I never imagined he'd be the type of man to take up with a child.'

'Ladies, please, we came here to talk about Sammy. He's what's important, not you two scoring points. I'm disappointed in both of you. You're behaving like children.'

'And you're as spineless as you ever were,' Shelly said. 'Control your new woman by all means, John, but thank God, these days I don't answer to anybody, least of all you. I can behave any way I damn well please.'

Marian tagged onto John's speech as well. 'Darling, just allow me one more swat at the tennis ball. Yes, we have your husband in common, but not for long. One of the reasons we came tonight is to tell you he's divorcing you.'

She heard John react but didn't look at him, she was focused on Marian's perfect smile.

John's pulse was visible as the blood pounded through the vein at his temple. She knew how to ease that. She pulled herself back because he was speaking.

'That was cruel. I said I'd broach the subject when I felt the time was right. You had no right.' John looked upset and Shelly was flattered until she reminded herself what a two-timing toe-rag he was.

'And when would that be?' Marian shot back. The smile was gone, lips tight and her eyes furious. 'When our child starts university?' She stroked her stomach and the single movement hurt Shelly more than any catty words could.

'Can you prepare Sammy, please? We'll be taking Marian's car. The clutch has gone in mine and it's in for repair,' John said.

John and Marian glared at each other. It wasn't all roses and sex in paradise, after all. Shelly was grateful for the reprieve. It gave her those few seconds to examine her feelings. Her husband wanted a divorce, presumably to marry his other woman. And she felt—what?

113

She prodded the emotion to see if it was real. It came as a shock. She wasn't expecting it. She should have been stunned and devastated. She felt none of those things. The closest she could come to defining her emotions was happiness. She was going to be her own woman with her own name, in her own right. Maybe she would meet somebody else. She could travel the world, her and Sammy. She couldn't break routine though, foreign postage costs and the dog made it difficult, but she could do it, and the thought pleased her.

'Shelly, I'm sorry about that. We'll get together at a more appropriate, time. It must have come as a shock,' John said.

'No, don't be daft. We'll talk now. I agree. There's no reason to draw it out. I've been waiting for the right time to broach that subject, myself. Aren't we both silly Billys? There's no need to pussyfoot around these things.' And the curtain call. She was going in. 'I want the house, by the way.'

She smiled a simpering smile at Marian. 'For Sammy, you understand.'

Marian answered her smile with one equally cool and picked up her glass.

'And we're going to have to sort out an ongoing fund for Sammy. Because of his disabilities, your duty of care won't end when he turns eighteen. That's the way it is, I'm afraid.'

'Of course. That all sounds reasonable. Naturally, I want what's best for Sammy. Anything else he needs, just let me know. We don't have to make this ugly.'

'Not at all. Ugly would be terrible. And, if anything happens to me, he'll come to you. So Marian had better get used to him.

Maybe you should take him every weekend and holidays. She might find herself playing Mummy to Sammy, one day. It's all for the best.'

Her hunch paid off. Marian looked horrified. Shelly knew the other woman didn't want to meet Sammy. John wanted her to. Sammy was going to tear that floozy to pieces on Saturday, mentally if not physically—maybe both. She felt warm inside and was glad she came. Let's see what a *soupçon* of Sammy can do to Romeo and Juliette's happy ever after, she thought.

'Nothing's going to happen to you, Shelly. You're always so morbid.'

'You'd better hope not, sweet cheeks. Because that would really screw up your plans. I hope, for Sammy's sake, it never comes to it.' She picked up her Coke. 'Cheers, by the way.' She took a drink and the bubbles made her eyes water. She hoped the effect was sparkling rather than panda. 'I think we're done here,' she said. 'Be at the house at ten sharp, and you don't let Sammy out of your sight. Your lady friend isn't used to him. So I'd rather you were in charge.' She rose. 'No offence, by the way.'

'None taken.'

'Shame. What colour's your car?'

Marian looked confused by the abrupt change in conversation, and Shelly was stomping all over her.

'Yellow, why?'

Shelly sucked air in through her teeth and shook her head. 'Yellow. Ouch. I hope it's well covered by insurance. Ciao.' She blew air kisses before turning away with a smile, but not before she'd seen the stricken look on Marian's face. She walked slowly, enjoying the new air in her step and the receding panic in their voices.

'Baby, what did she mean? What's wrong with my car?' She sounded common when she was upset.

'Nothing, sweetheart. She's winding you up. Of course, blue would have been better, but I'm sure yellow will be fine.'

CHAPTER 17

She led Sammy out of the house. For his sake, she had a huge smile on her face. Marian wore white jeans, size eight, ten at most, with a deep brown leather belt. Her designer blouse tucked into the waistband of her jeans highlighted her slim build above and beneath the overhanging baby bulge. The enormous, square buckle proclaimed that she was a *Hot Chick*. She wore six-inch stiletto heels. Shelly disapproved. She thought Marian's jeans were too tight, how could the baby have room to move? What if she fell over on those heels? A good mother would wear more appropriate clothing. Surely that kid was due by now.

Sammy saw the car and the two people standing beside it and despite one of them being his father, Shelly felt him tense. She wanted to save him from this, but his dad had rights. Sammy was silent, there was no barrage of questions, it was a good omen for a bad day.

'Sammy,' Shelly said, 'this is Marian, Dad's—friend. You remember? We talked about her. Now be polite and say hello.'

'Hello, Homewrecker Marian Anderson.'

Way to go, Sammy, Shelly thought. That has to qualify for

a ten-point start. John looked as though he wanted the ground to open up and swallow him. Shelly handed her son over to his father but she didn't go into the house. She leaned back against the garden gate and waited for the fireworks.

'What have you been saying to him? Why would you want to poison his mind against us? Jesus, Shelly.'

Shelly could think of several reasons. 'I haven't said anything negative to him. He must have heard me talking to Joan. You know what he's like for picking up loose talk. On the other hand, he might have made up his own mind about the situation.' She was unrepentant. If this situation had to be endured, the only feelings she cared about were Sammy's.

His eyes were pointing to the top right of his vision. he seemed to be focusing on a cloud that looked like a penis. Unfortunately, it wasn't positioned above his father's head. Sammy refused to take John's hand. He needed his free to make fluttering birds in front of his face.

'Yellow car. That is undoubtedly very bad. Yellow car people are very bad indeed.' Marian looked terrified of him and still hadn't uttered a word.

'Sammy, stop talking rubbish and get in the car.'

Sammy's response was making a dry humming noise in his throat, always the herald of a stressful episode.

'Come on. Let's get going, son, we're going to have a brilliant day.'

'Samuel May does not like Homewrecker Marian Anderson's yellow car.'

John turned on Shelly. 'Are you trying to make things as difficult as possible? Why didn't you warn him about the car?'

'Why didn't you warn him about the car?' Sammy repeated, picking up on the whiney vocal pattern. He mimicked John. Marian looked as though she wanted to run, high heels or not.

Sammy stood his ground and the only movement was in his hands. John opened the driver's door and pulled the seat forward so that Sammy could climb into the back. Sammy was used to four doors. Shelly didn't think he'd ever been in a car with two before. Marian owned a BMW 8 Series convertible—in canary yellow.

Pauline had given Shelly the weekly update about Marian over coffee that morning. Shelly had reciprocated with chapter and verse of the pub meeting. Apparently, the car wasn't available in yellow, and her father went mad when she'd had the original finish resprayed, instantly flooring its value. Her dad bought it for her for no other reason than she wanted it. He also bought the riverside flat that she and John shared in Lancaster. Despite being a successful woman in her own right, Daddy still paid her credit cards and gave her a generous allowance. His reasoning was that he did it for her brother, a useless layabout with a penchant for white powder, and it was only fair that he treated them equally.

'How do you know all this?' Shelly had asked.

'She's stuck up, but she's not so bad when you get talking to her,' Pauline said, and again Shelly felt betrayed. Her mother-in-law had seen Shelly's expression and defended her position. 'I have to get along with her, Shelly. For John's sake. And there's something else I've got to tell you.'

'What?'

'We were invited to dinner at the Anderson's the other night.'

'And you're only telling me this now? The day before she swans in and takes my son away.'

'You're overreacting.'

'And you went?'

'Of course, we did.'

Shelly sulked. Pauline was changing her mind about Marian. She could see it. They were quiet for a while, but curiosity got the better of her. 'What was it like?'

'I've never been in a house that posh.' She went on for the length of another coffee about what a great night they'd had. 'But you'll never guess what. George called Marian Princess. And she joked that it was because it was easier than having to get his secretary to remind him what her name was.'

Marian must have been pleased with her car and John was proud of her and the lifestyle she'd introduced him to. She imagined what he'd be like if Marian let him take the BMW into work, and he pulled into his private parking space, to the wonder of his workforce. It was a new world where John might belong. Sammy, however, didn't.

'Sammy get in the car.' John's voice was brittle. Shelly hated seeing her son distressed. She wanted to end this and take Sammy back inside. But she turned and went into the house before she started crying and caused a row. She wanted to scream at John for his harsh tone. It was on the tip of her tongue to tell Sammy not to get in the car. But Sammy needed a relationship with his dad and John had every right to discipline him. She shut the front door behind her and began the countdown of minutes until

Sammy came home.

Marian got in the driver's seat and started the car.

'Sammy, I mean it. Move. Now,' John said.

'Samuel May cannot get in Homewrecker Marian Anderson's yellow car because it does not have a roof.'

'It's a convertible, Sammy. It's fun.' He took a step closer and Sammy went rigid. Like a toddler having a tantrum, his arms were stiff and all his muscles tensed. Sammy's head and face shook with rage.

'I've had enough of this. Put the roof up, Marian.' He grabbed Sammy and made him move. He put one hand on his head, bent him in the middle and manhandled him into the car, pushing the passenger seat into position. He jumped in fast and slammed the door so that he couldn't get out.

'Lock the doors.'

Marian gave him a wary sidelong glance but did as he asked. The central locking clicked into position.

Sammy hit himself in the face with every scream. John moved fast. He had to hold his hands down to stop him from hurting himself and struggled to get his son's seatbelt on at the same time.

'I don't think we should do this, John. I'm frightened.' Marian had spoken for the first time. Her voice trembled and she looked close to tears.

'Just drive,' John yelled at her.

'Is he all right?'

'Just go, will you?'

Marian stalled on her first attempt to move and then pulled away with a screech of tyres.

Sammy didn't progress into a seizure, but he continued screaming. John fought to restrain him and prevent him from hurting himself or anybody else. Marian's driving was erratic but he didn't have time to pacify her. 'Just keep your eyes on the road and watch what you're doing,' he snarled as she missed a corner and drove over the pavement.

John knew Sammy couldn't scream forever. He'd have to stop at some point. Everybody they passed stopped to stare. He saw a woman grabbing her phone and wondered if she was calling the police. Sometimes, John had to fight Sammy to the ground and lie on top of him in public to keep him safe. Good Samaritans had called the police before.

'Come on, Sammy. Let's count it out, son. Count with me. One, two, three, four.' Sammy didn't count with him, but, although it took several minutes of craziness, he did calm down. His screaming became a hoarse rasp, and he lapsed into exhausted panting, narrowly avoiding a seizure. Ten minutes later, John was still counting. 'Six hundred and twenty-three. Six hundred and twenty-four.' Sammy's eyes were fixed on the sky. His hands were red, welts stark against the crimson where John had restrained him. His face was pale, his top lip swollen, and a bruise was turning purple on his left cheek.

Chapter 18

Sammy was calmer but still agitated. Marian was breathing hard, too. John took a chance and changed his focus from Sammy. He could look at Marian for the first time since getting in the car. She was shaking and had tears in her eyes. John stroked her cheek, and that was enough for the tears to fall. He tried for a grin and failed. 'I'm sorry, sweetheart,' he said. He risked turning in his seat to face forward. If Sammy was going to act up again his first action would be to hit himself or head butt the back of John's chair. He could move back to attend to him. He made do with putting his hand over Marian's, his finger tracing the outline of her thumb. She gripped the gear stick with white knuckles.

'I can't do this,' she whispered. 'I can't even speak in case I set him off again.'

'Please don't give up on him. He needs us. It's okay, the worst is over. Everything's going to be okay now. Isn't it, Sammy?' he said over his shoulder. 'We're all A-okay now, aren't we, big guy?'

'Samuel May does not believe that we are A-okay in Home-wrecker Marian Anderson's yellow car with no roof. Lightning could strike Samuel May while he is sitting in the back of Homewrecker Marian Anderson's yellow car with no roof. A bird could poo on Samuel May's head. A plane coming in to land could have an engine failure and come down on Samuel May's head.' Sammy listed all the improbable things that could happen to him while riding in a convertible, and every one of them included the awful name he'd concocted for Marian. His high IQ meant that his imagination was inexhaustible. John didn't try to reassure him because while Sammy was incanting the worst that could happen, he wasn't screaming or hurting himself.

'Sammy, I need to ask you to think about what you're saying. You know that isn't Marian's name. Can you please do something for me?'

Sammy didn't halt in his almanac of the worst things that can happen to a human being sitting in a convertible. When they got to decapitation and evisceration, Marian looked as though she was going to faint.

'Sammy, I know you're a kind boy. And I know you wouldn't want to hurt Marian, but you're making her feel bad, son. Can we be kind to Marian and sit quietly for a little while so that she can drive?'

'Okay.'

Sammy was silent for over ten minutes apart from his default humming noise, but his mind had been busy. 'I'll call Homewrecker Marian Anderson just Marian Anderson.'

John laughed. It took a while but they got there in the end. 'Thank you, Sammy.'

The rest of the drive to Alton Towers passed with quiet trepidation.

Sammy refused to go on any of the rides. He spent an hour, the length of time that they were in the theme park, listing every fairground accident he'd read about. The day before, he'd researched the safety of this kind of attraction. He also gave the names and ages of people killed or injured and explained their injuries in detail.

He wore his epilepsy helmet because people in high numbers upset him. The crowds were dense and the day wasn't successful. They paid a fortune and stayed less than an hour.

Sammy ate and drank. He had a burger and chips, a hot dog, candy floss, an ice cream, a large Coke and a Sprite. Shelly would never have allowed him to have that much food. John just wanted to keep him happy and resurrect what had been a terrible day from the start.

Sammy rammed the food into his mouth, washed it down with pop and barely took the time to chew before swallowing. At home, Sammy ate almost normally, too fast sometimes, and he had to be reminded to slow down. In social situations, the way he crammed food into his mouth was another symptom of his distress. Marian worried that he was going to vomit. John knew that he was and held a bag at the ready. As the half-chewed food in his gullet came back up, Sammy was still cramming more into his mouth. He vomited into the bag and over himself as he struggled against John. John cleaned Sammy's mouth with wipes and told Marian to take the remainder of the food away from him.

He could see that she was disgusted and embarrassed by the stares they drew. Marian took the last of his burger away from him. He reached for it, growling and glaring at her. John handed her the carrier bag with the vomit in the bottom and she screwed her face in horror before taking it in finger and thumb. She turned and put it into a waste bin behind them.

Sammy stood up so that John could wipe his trousers when he lurched towards Marian. He grabbed her wrist, his mouth still slick with vomit, and bit down on the flesh of her arm.

Marian screamed. Sammy had his teeth in her bicep and wouldn't let go and John prized him off.

In an automatic reaction as Sammy's face left her skin, Marian's arm came up and she slapped him across the face. The blow sounded as if a ringmaster had cracked his whip.

Marian gasped and her hands flew to cover her mouth. 'I'm sorry. Oh, God. I didn't mean to do it.'

Sammy covered the red mark on his face and whimpered. John shook his head at Marian and took his son in his arms. Sammy tensed his body and John rocked him until he relaxed. He stroked the side of Sammy's face and sang a lullaby. 'You hit my son,' he said, as though he was a man in a dream.

'I'm sorry. I didn't mean it. He bit me.'

'I can't believe you hit him. He's disabled.'

'What can I do to make it right?'

'Nothing. There's not a thing you can do. I'm going to take my son home now. I'll see you back at the flat after I've explained this fiasco to his mother.'

'Please don't go. How are you going to get home?'

'We'll take the train.'

'There's no need for that. I said I'm sorry. Let me drive you.'

'That won't be necessary. I need to get him back to his mother.

It's best if I take the train.'

Sammy had stopped holding his face. The clear impression of a handprint stood out in relief from his cheek. His hands fluttered in front of his face and he comforted himself.

'Where do we go from here?' Marian said.

'I don't know.'

Chapter 19

Sammy walked in and went straight into the kitchen to see Carthenage. 'Shelly May,' he said without a word of greeting or so much as a look at his mother, as John hung Sammy's coat up. 'Carthenage needs his walk now.'

'Hello, darling. What are you doing home?'

'Shelly May, Carthenage needs his walk now.'

'He's just been out, Sammy. Joan and I took him a little while ago.' She was by the sink peeling potatoes and was alarmed by the sound of the front door opening. She was already halfway across the kitchen when John stood in the doorway. Her voice rose in panic. 'What's wrong? Why are you back so early?'

'If you'll let me get a word in edgeways, everything's fine. We just had a bit of a tantrum, that's all.'

'Carthenage needs his walk now after Marian Anderson hit Samuel May.'

'She hit him?' Shelly screamed. 'She bloody hit him?'

'Oops. Bad word. Cathenage needs his walk now, Shelly May.'

'Calm down. It was an accident. Let me tell you how it happened.'

'Your bitch hit my son. Tell me, how do you hit somebody by accident?'

'Carthenage needs his walk now, Shelly May.'

'Just a minute, Sammy.'

'Take Carthenage into the garden, your mother and I need to talk,' John said. He turned back to Shelly but didn't speak again until Sammy had taken the dog outside. 'It wasn't how you think. Sammy was agitated. He bit her.'

'I don't care if he took the end off her turned-up nose. How could you let her hit him?'

'It all happened in a second. She didn't mean it. Marian was sorry. She was more upset about it than Sammy.'

'I'll be the judge of that. It's me that's going to have to deal with the fallout. I knew it was a bad idea to let him go.' She stomped into the hall, picked up her car keys, and was struggling into her coat. 'What's the address?'

John ran his hand through his hair. He looked tired. 'What have we come to, Shelly? How did this happen? We loved each other and we've been together for years but you don't even know where I live. Isn't that ironic? Sammy's fine. Come and sit down and I'll make you a cup of tea.'

'And let her get away with hitting him?'

'This isn't about Marian. She's sorry. It won't happen again.'

'Damn right, it won't. Sammy's not going anywhere near her again. I'll get a restraining order.' She ranted but at the same time, she took her coat off and hung it up. They went into the kitchen. She looked out of the window to check on Sammy while John filled the kettle. He made tea and they sat together, the way a

129

couple who know everything there is to know about each other do. But she hadn't known everything.

John talked Shelly through the events of the day.

'And she let you get a train home? You know how Sammy hates crowds. How could she be so cruel?'

'She had no option. I was reeling from what happened. It was my choice and she tried to talk me out of it. I take responsibility. Introducing them was too soon. I've apologised to Sammy, and I want you to know that I was wrong. I'm sorry.'

'How did he cope with the journey?'

'He was fine. There weren't many people in the quiet carriages. He told me all about trains and it was the best part of the day. We enjoyed each other's company.'

'How many trains?'

'Three.'

'And he was fine?'

'Mostly fine.'

'Mostly fine? How did my son react to being hit in the face by a mad woman and then getting dragged onto three trains?'

'He was stressed and frightened at first, but I managed to calm him down and I'd go so far as to say he enjoyed it. He didn't have a good day, and I messed up big time, but it ended well. We had ice cream at Preston station and he talked non-stop from Lancaster to Barrow. He even made friends with the lady across the table from us. He's home now. He's fine.'

'You're not taking him anymore.'

'I'm not going to ask. I realise that we've got to start again and I have to get your trust back. Perhaps my mum can take him, and

I'll see him there for the time being.'

'I'll think about it.'

'Thank you.'

'But I have a good mind to call the police over this.'

'There's no need for that. Please don't ring them just to punish me.'

'If I wanted payback it might be because my husband ran off with a woman half his age. Excuse me for taking exception to that.'

'We need to talk about what happens now. We have to find a way to make this work, for all of us.'

'She's nothing to do with him.'

'I'm not going to push for her to get to know Sammy. It was a mistake, but she's having my baby.'

'I won't have you rubbing my nose in it.'

John raised his hands in a placating gesture. 'Let's do this the right way. We love our son, so let's sort this out. It's not good for him to see us fighting all the time.'

She was quiet for a heartbeat. 'You hurt me, John.'

They'd never discussed his affair since the night he left.

'I know I did and I'm sorry.'

'Is she better than me?'

'You're asking me to compare apples and pears. I can't do that.'

'Is she better than me in bed?' He winced and didn't immediately reply. She could imagine his brain scrambling to structure the words that would cause the least fallout. Shelly could see his mind working and, in a different scenario, it would have been funny.

'I won't answer that.'

'Is she more than me?'

'Not more. Different. She wants me, Shelly. She wants me the way you used to before Sammy.'

'Before Sammy what? Replaced you?'

'Yes.'

She felt sick imagining Marian and John making love the way they used to. They had been good together. Sex was wild, life was adventurous, and they lived it to the full. And then along came Sammy. She'd heard more than she wanted to but it needed to be said.

John was right. She did put Sammy first. They drank tea and talked rationally, and she missed him. She watched him walk away and lifted Carthenage's lead from its peg. She'd already been out with Joan, but the house was stifling. It was too full of John. And Marian. She needed to get out, and she wanted to be with Sammy.

John went into the bedroom where Marian was lying on the bed rubbing lotion into her stomach to prevent stretch marks. The massaging was good for the baby. The little one liked it and it was part of the mother bonding experience. John wanted to bond with the baby, too. He wouldn't have another child that he felt distanced from. He'd always been left out with Sammy. He was

Shelly's child and no matter how hard he'd tried, he was on the outside looking into their relationship. Never mind Sammy, he was the awkward one. He had to learn from his mistakes and do better this time.

'Here, let me do that.' He reached for the bottle of oil.

Marian ignored him, covered her stomach and struggled to stand up. 'I'm sorry about today. How did it go with Shelly? Did you tell her I'm sorry?'

'It was okay but it's hard for her. I need a drink.'

'We need to talk.'

Bloody hell, another hormonal woman wanting to take a bite out of him. He didn't want to talk. He wanted to drink scotch over ice and watch Formula One to forget. He wanted to rub massage oil into his woman's bloated belly and make love to her while his unborn child kicked his stomach. Then he wanted to sleep. What he didn't want was to listen to another temperamental woman screaming at him.

'It's been a long day. Tomorrow, eh?'

'Now.'

'Before you have a go, I defended you after what you did, and it wasn't easy. I had to stop Shelly from coming here, so I've had a gutful today.'

'This isn't going to work.'

'Please don't overreact. Today was tough on all of us. I know it was awful for you, so I've brought chocolate and pickled onion crisps. Let me make you some supper, and we'll shut out the world and relax.'

He stood behind her and rubbed her shoulders. She tensed in a way she never had before. It wasn't tired tension or because she'd had a bad day. John knew it was more than that.

'It isn't fun anymore.'

'What isn't?'

'Us.'

She shrugged away from him. 'I've realised I don't love you. I never did. It was just, you know, trying someone older.'

'What are you saying?'

'Some of my workmates said older men make better lovers.'

It was so tragic, he couldn't even turn it into a joke. He sat on the bed.

'It's over, John,' she said.

Chapter 20

The window cleaner was due that morning, and Shelly had left seven pounds fifty on the coffee table to pay him.

'Oops, Shelly May.' She dried her hands on a tea towel and went into the lounge. Sammy was sitting at his computer desk with his back to the room. Carthenage looked guilty, his ears were down and his tail was between his legs. Sammy repeated the same phrase in his monotone without turning around.

'What is it?'

'Carthenage was eating Shelly May's money.'

'Are you sure? She went to the coffee table and saw the five-pound note ripped up on the carpet like confetti. Cathenage, trying to make himself small, snaked under the table. She heard his tail thumping against the floor. He was showing the whites of his eyes and knew he'd done wrong.

'Samuel May is sure.'

'And you didn't stop him.'

'No.'

'Did he swallow any?'

'Two-pound coins and one fifty-pence piece. Swallowed. Sure.

Oops.' He continued typing, and his fingers navigated the keys as he spoke.

'Jesus, Sammy. You just sat there and let him?'

'Samuel May said "No, Carthenage. Bad dog." Shelly May should not leave money lying around if she does not want Carthenage to eat it.'

'But you didn't get off your backside and stop him?' She coaxed Carthenage from under the table and forced his mouth open hoping he hadn't swallowed it yet. 'What's this?' she said to him, pointing at what was left of the money. 'You bad dog.'

Carthenage looked miserable.

'Carthenage is not a bad dog.' Sammy adopted Shelly's voice and mimicked her saying that puppies chew things and it's our responsibility to put things out of his way.

'Rules change, Sammy. When it's my money he's eaten, trust me, he's a bad dog.' She touched Sammy's head to show she wasn't angry and Sammy pulled away. She had a hopeless look around the floor for the missing money and stroked the dog, telling him it was okay. 'I'll have to ring the vet. If it's stuck, it could hurt him.'

'Stupid Shelly May.'

'You're really not helping, sweetheart.' Sammy ignored her and continued to give his opinion.

The veterinary assistant put her through to speak to the vet. He said there shouldn't be a problem and that the money would probably pass through the gastrointestinal tract and be processed normally. Probably. Was he a vet or a politician? However, he couldn't be sure and suggested that, because of the shape of the fifty-pence piece, she should bring Carthenage in for an X-ray. He explained that they had a walk-in surgery that morning, but as it wasn't an emergency, she might have to wait.

It couldn't have happened on a worse day. It was Saturday, and the surgery would be packed. She grabbed her phone to look for a sitter. Joan was with a client and Pauline answered her phone from the hairdresser's chair. She had a burnished gold colour on it and would be at least another hour. Brenda, next door, was out and didn't answer her phone. That was it, the sum total of her friends and family. John was at work—she'd heard that one before. Shelly had no choice and had to take Sammy with her.

The waiting room wasn't as bad as she expected. There were only four patients before Carthenage, a Staffordshire bull terrier, a retriever and two cats in a box.

Carthenage didn't like the vet after he had his vaccinations. He knew where they were before Shelly opened the door and the smell of disinfectant hit them. She pulled on his lead and Carthenage braced his front legs, stiffened his back and refused to move. He tried to sit down on the threshold, and Shelly had to drag him across the floor. He was a year old and a big dog. He shook like an earthquake and whined like a bitch.

Sammy had his epilepsy helmet on, signalling his difference. The woman with the retriever gave Shelly a faux-sympathetic smile. Shelly was reminded how annoying politically correct people were.

She signed Carthenage in and took a seat as far away from everybody else as she could, but after motioning Sammy to sit down it only left one vacant seat between her and retriever woman.

She saw them looking. All of them, and the receptionist. They judged Sammy and pitied her. Same old. After bringing up a disabled child she didn't get embarrassed by people anymore.

The staffy woman tried to talk to Sammy and spoke to him as though he was a deaf two-year-old. 'Is that your doggy? He's lovely, isn't he?' Sammy's reaction was to bring his hands up in front of his face and set them free to flutter. The woman turned to Shelly. She was a talker and felt the need to tell her the story of Tyson's sore paw. Shelly wished she'd shut up so Sammy could adjust to the noise and the voices. But she had a right to speak. Shelly couldn't prevent that.

Sammy didn't like people looking at him. There were too many eyes in the room, all risking their thinly veiled glances at different times. She'll look, then he'll look, and the unspoken universal language went in time-written circles. One would look away as another invaded his space. His eyes were up, the stress default, but he wasn't immune to the looks and the tension. He moaned. It began in his throat as a small noise and grew. Maybe his noise shut out all the others in his head. Soon he was putting on a show of his full vocal range with howls and screeches. He was on form today. She didn't say anything to calm him and didn't try and comfort him. He already had too much noise in his head. Her voice would only be another sound. His hands fluttered, his body rocked and he raised his fist and hit himself at the side of his face. Shelly took his hand and held it in his lap.

The cat man was doing his best to become invisible when Shelly caught his eyes straying to Sammy and met them with a cool gaze. She saw his discomfort in the way he shifted his buttocks on the seat. You wouldn't last two minutes, love, she thought. But, if he'd had a child the same as Sammy, in all probability he'd have to.

Sammy was threatening a fit. That was fine, there was a large surface area on the floor and nothing to hurt himself on. She wondered how many diseased dogs had peed there and how well it had been cleaned. But Sammy wasn't a snob, he'd fit anywhere, and had done it in worse places. His noise reached its climax.

The retriever woman gathered her dog lead and moved to the other side of the room to sit beside Staffy woman and the cat man who were glad to let her in. Solidarity was good, though Staffy tried not to let Shelly see her small smile of understanding for Retriever woman's discomfort. She had to be seen to be PC. Tyson strained at his lead to sniff the backsides of the retriever and Carthenage forgot his abject misery in the excitement. He stood up, wanting to play, and gave two curt barks to the three dogs on the other side of the room.

Sammy can divide a room, Shelly thought. It was a them-and-us situation. They were squashed on a row of seats at one side, and Shelly, Sammy and Carthenage had a row to themselves on the other.

The receptionist leaned over her desk. 'Mrs May, if you'd be more comfortable waiting in your car, I'll call you when it's your turn.'

Shelly considered it. She almost said yes to protect Sammy from the tension, but he'd refuse to come back in when she was called. And apart from that, why the hell should she? But she smiled as she thought about what John would say if he was with them. There's no way he'd ever allow Sammy to be ostracised to make things comfortable for other people.

'We're fine here, thank you.' She leaned down and stroked Carthenage. 'Quiet, you,' she said to the dog. 'Your socially unacceptable behaviour is going to get us thrown out.'

A lady with a cat came out of the surgery, paid her bill and left. Shelly wasn't surprised when Staffy woman gave up her turn and waved Shelly ahead of the queue.

Way to go, Sammy, she thought as she grabbed her dog, her son and her dignity and went in to see the vet.

CHAPTER 21

Stepping from the waiting room into the sterile quiet of the surgery was like walking out of a rave onto the moon. While they were sitting, the front door had been open, letting in the sounds from the street outside, traffic, people shouting and the general white noise expected of a busy Saturday morning. The receptionist's voice was shrill on the telephone, her fingers clacking keys. There was noise from the second surgery, where the sounds of staff dealing with an emergency seeped through.

Sometimes, Shelly listened to the noise around her and tried to hear it as Sammy did. She heard voices as sounds. They differed in pitch and tone and merged with every other noise that she usually blanked out of her conscious mind. No wonder Sammy was overwhelmed.

The outside cacophony was muted, but not gone. The whiteness of the room helped. Sammy saw noise in lurid colours. White was a neutral quietude for him. His body lost some of the tension and his racket reduced to a keening hum.

A new vet stood by the chrome examination table wearing a white lab coat and a smile. 'Hi, Mrs May. We spoke on the phone.

I'm Graham Langley and this must be Carthenage, the money box.' He grinned at his joke.

'Carthenage is not a money box. Graham Langley the Veterinarian is mistaken. Carthenage is a dog, a German Shepherd crossbreed.' Sammy spoke before reverting to his whining.

Langley looked up from the notes he was reading from a computer screen. 'And you must be the one who was making all the noise. We don't have any of that nonsense in here. So you can cut it out.' He looked Sammy square in the face. Sammy's eyes retreated to their usual focus, but Shelly was amazed when he shut up. His mouth was open. He gave a last rebellious squeak, allowing his fingers to come up to play in front of his face. Langley was a no-nonsense vet. He was used to calming skittish animals. Shelly reasoned that disabled children weren't so far removed from what he dealt with. She wouldn't have argued with him. His tone cut through the clatter in Sammy's head, he'd given a clear and concise direction and somehow he connected with the boy.

'That's better. I can hear myself think now.'

And that's all Sammy wants, Shelly thought, to hear himself think. Langley had looked at Carthenage. 'You're a bonny lad, aren't you?' he stroked him and then lifted him onto the table. He asked Shelly to hold him steady while he did an initial examination. 'What's your name, young man?'

'I am Samuel May.'

'Okay, Samuel May. You have a very important job. I need you to come here and stroke Carthenage's neck to keep him calm. That's it, good lad.' Carthenage had his haunches lowered in a half squat, his ears had dropped and his eyes were rolling. He was terrified and had his tail clamped between his legs, as he trembled violently.

'Graham Langley the Veterinarian must not hurt Carthenage.'

'Don't worry, Samuel May. I'm not going to hurt him.' He talked as he checked the dog's eyes then took a light and shone it into his ears. He opened his mouth, checked his teeth and gums, and said the gums were pink, with no signs of clinical shock or blood loss. Carthenage backed into Shelly's stomach trying to escape the indignity.

'Graham Langley the Veterinarian must not hurt Carthenage.'

'It's all right. I'm not hurting him.' He reached behind him and picked two instruments up from a tray on the counter. He winked at Shelly before looking at Sammy. 'I don't seem to have enough hands. I need you to hold these for me. Can you do that? It's very important that you don't drop them because they're sterile.' He offered them to Sammy, who ignored the vet.

'Sammy take the things, and hold them nicely for Mr Langley, please.'

Langley walked around the table to Sammy. He took hold of his hands and one at a time he pressed the instruments into them. Sammy's eyes flitted to the metal objects for a second and then returned. He held the instrument with the tube attached and the one that looked like some kind of probe. He didn't scream the place down, and Shelly was glad that he didn't bite the vet.

'Good lad,' Langley said. 'I like you, Samuel May.' Sammy smiled. He bloody smiled and Shelly didn't have her phone in her hand. He'd smiled for the first time in his life when they got the dog, but it was still a rare thing. The vet rubbed his hands down the dog's throat. 'There's nothing lodged in the thorax.' He wrenched up Carthenage's tail and inserted a thermometer into his rectum. The dog squealed and thrashed to get away while Shelly did her best to hold him still.

'Okay, boy. Be calm for me. You are a silly dog, aren't you?' the vet soothed.

'Carthenage is not a silly dog. Carthenage has a thermometer in his anus. Carthenage is telling Graham Langley the Veterinarian that his bum is sore.'

'It's not hurting him, it's just an unusual sensation. If he'd relax he'd probably even like it.' Langley told him in the same tone that he'd used to calm the dog.

'Bestiality is sexual deviancy and revolting behaviour. Attraction to animals leads to sexual relations between a person and a beast.'

'Sammy,' Shelly said. What the hell had her son been looking at on the internet? 'I'm so sorry, Mr Langley, he doesn't know what he's saying. Be quiet Sammy.' But Sammy kept talking.

'Bestiality is sexual activity between a human and an animal.'

'Sammy, that's enough. Stop it. We've talked about unacceptable conversations before, haven't we? I can't tell you how sorry I am, Mr Langley.'

Langley's face was screwed up and twisted. His eyes watered and then he let his breath out on an almighty guffaw. His professional demeanour crumbled and he laughed until tears squeezed out of his eyes.

'No, I'm sorry, Mrs May.' She could still hear laughter in his voice when he spoke to her. 'My joke was childish. It was juvenile university humour, and unprofessional. I do apologise but he doesn't hold back, our Sammy, does he?'

'Modern society is generally hostile to the concept of animal to human sexuality,' Sammy said. 'Peter Singer the author, argues that zoophilia is not unethical if there is no harm or cruelty to the animal. This view is not widely shared. Sexual acts with animals are generally condemned as crimes against nature and are seen as animal abuse.'

After years of bringing Sammy up, Shelly didn't often get embarrassed. She thought she'd seen and heard it all. Sammy had pulled some corkers in his time. He had no social filter. She'd apologised for him on many occasions but she couldn't remember a time when she wanted the ground to open up and swallow her as much as she did right now. She managed a weak smile. Thank goodness Mr Langley was taking it so well.

Under control, Langley tried to continue his examination of Carthenage. 'Well, after all that, you'll be pleased to know his temperature is normal.'

'That's good,' Shelly said, taking her lead from the vet and ignoring the monologue at the side of them. She hoped he realised that her response was in reply to what he was saying and not to her son.

'My opinion hasn't changed from what we said on the phone. I expect the money to pass through him without us having to be invasive.'

Sammy was still talking about bestiality.

'However,' the vet raised his voice above Sammy's drone. 'I'd

145

be lacking in my professional duty if I didn't warn you that complications could be nasty. I'd still like to get an X-ray done to be certain, but it's costly, and probably not necessary, so it's up to you. It's your decision.'

Langley was struggling to maintain his self-control again due to Sammy's ongoing facts. They knew everything written about sex with animals and Shelly was still horrified by the words coming out of Sammy's mouth. She had no idea that he'd been reading such literature. What the heck possessed him to look it up in the first place? He must have hit on the search by accident when he was looking up the dog's genealogy. 'Yes, please. We'll go with the X-ray.'

'I'm hoping it's going to be simple. If young Carthenage here plays ball, my nurse will be able to hold him on the X-ray plate and we can get a decent picture. But it's not always plain sailing. If he's too anxious and won't lie still we may have to sedate him.'

Sammy broke out of his echolalia. 'Shaking Carthenage is not to be put to sleep. Graham Langley the Veterinarian can take an X-ray of Carthenage, not too anxious, and bring Carthenage back to Samuel May and Shelly May in just a moment. Graham Langley the Veterinarian must not put anything in Shaking Carthenage's anus.'

'I won't be putting anything else in there. I promise I'll do my very best to get the X-ray while he's awake. It should be okay.' He turned his attention back to Shelly. I see from his notes that Carthenage hasn't been microchipped yet. Would you like me to do that while you're here today?'

After Sammy's reaction to a simple thermometer, she dreaded

to think what he'd be like with a huge needle. 'Not right now, thanks. I think we've all suffered enough for one day. I need to have him chipped, though. I'll ring to make an appointment through the week if that's okay.' She smiled at the vet.

'Sammy's delightful but that's probably for the best.'

He led Carthenage to the treatment rooms. A sign came on in the surgery saying *X-ray in progress*. She heard raucous laughter coming from Langley and a female. Her cheeks burned, and she could only imagine what he was saying.

Five minutes later, Langley brought Carthenage back and the dog went wild as he greeted Sammy. It was as though they'd been parted for weeks. He was given a clean bill of health. 'We located the deposit, Mrs May. It's well down in the bowel and you can expect a withdrawal from the ATM tomorrow at the latest.'

'Thank you, and I'm sorry again for—you know.'

'Don't give it another thought. Sammy's a character and you must be very proud of him.'

'Yes. I am.'

It had to be Sunday, didn't it? Shelly was up early to watch the dog in the garden while Sammy was working out mathematical complexities that Shelly didn't understand.

Carthenage had come up trumps and she was bending and

poking when she heard the back door open and stood up, hiding her hands behind her back. Joan was greeted with a guilty look that wouldn't even have fooled her son.

'Thank God it's you. I thought you were Sammy. He hasn't followed you, has he?'

'No, he's in the lounge. And hello to you, too. What the heck are you doing?'

'Prospecting for gold. And I hear tell that there's gold to be found in that there dog mess.' Shelly had bent over Carthenage's offering with her marigolds on and a stick at the ready.

'You aren't doing what I think—oh my God, you are. Shelly that's disgusting.'

Stripping off her gloves, she dropped them into the dustbin and followed Joan to the kitchen.

'Here. Coffee. I hope you're going to wash your hands, 'Joan said.

'Of course I am,' she said, going to the sink. 'You're spending too much time with Sammy. Will just the once do, Ma'am?'

'How did you get on at the vets? No operation, I see.'

'We coped—just. But I've never been so embarrassed in my life.'

'What did he do?' Joan looked amused and Shelly laughed.

'He only accused the vet—the gorgeous vet, by the way—of having sex with animals.'

'He didn't.'

'Good as.'

'Bless him.'

'Bless who, the vet or Sammy? And never mind them, what

about blessing me? It was one of the worst moments of my life. Graham—that's the vet—'

'Graham?'

'Yes, Graham. Anyway, he shoved a thermometer up Carthenage's bum and that was it, away we went on every dirty, perverted bit of text ever written on the charming subject of bestiality. And there's me telling the vet he's a good lad.'

'Graham.'

'Will you stop interrupting?'

'Never mind all that. Tell me about Graham.'

'Nothing to tell. Told me he was off to Marbella for a week and to keep Carthenage away from my purse in the meantime. Behave yourself. He's probably married.' She dunked a digestive in her mug, watching it to see it didn't drop into her coffee. 'But if he wasn't, I so would.'

'You fancy him.' Joan looked thoughtful. 'That's the first time I've heard you express any romantic interest in a man.'

'It's the first time I've seen one even remotely interesting.'

'It's time you got some action.'

'Don't be ridiculous.'

'Sammy's not a chastity belt. You can still have a life.'

'Like that's ever going to happen. You forget. We love him, but other people don't. I doubt there's a man on earth who would take me on with Sammy. Especially if he met him on a bad day.'

'Shut up, you sound like John,' Joan said.

'Maybe he had a point.'

CHAPTER 22

John looked at Marian. 'What do you mean it's over? You're having my baby.'

'I promise, I'll never stop you from seeing them. You can come and see them whenever you want to.'

'I won't need to come and see it because I'm not going anywhere. I live here, with you. This is just a wobble. Let's talk about this and deal with it like adults. Then we can move on.'

'I don't want to be with you anymore. I don't love you. I'm sorry. Let's not make a fuss. I've packed your things and I just want you to leave. Please.'

'You can't do this. Everything between us has been so good up to now, and I don't believe I was just an experiment in trying out an older man. You can't throw me out after one upset.'

'I can't be with you anymore. I'm sorry.'

'All this because of Sammy.'

She hesitated as though gauging his reaction before she replied. 'Partly.'

John let out a sigh of relief. 'Sweetheart, you've got it all wrong. He's not normally like that. That was my fault, and I messed up. I should have known he wouldn't cope with a theme park. You haven't seen the real Sammy, yet. He's a great kid. I promise you, love. Next time will be better. We'll take it slowly, and I won't throw you in at the deep end again. We'll meet up in a park. That's it, a nice, quiet park where he'll be calm and it'll be fine. Ten minutes, that's all, we'll take it ten minutes at a time and you'll learn how to deal with him. I'll teach you.'

'I don't want to learn how to deal with him. I don't ever want to see him again. Don't you understand? He terrifies me. I've never been around anyone like Sammy. I'm scared shitless of him. I know that's blunt, but I've got to be honest with you. I've been lying to you for long enough. I never wanted to meet him in the first place.'

'You're overreacting. He's my son. He's not a monster who's going to hurt you.'

'He bit me.'

'He didn't mean it. He was just scared.'

'I've never been physically hurt by anyone in my life. Nobody's ever laid a finger on me.'

'No, you're Daddy's Little Princess. You wouldn't know anything about the real world. Life isn't all about you, you know.' John was contrite after his outburst and rubbed his hand through his hair. His temper had come up and went down again in an instant. 'I'm sorry. I didn't mean it. That was a cheap shot, and completely uncalled for.'

'This is getting us nowhere. Just go. Leave.'

'No. I want us to be a family. You, me, the baby and Sammy. We've got to make it work, Marian. It has to.'

151

John was clutching at any straw strong enough to cling to. He was terrified of losing her. When it came down to it, what were they? A dolly bird and an older man. The only thing cementing their relationship was his baby.

'He'll never be part of my family. You don't get it, do you? I can't be around him. I don't want to get to know him. And he hates me.'

'He doesn't hate you. He was freaked out. He doesn't think the way we do. Sammy doesn't dislike anybody. He doesn't know how to. And apart from that damned dog of his, he doesn't know how to love, either, or laugh much for that matter.' He kept talking, trying to make her see that Sammy needed their love. 'When he was born, he'd cry. We'd pick him up and hold him close. And the closer we held him the more he cried.'

He could see from her expression that she didn't give a shit.

'We tried to wrap him up all cosy because we didn't understand it was our love that was hurting him. But as much as he can't stand to be coddled, he needs even more love because of that. More than other kids. He needs us, Marian.'

'This isn't about your son. It's us.'

'What does that mean? We're good together.'

'I don't love you.'

'You do love me. We're getting married. Let's go to bed. We'll sleep on it. I'll sleep on the sofa if you like, and give you some space. I'll bring you breakfast on a tray, the way you like it. We'll talk some more in the morning, and it'll all look different. You'll see.'

'I want you to leave. Now.' Her voice was a whisper.

'I see it now. You're just a bitch. I gave up my marriage so we could be together. I wanted to spend the rest of my life with you.'

'It wasn't meant to be like this. It was supposed to be fun. No strings, we said. Nobody gets hurt. And then I got pregnant and it's rocketed out of control. We're living together and picking out prams when I want to shop for shoes.'

'Not with those cankles, sweetheart.'

'Piss off. If you can't be sensible there's no point to this. We've been talking about beach weddings and inside my head I'm screaming for it to stop.'

'You wanted to get married. You said so.'

'I know. I tried to want it. I saw a friend of mine today.'

John tensed. 'Who?'

'Just a girl, John. Jeez, somebody I went to college with. We saw her the other week when we were shopping. Remember—tall girl, blonde hair.'

'The one you didn't introduce me to?'

'I was talking to her about us. And she told me she thought you were my dad.'

'Does that matter? Does it really, when you're carrying my baby?'

'Yes, it matters. Not what she thinks, not what anyone thinks, but it matters that I'm not ready for this,' she spread her hands in a gesture of hopelessness. 'I'm not ready for you, or the baby, or all of this bloody responsibility. I'm twenty-three years old.'

'Not in your head. Not in the boardroom. And not in our bedroom. Marian, listen to me. You're the most grown-up twenty-three-year-old on the planet. That's what drew me to you. You blew me away with your confidence and maturity. We said all along that the age difference doesn't matter. We don't notice it, do we? Is there somebody else? Is that it?'

'Not really. No.'

'Not really?' John exploded. 'What does that mean? Either there is, or there isn't.'

'There's a man. We hung out a bit before I met you. He's got tickets for a gig in Milan, a music festival. We're leaving tomorrow.'

'Are you mad? You're not going to a bloody mosh pit with my kid inside you.'

'It's a folk festival. They'll be fine. My body is robust and designed to keep them safe.'

'Full of hippies and drugs. And you're having one baby. One. Have you any idea how annoying that is, and how many times I've had to explain to people that you're not having a bloody quintet.'

'Goodbye, John.'

John sat alone in a dimly lit corner of the pub, nursing a pint of lager. The hum of conversation around him only left him more detached. His mind was a whirlwind of regret and self-recrimination.

Marian's angry face lingered in his thoughts. He didn't blame her for throwing him out. But he'd left his wife for her, to chase a fleeting memory of youth and excitement. Sitting in the gloomy atmosphere of the pub, he realised he'd been running from the truth for too long.

Couples laughed and flirted. The vibrant energy of their youth was a contrast to his life. He'd chosen a wine bar frequented by people under twenty-five. What was wrong with him? Marian was half his age and a midlife infatuation that had gone horribly wrong. She'd made him feel vibrant again, but he was still beige, and now he was paying the price. There was a mirror across from him. It reflected his vanity.

The reality of what he'd done hit him like a shattering mirror. Leaving his family was the biggest mistake of his life, and he couldn't undo it. Sammy was left with a void where John used to be—albeit a smaller one than Shelly would have caused. And now there was a baby, a tiny innocent life, caught in the crossfire of his selfish choices.

John took out the family photo he had in his wallet. Point proven. Nobody carried printed pictures anymore. He stared at the snapshot of happier times. His wife was smiling at the camera, his arm draped around her shoulders. The contrast between that picture and his current reality was painful. He missed the old days.

He had to find a way back into his family's life and to do that, he had consequences to face. The pub was a brief refuge for his wounded ego. He couldn't go home and still had to find somewhere to stay. With determination born from remorse, he pushed his glass away and left the pub.

He was going to be a better man.

Chapter 23

The weeks flew by fast and Shelly was looking over the expanse of the six-week Summer Holiday. The two weeks at Easter were bad enough, but John had left soon after, and as much as she hated to admit it, things were easier without him. Routines were better maintained, and sometimes even adapting them was calmer without him around. It saddened her to think life was smoother for Sammy without his father, but it was true. John had booked a week off work halfway through the summer holidays. He said he'd be going away for a few days, and thank God he didn't mention taking Sammy, but after that, he said he wanted more access to his son.

He'd come in, mess the routines to hell, breeze out again and leave Shelly to sort out the aftermath. That was the price she paid for her husband running out on her.

Shelly was sending some information to her solicitor by recorded delivery. While Sammy understood the logic behind queuing and agreed with it in principle, he believed that other people should queue while he should have a golden ticket to take them straight to the head of any line they joined.

He was agitated, eyes up, hands fluttering, as he tried to block out the noise with his cow-like moan. It grated on Shelly's nerves because she was tense about the divorce. Normally, as Sammy tuned out the white noise, she could do the same with him.

He had his helmet on, but other customers gawped at him with or without it. Because he always wore it when they were in public, Shelly felt that ignorance was divined through the power of the helmet. She hated it and often thought about burning it and letting Sammy take his chances with the fits. After all, he didn't wear it in the house and had several seizures a week.

The decrepit old lady behind them pulled her out of her thoughts. 'I hate queuing.' Shelly smiled at her. 'Your little man doesn't seem too keen on it, either,' the woman said.

'He's all right. Aren't you, Sammy?' Shelly gave him a nudge and felt him stiffen.

'If you don't mind my asking, what's the matter with him?'

'I don't mind at all. I'd rather people asked than just stared.' Several people lowered their heads to examine their footwear. 'He's autistic.'

'Well, I never. We didn't have anybody autistic in my day, they were either spastics or mongrels, no such things as autistic. I've never met anybody autistic before. Can he hear me?'

Shelly bit back a retort, 'Yes, he's got great hearing. And we don't use those words anymore.'

The old lady raised her voice to a shout and separated every word, 'How. Are. You. Today. Little. Man?' she flapped her hands as though she was trying some form of unrecognised sign language.

'Sammy,' Shelly said. 'The lady's speaking to you.' She caught the eye of a young man three people back who was trying not to laugh. She recognised him as the brother of a boy at Sammy's school. She saw his shoulders jerk with the effort of containment. Shelly was amused that the old lady was more entertaining than Sammy. On another day, she might have been rude and told her how offensive her language was. It was no business of hers what was wrong with him. She might have yelled, 'What the hell are you laughing at?' to the teenager. Her moods could be as erratic as Sammy's. Today she was just amused.

'Are you having something nice for lunch?' the woman asked.

'Spastics and Mongrels are not eating lunch in the post office queue. We are queuing in the post office queue,' Sammy said in the same voice the old lady used. 'What's the matter with you?' He resumed his moan, but it was quieter. He was listening. The old lady's smile was painted on like a mask over her discomfort. It was as if she'd made initial contact with the missing link.

'Samuel May is going to be a veterinarian.' This was the first Shelly had heard of it.

'Who's Samuel May?' She was still shouting, enunciating, and wherever possible doing the actions. When she got to the word May, she steepled her hands over her head which didn't seem to equate to anything. The lady was oblivious to everything around her because she was having her first conversation with a real autistic person.

'Samuel May is Samuel May. Samuel May can communicate.'

At a loss, she looked to Shelly for help. 'What's he saying? I can't understand him.'

'He was just saying that he wants to be a vet.'

'Oh, that's so sad. The poor little mite wants to be a vet. What a shame.'

Shelly wasn't laughing now. The woman was right. It was a shame. Sammy was never likely to function as a vet. Her ignorance had amused Shelly. Her pity angered her. She felt the need to poke the woman. 'Why is that a shame?' She kept her voice pleasant.

'Well, love, no offence intended, but because of his poor little mind, he won't be able to work, will he?' she tapped her forehead and Shelly wanted to take hold of her finger and snap it.

'My son will be anything he chooses to be. He has an exceptionally high IQ. It's probably the highest of anybody in this town.'

'Samuel May's Intelligence Quotient is one hundred and twenty-eight, taken from the last reading.'

'And that's only because it couldn't be recorded because it went off the scale. Your consultant thinks it might have been two hundred or more. Go on, Sammy. Do your party piece.' Why did she feel the need to say that? She didn't have to answer to this line of no-hopers.

'Party piece?'

'Yes, he's a living, breathing, Speak-Your-Weight machine.'

Sammy looked at the old lady. 'Your light summer jacket weighs one pound. Your blouse equals half a pound. The skirt is half a pound as well. And your shoes are one and a half pounds for the pair.'

'What dear?'

Sammy paused for a moment, his gaze unwavering. 'You are sixteen stone and ten pounds, including your clothes. Without them, you would have a lot of loose skin but Samuel May has taken the weight of that into account. You are sixteen stone and six point five pounds.'

The lady shuffled as the man three people back snorted and laughed out loud. She looked relieved that the awkward conversation had come to an end. But the woman was the one who'd invaded their privacy. Shelly moved to the teller's window and heard the old lady say to the person behind her, 'I didn't mean to cause offence. I was only making conversation. Some people are too sensitive if you ask me. I was just saying to my Bert this morning, you can't say nothing these days.'

When her business was complete, Shelly turned away from the counter and Sammy stopped at one of the rotating displays. 'Come on, Sammy, you're holding up the aisle,' she said.

'Shelly May. Samuel May needs three Ian Sutcliffe: Photographs of Whitby. Samuel May needs Ian Sutcliffe: Photographs of Whitby right now, Shelly May.'

'What do you want some old postcards for? We're in Cumbria, honey.'

'Samuel May needs Ian Sutcliffe: Photographs of Whitby right now, Shelly May.'

'No, Sammy. I'm not going to the back of the queue to stand for another twenty minutes.' She took him by the hand and managed to get him out of the Post Office without him trashing the place. When they got home he went straight to his computer to research Whitby.

When Shelly had made coffee, she took out her phone to sneak a look at the new baby. Marian had posted more pictures of her two-week-old daughter. She had her daddy's eyes, and they looked as they should.

That afternoon, there was a knock on the door. A young man stood on the step looking awkward. He seemed familiar and it took Shelly a second to realise it was the teenager who was trying not to laugh in the Post Office. 'I'm sorry to bother you. I've seen Sammy getting off the school bus here.' He shuffled his feet and held out a paper bag to her. 'My brother goes to the same school. He's autistic, too.'

Shelly took the bag.

'It's the postcards he wanted.'

She was touched and didn't know what to say. 'Thank you. That's so kind. You're Danny's brother Aren't you?'

'Yes. We're taking him swimming—that's always fun. Not.'

They both laughed, understanding.

'I just wanted you to know we aren't all dickheads.'

She smiled as she watched him walk down the street. Sometimes small gestures were warm things.

Shelly waited for Sammy to go to his room and treated herself to a soak in the bath, praying that she wouldn't be disturbed by some triviality. It had taken a while, but she'd got Sammy out of calling

162

her to turn his light off. She was lying in bed watching TV.

It was almost half past ten that night when they had another visitor. Shelly hurried to answer the door because Carthenage was barking and would wake Sammy.

'What are you doing here at this time of night?'

John had been drinking. 'Can I come in? I need to talk to you.' His voice was loud and his words slurred.

'Shush, you'll wake Sammy. What's the matter? Can't it wait until tomorrow?'

'No, I need to talk to you now. It's important.'

She let him in and went to the kitchen on auto-pilot to make tea for them. Then she put John's mug on the table in front of him. *World's Greatest Dad*. Neither of them had spoken again. John was sitting with his head in his hands. She took her place opposite and pulled her dressing gown around her neck to cover herself. 'It's late. What do you want?'

'I've made a terrible mistake, Shelly. I hurt you. How can you ever forgive me?'

'I can't. And don't see why you've come round to rake it up again. You've got Marian and the baby now. I have to be up with Sammy in the morning, and to be honest, John, I'm not interested in your problems.'

'There is no Marian. We're over. Daisy's two weeks old now, and Marian kicked me out the night before she was born.'

Shelly was determined not to let him see her reaction so she went to the counter and came back with the biscuit barrel for him.

'Jesus wept. I wondered why none of the baby photos had you

in them.'

'I wasn't even there when she was born. I've been staying in a B&B. But I've been such a fool. I want to come home.'

'I'll give you one thing. When you mess up you do it in style.'

She took a second to process. What did she feel? Poor John. He'd messed up big time. All she had to give him was a kind of amused, ironic pity.

'You're delusional. Have you hit your head? You split up with her, lick your wounds, and come running back to me to make it better. What am I—your mother? I haven't got time for this. Sober up, go home and sort it out with her.'

His endearing hair-touching tic was annoying. 'It's not an argument. It's over for good. I didn't come straight here. That wouldn't have been fair to you. I've had a lot of time to think.'

'Mr Considerate. You've got a cheek. I'm yesterday's chip paper, remember? It's her you should be talking drunken shit to. Tell her you're sorry and buy her a diamond or something. Sort it out.'

'I don't want to sort it out. I don't want her back. I belong here with you and Sammy. I'll get down on my knees and beg if I have to. Please, let me come home. I want you back.'

'Are you mad? Our decree nisi is due any day. We're getting a divorce.'

'It can be stopped. I'll cancel it first thing tomorrow. Please. We'll go away for a few days, just the three of us, somewhere nice. We can put all this behind us and start again. I'll do anything. Just let me come home.'

'What about the baby?'

'It's a mess. I don't know what to do. I need you. Please just let me come home and we'll sort it out.'

'Grow up, John. I'm not taking you back. You've had a tiff, go home. Marian's just had your baby and her hormones will be all over the place. Your responsibility lies with her.'

'I can't go back. She went abroad as soon as Daisy was born.'

'But she's just had the baby, why would she do that?' Shelly let the disapproval drip from her tongue.

'It's worse than that. She had the baby and left her the next day. I don't think she's going to take to motherhood. She dumped Daisy on her mother, and swanned off to Milan's answer to Glastonbury.'

Shelly couldn't help laughing. John had slumped over his cold mug of tea and looked as though he was going to cry when his digestive plopped into the drink.

'God, you can pick them. That poor baby. Who did she go with?'

'I don't know, a man she's known for a while. Probably some hippy with long hair and denim flares who says, "Yeah man," a lot. That doesn't matter. I'm not bothered about her. She's back now anyway. It's made me realise what an idiot I've been. I want you. I had a mid-life crisis and wasn't thinking straight.'

'How straight do you have to think to make a baby?'

'Let me prove how sorry I am.' He reached for her hand across the table and she pulled away from him.

'You can't leave it like that. You have responsibilities. You need to sort it out with her for the baby's sake,' Shelly said.

'I have access to Daisy and arrange everything so I can see

her. But I'm here to talk about us. Marian's probably shagging another man and I'm not even jealous. It's a relief. I just want to come home. Please, Shelly.' He slid from the table onto his knees. She thought he'd passed out until he clasped his hands together in front of him. 'Please take me back. I'll never hurt you again.'

'Get up, you fool.'

It would be so easy. They could slip back into their marriage as though he'd never left. She felt sorry for him. He was an idiot, but he'd always been her idiot. She looked at him, drunk, pathetic and on his knees. She felt pity and sadness. He'd had his head turned by a pretty woman giving him attention. How would she have reacted if the tables had been turned? She realised that she was ready to forgive him. They didn't have to hurt each other anymore. It could stop. She held out her hand to him. He grabbed it with both of his and kissed her fingers, the back of her hand, and her palm.

And she put her arms around him and smiled.

She'd never take him back. She didn't want him. It was her turn to say, 'It's over.'

CHAPTER 24

Shelly was glad when the summer holidays were over and Sammy was back at school. She'd woken late this morning and was having to rush for John's Saturday visit. 'Hurry up, Sammy. Your dad will be here in a minute,' She called out. Sammy was tying his shoelaces in bunny ears, and that could take a while. His deep-set eyes and mop of unruly hair, melted her heart as it did most mornings. Today's outing to Heysham cliffs had been planned for every eventuality, and she'd packed what they'd need to en-compass all weather conditions.

'Samuel May is getting ready.' His words were measured and deliberate as he finished tying his shoes.

Shelly smiled at her son's dedication to the task, but time was getting ahead of them. It was two o'clock. She looked out of the window, watching the grey clouds hanging low over the street. It was the last weekend of September and the promise of a chilly, windswept afternoon at Heysham was something they were looking forward to—though a sunnier day would have been better.

John pulled up in his blue Vauxhall Astra, its fading paint

a testament to countless adventures. He stepped out, wearing the jacket he used for rambling, walking boots and a smile that held warmth and nostalgia. But today was a family trip and they were walking alone. Despite their separation, Shelly and John had worked hard on their post-break-up relationship through the summer. John brought up the subject of them getting back together a couple of times, and Shelly was quick to put him back in his box. Any romantic feelings she had towards him were long gone, leaving a wistful memory of better times and the wish that things hadn't gone so bad between them. John had grown into a better parent for both of his children and made a point of getting together at least once a week, for Sammy's sake. For now, it created a harmonious co-parenting bond that Sammy was thriving on.

John greeted him. 'Ready for the off?'

Sammy nodded. He'd talked about it all week and was having one of his better days.

'You look nice,' John said to Shelly.

She looked the way she always did when they went out walking. It was sad that he'd never said that when they were together, but she smiled. Sometimes being with John was still an effort, but she was learning to bite back any sarcastic remarks before they went as far as being spoken.

Sammy was buckled into the backseat with Carthenage, and they set off for Heysham. The drive through the picturesque Cumbrian countryside was a calming prelude to their outing. Fields of lime green stretched out on either side of the A590, dotted with grazing sheep and ancient stone walls.

John said they'd take the old road rather than the motorway and drive through Carnforth and Morecambe. As they turned right at Bolton-le-Sands and drove down the hill, they had their first glimpse of the receding tide. The ocean scent hit them first—a briny tang that filled the air through the partially open windows. They parked near the entrance of the coastal path, and Carthenage wagged his tail and frolicked.

John had to work a half-day before picking them up, and despite it being after three in the afternoon, they were in no hurry. The leisurely walk along the rugged cliffs was invigorating. The coastline stretched out for miles, a stunning blend of rocky promontories, green hills, and the shimmering waters of Morecambe Bay. Gulls cried overhead, riding the coastal breezes, and Sammy watched them with interested attention and only worried about them pooing on him when they flew directly overhead.

They walked for several miles before turning back for their picnic. They'd built up an appetite but were enjoying their walk, too. Ramblers had made them fit, and they'd done the entire cliff walk and dropped back onto Morecambe's promenade.

Because it was so lovely out, they decided not to walk back yet and to carry on to the end of the prom by Happy Mount Park. It was a long trek and they still had to walk the five miles back.

On the return leg, they stopped near the Eric Morecambe statue and crossed the road to have coffee and cake outside the King's pub as all the seafront cafés had shut by that time.

'Our time's our own,' the new and improved John said. 'It's been a great day, and there's no rush to get back.' Shelly loved that he was more involved with Sammy and they enjoyed getting out and walking at the weekends since they got Carthenage. The marriage was dead in the water, but the dog helped to save them and bring them back as a family. Shelly could even talk about Daisy without resentment.

By the time they were near the car, they were exhausted and starving. The path led them past St. Patrick's, an ancient stone ruin that stood sentinel on the cliffs. Sammy explained its history to them, his eyes lighting up as he passed on every detail. 'St. Patrick's Chapel is a ruined structure dating back to the eighth century. St Patrick's Chapel stands on the headland above St Peter's Church, in Heysham, Lancashire, England. It is recorded in the National Heritage List as a designated Grade I listed building and is a Scheduled Ancient Monument.' He had much more to say about it and they let him talk as they walked, enjoying the view.

The ruin was perched on the cliff's edge, overlooking the Irish Sea. And Shelly was happy. Life didn't get much better than this. She watched the ocean and was silhouetted by the setting sun. John and Sammy went back to the car to get the picnic, some throw blankets, and the halogen camping fire they'd brought with them. Shelly unpacked sandwiches, cakes, fruit, and a flask of hot tea, while John and Sammy explored the chapel's secrets. When they came back and Sammy was busy washing his hands from a water bottle and then using his antibacterial handwash so he could eat, John said he'd been going to tell him some of the ghost stories related to the ruin. But he'd remembered how literal Sammy was and thought better of it. Shelly saw a look of sadness cross his face and knew he longed for the father-son relationship that other dads had.

They ate with the sea breeze tangling their hair and the sound of waves crashing against the rocks as the tide came in. It was chilly and they cooled quickly after walking so far. But it was cosy in front of the fire, wrapped in their blankets. Shelly said they'd have to go soon because the night was coming in and the air was damp. She didn't want Sammy catching a chill. He was hard work when he wasn't well.

Sammy's strange laughter, mixed with the cries of seagulls as he tossed a ball for Carthenage to chase, was the best sound Shelly had heard all day. He even laughed in a monotone, but he'd never done it in his life until they got the dog. Carthenage had given his laugh to him.

The last of the sunlight cast a burnt umber luminescence over the cliffs, and John and Shelly watched in silence. The beauty of Heysham eclipsed the problems they dealt with but even Sammy would agree that it had been a good day.

Shelly called Sammy away from the edge as an excuse to inch away from John. He was making his simpering doe eyes at her again, and in other circumstances—with another man—the romance of the evening would have affected her, too.

But then there was Sammy.

And John was the last thing she needed in her bed.

CHAPTER 25

The moonlight cast long shadows across the cliffs, as they packed their picnic. Shelly stowed the empty tea flask away, and John folded the blanket. Sammy helped by picking up any stray wrappers and putting them in a rubbish bag.

'We must leave the countryside as we found it. Slam dunk the junk,' he said, quoting a slogan he read online.

They loaded the car and John turned to fasten Carthenage into the back seat but he was still off his lead and they couldn't see him. The realisation that their beloved dog was missing sent a pang of worry through the parents, and they tried not to show it. They weren't too concerned, he wouldn't be far, but he should have been beside them.

'Carthenage?' Shelly called, her voice carrying over the cliffside. 'Here, boy.'

John joined in, shouting the dog's name as he reached for the whistle hanging from his keychain. He blew it, and the shrill sound cut through the air. Carthenage had an excellent recall to three sharp blasts, but he didn't come galloping over the headland as they'd expected.

Sammy had gone beyond his cow moan and straight into the high-pitched continuous whining.

'We'll find him, Sammy,' John reassured his son, but there was a hint of unease that he tried to keep out of his voice. Shelly picked up on it and made sure she sounded bright.

'Don't worry, Sammy. He'll be back in a minute.'

As they searched, Heysham had dissolved into darkness. What had been visible a few minutes before was gone, as if a switch had been thrown. It was a clear night and the moon and stars were visible, but at ground level on the rough land, they offered no light. They took their phones out and turned the flashlights on. The cliffside, which had been so inviting and picturesque, took on an eerie foreboding as night enveloped it. It was after half past eight, and it was freezing with the loss of the sun.

They moved with urgency, scanning the uneven terrain, and called out for Carthenage. The open cliff edge was a looming, shadowy void. Shelly was terrified as she edged closer to the precipice, peering into the inky blackness and the rocks below.

'Carthenage.' Her voice cracked with anxiety as she shone her light over the edge, revealing nothing but a furious crashing ocean and rocks that looked like a razor back.

The cliff was known for its treacherous drop and it had taken several lives. It was a hundred and thirty feet to the sharp rocky shore. Panic crept into their voices as they called for their dog, desperation mounting with every second.

'Carthenage, come back.' Sammy's voice was filled with distress as he echoed his parents' cries. He ran in circles with his hands flapping out the Morse code of his panic. He was getting closer to the drop. Shelly stood in front of him with her arms spread to stop him from running headlong over the cliff like a lemming.

The cliff, a picturesque backdrop to their outing, had turned into an ominous presence, shrouded in darkness. With the cold, biting wind intensifying and night closing in, they needed help.

'We have to call the authorities,' John said. 'And we need proper lights—searchlights or something. We won't be able to see a thing in this darkness.'

Shelly's phone died, so John took charge and made the call. Their sense of unease grew, and neither of them confronted the prospect that their dog had fallen over the cliff's edge and might be lying horribly injured, or dead.

Shelly held her breath, expecting the nightmare to get worse by John having no signal. But his phone was okay.

'Which service do you require?' The impersonal voice on the other end answered.

'Police, please.'

It was probably three seconds but it felt like an age for the call to be connected. It didn't instil a lot of hope in rapid response.

'Police.'

'Our dog's gone missing on Hesham Cliffs.'

'This is the emergency line, sir. Perhaps you'd like to redial and call your local police department.'

'You don't understand. We're on the top of a cliff, with a huge drop and it's pitch black.'

Shelly had learned her lesson about not giving full disclosure after Sammy went missing in Keswick. She motioned for John to give her the phone and explained to the police that Carthenage belonged to their son who was deeply autistic and couldn't function without him.

'Is it a service dog?'

'Yes.' Shelly lied. Technically, he wasn't. 'Help us, please,' she said, giving way to the anguish she felt. It had been over fifteen minutes and Carthenage hadn't come back to them. 'I have my autistic son with us, he's cold, he's frightened and he's going to melt down. The dog is his life.'

The desk sergeant didn't hold much urgency in his voice, but he took some details and said they'd send a car out to them, but with it being Saturday night they were very busy and it might be a while.

They couldn't leave and drive home and they had no choice but to carry on looking. A vicious wind had picked up and was tearing at their clothing. Sammy was two minutes away from having a fit and everything felt hopeless.

'It's getting late, Shell. You take Sammy to Mum's and come back. I'll stay here and keep looking.'

'That's nearly two hours, John.'

'I'm going to take the path to the bottom and get to the shoreline.'

'The tide's in. It's too dangerous. You'll be swept away.'

'What choice do we have?' They were going through their options when John's phone rang, breaking the tension-filled silence that had settled around them. He fumbled for it and answered the call.

'Hello?'

The voice on the other end was gruff and angry. 'Have you got a German shepherd?'

John's voice rose with excitement and fear, and Shelly reached for Sammy's hand.

'Yes. Have you found him?'

'We've just fished it out of the dock,' the man said. His tone was harsh and accusing. 'Nearly drowned one of our men in the process.'

Shelly's heart sank. It was over half an hour since Carthenage went missing, and the dread gnawing at them made Shelly tremble with more than the cold.

'Is he okay? We lost him on the cliffs.'

The dock worker sighed, his breathy voice clouded with frustration over the phone. 'He's alive. He stepped off the dock and fell in. You're bloody lucky, it wasn't Drydock or he'd have been killed instantly. Dave risked his life jumping in to pull it out.'

'Thank you so much.'

'You should have been looking after him. And another thing, you need a new identity tag. It's scratched and we could hardly read it to call you.'

'We're very grateful. We'll come and get him now. Thank you again.'

The man gave him directions, and as John was hanging up he heard him say to somebody in the background, 'People like them shouldn't be allowed dogs.'

Shelly's stomach clenched and Sammy's wail had intensified. She couldn't believe how close they'd been to losing Carthenage for good.

Sammy's eyes were flying all over his sockets, the fit that had threatened since Carthenage went missing wasn't far away. They got in the car and John put the docks into his phone. Shelly wrapped Sammy in her blanket as well as his own and tried to hold him but Sammy was too agitated. The engine hadn't warmed the car yet and their breath rose in billowing clouds.

When they got to the dockside they found the workman's hut and ran from the car. A man stepped out and closed the door behind him.

'Where is he?' John asked, his voice flooding with relief.

'Sorry, mate. It's gone. One of my men opened the door to go on his rounds and the dog bolted.'

It was too much for Shelly and Sammy. She caught him as he fell to the floor in a seizure.

The tension intensified and the man looked stricken. 'What the hell.'

'He's having a seizure,' John shouted.

'Sammy?' Shelly cleared the area of any rough stones and gave him room to move.

'Hold him down,' the man said. 'He's going to hurt himself. I'll call an ambulance.'

'No. We're used to this. We don't need an ambulance,' Shelly shouted and the man hesitated.

'The days of holding people tight, and putting things in their mouths are gone. Forced restraint only intensifies the strength of a fit and prolongs the length. It can cause more harm than good. He doesn't need an ambulance. He'll come out of it in a minute.'

Sammy's body convulsed, and his limbs trembled as he writhed on the ground. Shelly knelt beside him, and as he showed signs of returning to her, she cradled his head.

Panicked dock workers rushed over to help. They were still reeling from the harrowing scene with Carthenage earlier and spoke about both dramas in excited voices. One of them stood beside Sammy, his weathered face etched with concern. 'Is he okay? What can we do?'

Shelly, had tears streaming down her face. She stroked Sammy's hair, whispering soothing words to him. 'Just give him space, please. He's autistic and can't cope with a lot of noise.' Sammy stopped thrashing. 'It's okay, Sammy. Relax, sweetheart.' She held her son close, praying for Carthenage's safety.

When he came around, Sammy was quiet. It was often the case after a fit. It sapped his energy and left him tired and listless. He was shaking and his teeth chattered.

'Here, get him inside. We've got a fire on,' The man in charge said. Shelly thought it was the one on the phone who'd been so angry. Now he just looked terrified.

Although they called it a hut, the building was large and insulated. It was warm in there and the man guided Shelly to a large armchair for Sammy. He was biddable and didn't scream or fight them. The man brought a quilt and Shelly wrapped it around him. Sammy was conscious but his mind was still elsewhere in the aftermath of his seizure. She estimated that they had another ten minutes before all hell was let loose when Sammy realised the dog was gone.

'Can I get him a hot drink? We only have tea or coffee, I'm

afraid,' the man said.

Shelly shook her head. She looked around the grimy hut. Sammy would never cope with drinking from their mismatched and chipped mugs. He'd have something to say about the warm quilt that didn't belong to him when he had his wits about him, too.

'No, he's fine, thank you. I'll get him back to the car and give him some water there. You've been very kind. Thank you.'

'Let me at least get you and your husband a drink. You look frozen.'

'We've got to find Carthenage. He's out there somewhere,' John said.

'Why don't you give the lad another few minutes? You'll search for the dog more efficiently with a hot drink inside you.'

'How was he? Is he okay?'

The dock worker said, 'Your dog, must have got lost in the dark and when he couldn't find you, he ran blindly, ending up here. It was touch and go. I've no idea how long he was in the dock, but the freezing water weighed him down. He was tiring and going under when we got there. I saw him sink three times and each time I didn't think he was coming up again. It was a miracle that we heard him. It was only that one of the lads went out to the loo and heard splashing.'

'One of us had to jump in,' another worker said, his voice filled with anger and concern. 'We tied a rope around his waist and he dived into the waters. It was pitch black out there. Your dog kept pulling him under, mate. We nearly lost a good man.'

Shelly imagined the terrifying struggle that had played out in the darkness of the water. Her eyes stung with tears of gratitude for the dock worker who had risked his life to save Carthenage.

'We got him to safety and warmed him up by the fire. But the first crack in the door and he was off like a whippet. We tried to grab him, but he was gone.'

Shelly couldn't find the words to express her gratitude and remorse. But all she could think about was finding the dog and making sure he was safe. They apologised to the men, and seeing that it was just an unfortunate accident, even the man who had sounded so angry on the phone was friendly and said he hoped they found him soon.

Chances were, Carthenage was away from the cliff and the docks. They only had the roads to worry about—and getting him home. That night, they'd narrowly escaped a tragedy, but their family was intact. Shelly told John that she hadn't had time to go back to the vet to have Carthenage chipped and she was furious with herself. If he'd made the same mistake, she'd have gone mad with him.

'This is all my fault.'

'No, it's not, Shell. You weren't to know something like this was going to happen. Don't be so hard on yourself. When we get him home I'll take him for you next week. That way, you can look after Sammy.'

Sammy must have been feeling better because he spoke for the first time and wasn't as forgiving as his father. 'Shelly May should have taken Carthenage to Graham Langley the Veterinarian to have Carthenage microchipped.' He started moaning and rocking. Shelly was sitting in the back with him, knowing that there would be trouble at some point.

Here we go, she thought. The rest of the drive home was a nightmare. Soon, Sammy was wailing and fighting. He tried to headbutt his mother and punched her whenever he could get his hand free.

'Sammy, stop that,' John shouted. 'Are you okay, love?'

'Just hurry up and get us home.'

When they got back, they called the doctor out and he sedated Sammy to ease his agitation. 'He'll sleep now. If he's no better in the morning, call me,' the doctor said. Shelly was glad that the medication was already taking effect.

John stayed for a cup of coffee, and long enough for Shelly to fill him a flask, and he set off to go back to Heysham.

Chapter 26

Shelly didn't want to wake up. Her body was heavy with exhaustion. She rubbed her eyes and winced as her fingers brushed against a tender spot on her cheek. The morning sunlight streamed through the curtains, casting a warm glow across the room. Her memory from the previous night came rushing back in a whirlwind of chaos.

Bruises covered her face and arms, and a dull ache radiated from the bite mark on her shoulder. She tasted the acrid remnants of last night's terror in her mouth, and she swallowed, willing herself to push through the pain and anxiety clinging to her.

She sat up and looked at the space beside her in the bed. She hated to admit it, but this morning she missed the comfort that John being there would have brought. She hadn't heard him come back and it was as though she sensed the bed in the spare room was still empty. She wondered if he'd been out all night searching for Carthenage. The worst part of this morning was not hearing the dog demanding attention from her and Sammy. Until Carthenage was found, it was going to be a tough day.

She swung her legs out of bed, ignoring the sharp pain in her side, and went to her son's room. The door creaked open, and she flicked the light switch to reveal the familiar surroundings.

Sammy was gone.

The bed was made. Panic clawed at her chest. It was rare that she hadn't been woken by him shouting for her and needing attention. Her maternal instinct should have kicked in and told her he wasn't there. Just as it was telling her that he wasn't in the house or garden. She hadn't worried because he'd fallen into a deep sleep the night before. She'd expected him to be asleep after the ordeal of the previous night and the subsequent sedation to knock him out.

She scanned the room, looking for any clues to where Sammy might be, despite it being obvious. She didn't want to confront that thought—not until she had to. The window was closed, and when she ran downstairs, the doors were still locked. It was as if Sammy had vanished into thin air and she was surprised that her son, with the footfall of an elephant, could summon such stealth.

Tears filled her eyes as she called him. 'Sammy? Are you there?'

The house was silent. It had never felt like this before. There was always something going on. Her son's absence was a painful void that consumed her. She needed to find him, to know he was safe and bring him home.

The bruises on her body and the bite on her shoulder were a clear reminder of his outburst last night. But worse, it showed that Sammy had built muscle and had the strength to overpower her. He was strong and could hurt her. But nothing compared to the terror of waking up to find Sammy gone. He was alone in a world that didn't make sense to him.

Shelly checked the house and garden. She opened the cupboard under the stairs and checked his wardrobe in case Sammy had sought escape in the closed spaces. He never had, but he'd never lost his dog before. She checked every room and small space, calling for him. It was like a macabre game of hide and seek, and she was the loser. She stood in the eerie silence, and the night's events crashed down on her like a crushing boulder.

She looked out of the window, her eyes scanning the horizon, hoping to see Carthenage returning with John and Sammy. But the world was empty, and her family weren't in sight. She ran into the street, shouting for him, but had no idea where to go and gave up. She needed to search for him in a proper manner rather than flying into the early morning without even dressing. She'd get back, call the police and get out again.

She made coffee and put two slices of bread into the toaster on autopilot. But when the toast popped, she couldn't face anything to eat and threw it in the waste bin.

The sound of the front door creaking open made her jump up so violently that the barstool crashed to the floor. John came in and his face was haggard. His eyes were puffy and bloodshot from the night search. He didn't need to say anything. She got the story from his lone arrival. He'd been out all night scouring the darkness for Carthenage, and the fatigue etched deep lines on his face.

John said, 'How are we going to tell Sammy?'

Her voice was filled with dread, and she managed to spill the words that had been threatening to make her crumble since she discovered the empty room.

'Sammy's gone,' she whispered.

'Damn.' Shelly watched his face clouding as he took a second to process it. 'Have you rung my mother? He'll have gone there.'

'Not yet. But you know he hasn't. This is Sammy. He's gone to find the dog. And Pauline would have rung to let us know he was safe.'

'I've got to get back out there. He can't have gone far.'

'Can't he? We don't know how long he's been gone.'

'Jesus. Tell me he hasn't left in his pyjamas. It's freezing out there.'

'No, they were folded on the chair beside his bed. He's dressed.'

'Either that or he's single-mindedly wandering the streets naked.'

'You can joke at a time like this?'

'No. I'm sorry.'

'He's got his warm coat and boots.'

'See, he's thinking. He'll be okay.'

The world outside had disappeared. Then, with a sense of urgency that matched Shelly's growing panic, he took a step closer and put his arm around her. 'We have to call the police.'

Shelly had been putting it off. Speaking to people in authority made this nightmare real. 'I know.' She sat on the edge of the sofa, as she clutched the phone to tap in the emergency number. Her gaze was fixed on the clock. Its ticking was too loud. The room was oppressive and closing in, threatening to suffocate her. She needed to get out and look for her son again but realised she

185

hadn't even put her slippers on when she got out of bed. It was the first time she'd been aware that the cold laminate floor sent ice through the soles of her feet to rise up her calves.

After Shelly explained the seriousness of the situation, the police said they'd send somebody. 'I need to get dressed.' Even to her, the voice that left her mouth sounded as though it belonged to a robot.

John had kissed her on the cheek as she'd left the room. He said he was going. He left while she was in the bathroom and she heard, the tires of his car screeching into the distance as he sped off. Go, Starsky, she thought. Her husband's determination to find their son was palpable, but so was the dread that threatened to consume them.

She had to sit and wait for the police and put the kettle on to make them coffee when they arrived. But after half an hour nobody came. Pauline was frantic and on her way over. And Brenda had called for their usual morning coffee, oblivious to everything that had happened the night before and this morning. She sat beside Shelly, holding her hand and muttering all the obvious platitudes. 'He's a sensible lad. He'll be fine, you'll see. He won't have gone far. He'll give up and come home when he's hungry.' Blah, blah, blah. Shelly tuned her out and gave in to the tears. And then she got angry.

'This is bloody ridiculous. Where are they?'

'They'll be here,' Brenda said.

The door opened and Shelly ran to see if it was Sammy, or the police, not that they'd let themselves in, but her mind was all over the place. It was Pauline, and she had to go through the story again. It irritated her when they should be out looking.

'I'm ringing the police again.'

The call connected, and Shelly struggled to hold back her tears as she yelled the situation to the operator, a different person to last time. 'Why aren't you here? You said you were coming and that's half an hour ago.'

'Calm down, madam. I've got your call logged on the system, and I can assure you we'll get officers out to you as soon as we can.'

'That's not good enough. My son has gone missing. He's severely autistic and vulnerable. Please. You have to help me find him.'

Minutes felt like hours as she listened to the operator's assurances. She was still on the phone and giving the woman hell when a knock at the door shattered the tension, making her jump in her seat.

She rushed to answer it, her trembling hand fumbled with the handle, and she was met by two female officers in crisp uniforms. Their expressions were etched with a sense of urgency as they introduced themselves.

'Mrs May? I'm Detective Inspector Brown. And this is PC Jackie Woods.' Her voice was firm, but there was empathy in her eyes as she spoke.

Shelly nodded, but couldn't trust her voice as she ushered them into the living room. The officers looked around, assessing the home situation, before focusing their attention on her.

'We've been informed that your son, Samuel, is missing,' DI Brown said.

With tears pouring down her cheeks, Shelly said, 'He's autistic, and he's never wandered off before. We don't know what to do.'

Detective Brown crouched in front of her and took her hands, and PC Woods sat in the seat opposite. Pauline offered them coffee and went to make it. Brenda said she'd give her a hand.

'We'll do everything in our power to find your son, Mrs May. But I need you to tell us everything about Sammy, any routines, any special places he might go. Every detail could make a difference.'

'Don't you people talk to each other?' Shelly was furious. They should be out there by now, not here going over old ground. 'I told the woman on the phone. He lost his dog in Heysham last night. He's gone to find it. But he can't cope with people or situations—or anything.'

'I understand that, Mrs May. And I promise you, every officer in the district has been given a description of Sammy. They are already looking for him. I need a more detailed description, and a recent photograph of him to scale up the search. We understand how vulnerable Sammy is.'

'I'm sorry. I just want to know that you're looking for him.'

'I assure you, we are. However, I'm not convinced that Sammy will be heading for Heysham. Our experience in these matters would indicate that he's probably less than half a mile from the house. I doubt he'll have gone far.'

'You underestimate my son. Sammy can't make a sandwich, or run his own bath, but you will never meet anybody more single-minded. His brain doesn't work like yours and mine. He'll get an idea in his head and make it happen. I promise you, he's gone to look for Carthenage.'

Detective Brown squeezed Shelly's cold hand and then got off her knees and sat beside her on the sofa, but she took her hand again. 'Let's work together. We might not understand Sammy, and that's where you come in to guide us with your expertise. Nobody knows your son like you do, we get that, but we are very experienced and good at what we do. We're going to find your son.'

'You promise?'

'No. We can't make promises but we'll do our best. We'll appoint a family liaison officer to be with you as much as you need so that we can get out there to look.'

'I'm sorry I shouted at you.'

Brown laughed. 'You shout as much as you want to. Now, tell me about this boy of yours.'

Shelly took a deep breath. She described Sammy, his routines, his favourite places, and the challenges he faced as somebody who was neuroatypical. The officers listened and only interrupted when they didn't understand something or needed clarification.

Shelly clung to the hope that the police would bring her son back safely, but the drama that had gripped her life intensified with every tick of that damn clock.

CHAPTER 27

That morning, Samuel May's eyes were sticky with rheum. They were heavy with the sedation that had pulled him into sleep against his will. He tried to make sense of his surroundings. The room was dark with the curtains drawn to keep out the morning light. The familiar objects took shape—his writing desk, the books alphabetically arranged on the shelf, and his carved elephants sitting by the window.

But Carthenage was missing. He was lost and Sammy ached to have his personal needs in their relationship met by the dog. He'd grown accustomed to a new routine that included him. Now that Carthenage was gone, his life was altered and he didn't like it.

The haze of sleep left him, and he remembered the freezing night before. 'It was a very bad night.' The memory made him shiver and he needed to find Carthenage. Samuel May would go and get Carthenage right now. With default focus, he got out of bed and moved with automotive precision. He was careful not to make a sound that could alert Shelly May.

He went into his wardrobe and drawers for clean clothes, his fingers selecting items by order of arrangement as per the day of the week. And then he calculated how cold he'd been the night before using the expected temperature for that time of year. He relived the bone-numbing wind and the way it made his lower back ache. He added his warm rambling clothes, sturdy walking boots, and his blue hat, scarf, and gloves for a Sunday—all chosen with the purpose of facing the unpredictable weather outside. It was only September, but after last night, Sammy knew the importance of staying warm.

His attention shifted to his belongings. His wallet, which held his emergency twenty-pound note, went into his left-hand pocket with a zip. Then he took it out again to check that his disabled person's rail card was in the see-through pocket. It was another necessity to complete his plan. Sammy was prepared for whatever he had to do.

He crept downstairs and picked up Carthenage's lead. The worn leather handle was a comforting weight in his hand. It was a link to his dog and Carthenage would see that he had it and come back. He grabbed the training whistle from beside the front door and put it around his neck. For a second he worried that it might tighten and choke him, but without Carthenage, Samuel May didn't mind if he went blue and died.

With his other pocket overflowing with dog treats, Sammy went to the door, being very quiet indeed. The house was still, and Carthenage was out there, somewhere around Heysham when he should have been jumping on Samuel May's bed. And Samuel May should have been shouting, 'Get down, Carthenage.'

He unlocked the door and stepped into the unknown, set on the blinkered tramlines of finding his dog.

He waited until he got around the corner away from the house before making a sound. Then, as he walked along the quiet streets on his way to the train station, he gave three sharp blasts on the whistle. Counted to five and did it again all the way to the station in case Carthenage had come back to Barrow. It didn't cross his mind that people in the surrounding houses might still be sleeping. His dog was lost. 'That was a very bad thing.' He spoke softly to himself, the words flowing in a stream of consciousness.

'Samuel May must find Carthenage. Samuel May and Carthenage live together at 57 Summerfield Lane, Barrow-in-Furness. Carthenage does not live in Heysham attached to Morecambe. It is too cold for Carthenage to live in Heysham attached to Morecambe.'

His fingers clutched the lead. It was his lifeline to Carthenage. He walked with his peculiar gait, his boots clicking on the pavement in accompaniment to his thoughts.

'Shelly May must not worry. Samuel May will find Carthenage May.'

The train station was a place of familiarity and trepidation. Sammy adjusted his scarf and checked to see that he had his rail card in his pocket. Samuel May knew trains. His special needs support worker had taken him on trains during their one-to-ones. It taught Samuel May how to be independent. And when he got really good at saying, 'A single ticket for the train to Ulverston, from Barrow-in-Furness,' she drove her silver car to meet him and Samuel May rode the train by himself.

'Get on the train. Go to Heysham. Carthenage is there, maybe. Samuel May will find him.'

At six o'clock, the platform was deserted, and the ticket office was closed. He knew that when it was closed you could still get on the train and buy a ticket. You got it from the man or lady—or transexual or non-binary person—who walked up and down the carriages saying, 'Tickets, please.' Sammy waited some more for a long time. The anticipation built in his chest and his eyes took to flicking around. He checked his wallet, ensuring the twenty-pound note was there and then he checked his rail card.

'Heysham, cliffs, water, Carthenage. Sammy's best friend.'

Sammy's voice was softer, a whisper of hope buffering against the uncertainties of his mission.

'Carthenage, Samuel May's coming.'

Confused and overwhelmed, he stood in front of the timetable board. His fingers traced the unfamiliar schedules without touching the glass. The letters and numbers on the notice were a jumble until his brain clicked in and they were clear to him. He memorised the complete timetable and knew the destinations and times of all the trains. And then he learned all the stations they stopped at.

A group of teenagers burst onto the platform, their laughter echoing through the station. They were loud and Sammy didn't like teenagers very much. His hands came up in front of his eyes and made butterflies. One of the boys nudged the one next to him and grinned. They shared sly glances.

'Look at him,' a girl sneered, nudging her friend with an elbow. 'He can't even figure out the timetable.'

'Samuel May knows all the timetable.' He reeled off the information he'd taken in and they roared with laughter.

'Hey, Jack. He's like Wikipedia. I bet he can even tell the time.'

'Tick, tock. Tick, tock. What time is it Mr Retard?' Jack said.

Sammy was still reciting the train times but changed subject like a locomotive when the tracks were switched.

'Samuel May is not a retard. This is a very politically incorrect thing to call Samuel May according to societal norms and guidelines.'

'What are you doing out of the mental home?'

'Samuel May has not come from a mental home. Samuel May lost his dog last night and must find him. Carthenage is Samuel May's dog. He is a German shepherd crossbreed.'

Jack grinned. 'I stand corrected, Samantha May. Hey, Jamie, didn't we see a German shepherd this morning? Where was it, now?'

Jamie gave Jack a knowing wink. 'No, we didn't see him this morning. It was late last night, remember? While we were on our trip, we saw him outside London Tower.'

'London Tower is in the City of London. Carthenage did not get lost in London. Carthenage got lost in Heysham attached to Morecambe, Lancashire. The boy called Jack Who-is-Very-Rude must be mistaken.'

'Yeah, that's right. He's gone to visit the King. Hang on, though, maybe it was Blackpool Tower, not London,' Jamie said.

'No, I'm sure it was London.'

Sammy felt very upset at the mention of London Tower. The thought of Carthenage being so far away sent a surge of fear through him. He turned to his tormentors, his voice trembling with anxiety.

'Carthenage must not be in London. London is two hundred and twenty-two miles from Barrow-in-Furness, Cumbria. That is a long way for Carthenage to walk. Carthenage must have very sore feet.' Desperation laced his words and the four kids laughed so hard that the girl nearly fell off the platform.

'Oh, yeah. He was barking at the King. I remember because he was wagging his tail and everything.'

'Carthenage wags his tail.'

'There you go then, that proves it. London.'

'Or Blackpool Tower?' Sammy said.

'Yeah or Blackpool Tower. Come to think of it, it wasn't London it was definitely up the tower, right at the very top. He was barking at the fishermen in their boats.'

Their laughter was harsh, and Sammy's face fell in confusion. He clutched the dog lead and checked the rail card in his pocket. As he opened his wallet the girl noticed the twenty-pound note.

'He's got a twenty in there,' she said.

'Lend us some money, mate.' Jack moved closer to Sammy and Sammy backed away. He heard a train coming down the track.

The cruel ruse left him torn between the hope of finding Carthenage and the fear of him being lost in a far-away city.

Jamie made a grab for Sammy's wallet as the train pulled in and the bully withdrew his hand fast when people crowded onto the platform. The doors slid open with a mechanical hiss. Sammy knew that every train from Platform A out of Barrow took him as far as Lancaster. He'd planned to take this train anyway, transferring to Morecambe at the end of the line.

With the memory of Carthenage's happy bark ringing in his ears, Sammy climbed onto the train with single-minded resolve. He checked the lead, railcard, and his money. The cruel kids watched, still laughing at their mean-spirited games. The girl spat at him through the closing doors, and Sammy was glad that it didn't reach him.

As he settled into a seat near the window, he couldn't escape their taunts. They tapped on the glass.

'Say hello to King Charles for me,' one of them jeered.

'And bring me a stick of Blackpool rock.'

Sammy's face reddened with humiliation, his fingers gripping the dog lead so tight that it dug into his palm. He realigned and focused on the journey, to block out their voices, but their laughter lingered over him and made him moan.

Sammy was glad that the train only stopped for a couple of minutes and then pulled out of the station. He recited the stops he would make and watched the familiar landscape pass by. The fields and towns blurred together as they took him closer to Carthenage.

The ticket collector came down the aisle, in her crisp and authoritative uniform. She stopped at Sammy's seat.

'A single child's ticket to London Euston, with a third off from my disabled person's railcard.'

'Twenty-seven pounds, please,' she said.

Sammy fumbled through his wallet. His face was blazing. He held up his twenty-pound note. Panic welled in him, and he could feel the ticket collector's gaze, waiting for him to produce the correct fare.

'Twenty-seven pounds, please.'

Sammy made his cow noise.

'Are you okay, love? Are you travelling alone?'

'Samuel May is not okay. Samuel May has lost Carthenage.'

The train and her stare were overwhelming, and he struggled to make sense of the situation.

In desperation, Sammy made a split-second decision. He handed the note to the ticket collector. His voice faltered as he said, 'A child's ticket to Blackpool.'

The ticket collector accepted the money and issued Sammy's ticket. 'Do you have somebody with you?'

'Samuel May is not with Shelly May. Samuel May has taken the train before. Samuel May is an independent individual with a disabled person's rail card and an eight-pound twenty-pence ticket to the station called Blackpool North.'

'Fair enough, young man.' She gave him a curious look but didn't say anything else, and moved on to the next passenger.

Sammy clutched the ticket and put it carefully inside his wallet with his change. He checked his rail card was still in the see-through pocket on the other side. His decision to find Carthenage settled heavily on him. The uncertainty of his limited funds led him to choose a different path. Samuel May didn't like changing course. If he didn't find Carthenage at Blackpool Tower, he would walk to London.

CHAPTER 28

It was late and there was little light over Heysham, but Carthenage was in a built-up area with street lighting, which wasn't as frightening as running in the dark. The night was cold and damp and the dog was terrified after falling into the docks. He was wary of everybody and everything as he searched for his family. His home was too far away.

His coat had been matted with silt and soaked from the experience. The dock workers had taken his collar off to rub him with a towel and when he'd run away it was still on the table. The dog had no identification and wasn't microchipped. He just wanted to find Sammy.

Carthenage had managed to escape from the hut at the docks. His frantic search led him through the streets of Heysham. Every corner was a potential hiding place for his humans.

Desperation coloured his pace as he sprinted down the unfamiliar roads. His paws splashed through puddles and his breath came in ragged gasps from exertion and anxiety. After running for several miles, tiredness got the better of him and his frenetic pace slowed to an aimless trot.

He was so dirty that he might be mistaken for a stray—but anybody could read his expression. He was a hangdog and miserable.

The clock on the dashboard read 10:38 p.m. when Maura, weary from a long day of work as a waitress, turned onto Heysham Road. She was crying. She'd cried a lot. She had to go home—there was nowhere else to be, but it held no joy for her. Her husband was there and she loved him, but the house was still empty.

The night held no promise of an unexpected encounter, and she was driving on autopilot and only paying scant attention to what she was doing.

A dishevelled dog ran into the middle of the road. Even in the dipped rays of her headlights, she could see that he was distressed. Maura slammed on her brakes. The car screamed in protest and she had to steer hard to avoid hitting the dog. The car was out of control and she swerved it as she brought the car to a stop without any damage. The dog was running. It moved onto the grass verge and set off at a gallop. The road would be busy in another half hour when the factory changed shift and all the taxis were out for the Saturday night pubs emptying. The poor animal would be killed.

She drove ahead of the dog and pulled up a hundred yards

in front of him. Opening her car door cautiously, her voice was gentle and soothing as she called out to him. 'Hey there, fella. Come on, it's all right. I've got something for you.'

The dog stopped and his ears flattened to his head. His tail was tucked between his legs. The instinct to flee was clear in his body language and she saw him gauging the gap to run clear of her and the car. He approached the woman's outstretched hand, the aroma of her chicken supper from the restaurant where she worked wafted in the air and she heard her stomach growl.

He whined as he came closer and took a piece of meat from her hand. Maura resigned herself to losing her supper and let him eat his fill. The dog was hungry, but as she ran her hand over his flank, she realised that although he had no collar, he wasn't starving.

He was resistant to getting into her car. But Maura's patience and kindness won him over, and with a nudge to encourage him, she persuaded him to jump into the warmth of her vehicle.

Her house, a large semi-detached 1960s build, sat at the other end of Heysham Road. She coaxed the dog out of the passenger seat and saw him eyeing freedom. His intentions were easy to read. Holding the ruff of his neck she got him out of the car and through her front door. 'I'm home,' she shouted. The warmth of her house was welcome, but coming home to Paul didn't make her happy the way it had less than two weeks ago.

The dog growled a warning as Paul appeared from the living room. 'What the hell?'

'He was in the road. I nearly ran him over.' She burst into tears and Paul wrapped his arms around her and held her close.

'I almost killed him. It was awful.'

'It's okay. He isn't hurt. I'll make you a brew and put your filthy friend in the kitchen, then you can tell me all about it over supper.'

She managed a snotty laugh. 'The dog ate it.'

'What? I've been looking forward to Bertie's chicken and chips all night. It was the only good thing about you going back to work so soon.' He laughed, but it wasn't his old laugh. He hunkered down in the hall.

'Wow, aren't you a good-looking boy? Come here, lad. Come on, I'm not going to hurt you.'

The dog dropped onto his belly and growled as he slithered commando style to Paul who kept his hand steady and his voice soft. As he petted the filthy dog he rolled onto his back and let Paul stroke him.

'We'll have to ring the kennels tomorrow. He's soaking and two of his pads are bleeding. Do you think it'll stress him out if I put him in the shower?'

'Yes. Don't, Paul. Let's just towel dry him and let him rest.'

They cleaned him up as much as they could and he looked a lot better so they took him to their living room. The dog was so exhausted that he fell into a deep sleep with his head on the man's lap until they moved and prepared for bedtime. The dog went to the front door and whined to get out.

'Have you put a notice on Facebook to find his owners?'

'Yes, a couple of people have responded saying that they saw him running on the road too, but they couldn't stop.'

Paul guided him to the back door to let him into their enclosed garden while he made a comfy bed in the kitchen for him. Maura donated a spare quilt that they only used when they had guests. She could buy a new one.

He howled all night.

The next morning, Maura O'Neil stirred in bed, her mind already heavy with the familiar weight of grief that had haunted her since the loss of her week-old first child. Every day was a struggle just to get out of bed, a painful necessity through the endless abyss of grief.

Today would be another battle, just like yesterday. Paul had already gone to work. He'd left a cup of tea beside the bed for her but it was cold. His grief cut Maura to the quick, and his pain added to hers. Maura didn't blame him for escaping the house and her blanket of depression.

She'd let the dog come up through the night and brought his quilt. She felt him lying beside her on the bed and remembered. His head rested on his paws and his three-quarters of the king-sized bed was well used. Like her, he'd had a restless night, and she didn't know which of them had kept the other awake. Having him here made it a single increment better than it was before and a bond had grown from their shared grief. The dog understood her loss.

Maura stroked his fur and took comfort from his presence. She had no choice and had to get up. But for the first time since Nuala's passing she wanted to. He was depending on her, even as a temporary measure, for his comfort. His sad eyes met hers, and she felt a kinship with him.

'I know, boy. It hurts doesn't it?'

The dog cocked his head and licked her hand. They were both missing somebody they loved.

Maura had a purpose and a task to complete. She had to make posters to put up, saying that she'd found the missing dog. It was a small thing, but it gave her focus.

She got out of bed and went downstairs. The dog followed, pushing ahead to stand at the front door whining to be let out. 'Come on, you sweet button, you can't go out there.' She went to the kitchen and made a fresh cup of tea and two slices of toast with jam. She offered some to try to get the dog away from the front door, but he wouldn't take it. He had an agenda. She called him away and put him in the back garden to do his business while she gathered supplies—paper, markers, and a photograph of the dog taken on her phone. She created posters, determined to do whatever she could to help him. Her pain wasn't going away, but he could go home if she found his owners. She put some music on while she created the posters and it calmed the dog. Maybe it had a semblance of familiarity for him, like being home.

Maura left her house, using one of Paul's belts to hold the dog. At first, he pulled and whined, but when he realised he couldn't escape, he settled down and walked nicely for her. She enjoyed the feel of the brisk morning wind, on her face. Yesterday was the first time she'd been out since losing Nuala. Her state of mind was ragged and she was hanging on by a thread.

Button trotted by her side and was distracted by the new smells and bustle of the town as they walked to Blanco's Pet Shop near the precinct. The daft mutt responded to the name and, as she had to call him something, it would do because he didn't belong to her. Giving him a name that didn't suit him was her way of stamping and sealing the fact that he'd leave her soon.

She bought essentials for him—dog food, a collar and lead, and whatever else he needed that she wasn't aware of until she looked for them. She was sad when Emilio told her that they would be closing the doors forever soon after forty-five years. Everything dies eventually. Her time with Button was limited, but the responsibility of his care had been forced on her.

There was only one partner in the business now. There used to be two. Too much sadness, she thought. Everywhere you look, somebody is hurting. She chose a bag of dog food with a higher protein percentage. She felt an attachment to the dog who was an unexpected source of comfort. She looked at a huge furry dog bed. Did he need one? He'd seemed content enough taking up all of their bed when he finally settled. She had to remind herself that he wasn't staying and walked away from the bed.

Button waited by her side. His tail wagged once when she returned his gaze, and again when the man offered him a treat. He sniffed but didn't take it. Muara saw his thought process as he whined and looked at the door. Maybe this man would let him go.

She couldn't stand the thought that Button was so sad. She'd told him she was going to help him find his loved ones and they had a silent understanding that transcended words. But Button was impatient. He was a dog with somewhere to be, and he made that very clear to Maura.

It had only been eight days for her. She still felt the impression of her little girl's tiny body in the crook of her arm. She smelled Nuala against her breast and, knowing that Button was as temporary as everything else, the pain hung over her until she had to push the thought away. For now, he was her friend, however reluctant on his part. They walked home together, with Maura carrying the bags of dog supplies and Button carrying his new ball. She laughed when he turned his head to face everybody they passed to show them.

Chapter 29

Button paced, matching the chaos in Maura. She'd offered food and soothed him, but nothing eased his need to be let out of the front door. His unhappiness was a mirror image of hers, and their losses made them damaged souls.

She couldn't tell him off for wanting to get out. She remembered how he'd responded to music earlier and settled for a while.

She took him into the nursery. It was Maura's torture chamber and she was pierced with sharp knives every time she opened the door—but she couldn't stay away. As much as it hurt, the intense pain of being there helped. The walls were papered with her dreams and she had memories of a child who never had the chance to sleep there. Nuala never came home from the hospital.

The room was decorated in peach and lemon. Delicate voile curtains billowed in the breeze flowing through the window, open a crack to keep it aired. A crib stood in the centre, its yellow quilting and bumpers plush and covered with decals of bunnies.

Maura settled into her rocking chair. Paul had bought it for her Birthday in poor condition and spent hours sanding and painting it. She'd made the cushions herself. It was where she'd feed Nuala when she came home.

Button lay at her feet with his ball between his paws. It was his and he wouldn't be parted from it. She understood his attachment to it and smiled. Maura cradled her daughter's teddy bear. Nuala was named after Paul's mother and her name was stitched into hours of work in a cross-stitch picture on the wall. It had kept Maura busy when she had back ache in the night and Nuala had kicked her, keeping her and Paul awake. She'd come in here to stitch and the empty cot was a happy gift waiting to be filled. It was still empty and the colours were cold—the warm yellow felt as cold as dark ocean blue. The room resonated with broken promises but a poignant frozen beauty, a sanctuary for a mother without her child.

She asked Alexa to select some sad music and it filled the room with soothing notes. Button relaxed, his energy easing as he curled at her feet.

Maura closed her eyes, rocking in the chair as she held the teddy close. The solidity of grief felt lighter, as she imagined her little girl in her arms again. In the company of the dog who had wandered into her life, and surrounded by the memories of a daughter who never came home, she found fragile solace. It was a respite from the sorrow engulfing her.

With the afternoon sun sending shadows across the bunnies on the wall, making them frolic, Maura and the dog slept, finding peace in their respective dreams.

When Paul came home that evening, Maura mustered the courage to broach an idea. She missed her child, and the pain that consumed her was unrelenting. Button had come into their lives on the day of Nuala's funeral. Maura had returned to work to regain some normality even though everybody told her it was too soon. 'Time is a great healer,' and all that bullshit. They spouted every tired platitude. Nothing was normal anymore.

Sitting in the living room, she looked at Paul. Keeping the raw emotion out of her voice, she gauged his mood. 'Do you think Nuala sent him for us?'

'What?' His incredulity made her nervous laugh bounce off the tension.

'Paul, I've been thinking about Button. I think our little girl sent him to us.'

'Honey, come on, now. I don't think that's the case. He's a lost pup that somebody is missing.'

'I know he's not ours, but maybe we could keep him. I miss Nuala so much, and she sent Button to us. I know she did. Open your heart and you'll feel it, too. He's special, Paul. The way he looks at me isn't like other dogs. What if Nuala is in there? I can't send her away.'

'You think our little girl's inside that dog?'

'No. I don't know. When you put it like that it sounds stupid. But is it so hard to believe? He came to us after laying Nuala to rest yesterday.'

Paul grabbed her hands and she watched him working on what he was going to say so that it didn't come out wrong. 'Darling. Another second and you said yourself, you would have hit him.'

'But I didn't. Don't you see. That was Nuala, too. She stopped me having an accident.'

Paul stroked the dog's head. He felt the pain of their shared loss and Maura knew she'd shut him out.

'Let's try and find his owner first. They must be missing him. We'll ring the vets again to see if anyone's reported him missing.'

'I've already done it,' she lied.

She was grateful for Paul's understanding. He hadn't said they couldn't keep him. They had a responsibility to try to reunite Button with his owner, but she had a glimmer of hope that he could stay with them. That night, Button was less agitated, and his restlessness diminished. He still went to the door, but not as often.

As they waited for news, Maura's conviction that he'd been sent to her by Nuala, as a guardian to help her heal, increased. In her most irrational moments, she thought Nuala's soul was inside the dog. She talked to Nuala and Button responded positively to what she was saying, proving her point.

That night the evening news was on. Paul went to make them a coffee as the anchor's voice filled the room with a report about a missing boy from Barrow taking the headline.

'In a developing story tonight, a vulnerable fifteen-year-old boy with autism has gone missing from Barrow-in-Furness. Due to his condition, his disappearance has raised concerns about his safety.'

The screen displayed a picture of the missing boy. His eyes held a sense of innocence, but the vulnerability inherent to his autism was apparent.

The anchor continued, 'The boy was last seen at his home in Barrow. Authorities do not believe foul play is suspected, and think he may have run away and could be heading towards the coastal town of Morecambe.'

Maura's heart sank as she listened. The mention of autism touched her. She understood the challenges faced by autistics and the need for routine and familiarity. The thought of a young boy, alone and vulnerable, hurt her. But only for a second. The next photograph showed the same boy with his arm around Button.

The anchor concluded the report with a plea for information. 'The family dog went missing on Heysham cliffs last night, and it's believed that Samuel is looking for his dog. Barrow police station is leading the search efforts, and authorities urge anyone who may have seen the boy, or has information about his whereabouts, to come forward.'

Maura looked at Button and knew where he belonged. The image of the missing disabled boy lingered in her mind. She knew the anguish of losing a loved one, and the thought of that family enduring a similar ordeal filled her with sympathy. She felt for them—but not enough. With guilt filling every nerve ending in her body, she changed the channel on the TV before Paul came back in.

She hoped the missing boy would be found safe and reunited with his family, but he wasn't taking her dog away. What began as a vague idea, had taken hold and with that awful decision to hide Button's whereabouts, an obsession consumed her.

'It's okay, Nuala. I understand.'

CHAPTER 30

It was ten in the morning when Sammy left the station and walked down Blackpool's bustling seafront. His senses were bombarded by the cacophony of sounds and sensations around him. His fear governed everything from his posture to the way he shuffled along the pavement. There was too much noise in his head. Everything bombarded him at once. People talked to him and he didn't like it. They had muffled voices that came down long distorting tunnels. He pushed them away and barged through without stopping. The sensory overload drove him into a single-minded headlong need to get where he wanted to be.

He was at a busy junction waiting for the man to turn green and somebody spoke to him again. People kept asking if he was all right.

'Where is Carthenage?' he asked. The light changed and the man hurried across without answering him. He hesitated too long and the light was red again. He wanted to run across the road in front of the cars and buses but knew he had to wait and it made him moan.

The dazzling array of lights was a torment. Neon signs, flashing billboards, and colourful decorations adorned the buildings, casting a mesmerizing glow to dance in front of his eyes and blur into a nightmare blaze of random colour. Fixating on the garish, swirling characters, the too-bright stalls with coloured bags of candy floss and rock, and people dressed in costumes handing out flyers, he hurried on. A girl tried to thrust a poster into his hand, shouting something about Tussauds at him, and his fingers came up to his face while he wailed in reply. His attention was drawn to each new display capturing his gaze but nothing made sense—the world was a nonrepresentational Pollock. The lights turned in a kaleidoscope of merging interchange, painting the world to perplex him.

The sounds of Blackpool were overwhelming. Laughter and talking from passersby, the distant roar of the ocean, car horns, and the blaring music from amusement arcades suffocated him. Sounds colliding with each other created a symphony of noise that Sammy couldn't decipher. Clutching his ears with his gloved hands, he filtered out the auditory assault as he pressed on.

The aroma of street food wafted through the air as he passed hot food stalls, tempting him with their array of scents. From candy floss to fried doughnuts, the smells beckoned him, making his stomach rumble with hunger. But even the scents from stands amplified like a noise in his head. The aromas blended and mingled, overwhelming him.

People's rapid footsteps were a steady rhythm on the bustling street. Everybody was in a hurry. Sammy mimicked them, making every step a deliberate effort to navigate the crowded holiday pavement. His woolly hat shielded his face from the glare of the streetlights and the too-bright sun. He pulled it low, giving him a small oasis of shadow in the midst of the overload. Clutching the lead made Carthenage a grounding force in the sensory whirl-wind.

Despite the overwhelming stimuli, Sammy's determination was unwavering. He was here to find his dog and return to the familiar comfort of their home. Sammy drew strength from his need and it helped him through the maelstrom of Blackpool's vibrant seafront.

He saw Blackpool Tower, its iconic presence brought famil-iarity to the madness. It was close. He kept walking but didn't seem to get any nearer. His frustration welled in a surge of tur-moil.

He tried to run but it was a never-ending obstacle course of people. They were oblivious and materialised in his path, obstructing his way and barging into him. Sammy shrank from the touch of people and couldn't stop his high-pitched don't-touch-me screams. It gained him more space on the pave-ment as people gave him a wide berth and stepped into the road rather than get too close as they passed him. Every person block-ing his progress increased his anxiety.

Reaching Carthenage outside the tower was an all-encom-passing obsession. His dog was waiting there, cold and fright-ened, looking for him. He couldn't be in London, it had to be here. Sammy felt it, and logic told him. Carthenage being lost here pushed him harder.

The promenade was an ocean of humanity. He hyperventi-lated, his breath coming in short bursts. 'Sit, Carthenage. Stay.

Samuel May is here.'

Sammy was shouting for Carthenage with more urgency. He blasted three toots on his whistle between yelling. He didn't notice people staring at him and pointing. Looking up, he couldn't see the top of the tower from the pavement. Its grandeur and stability were a contrast to the swirling torrents of worry inside him. He was consumed by his persistent fear.

A lady said, 'You look upset. Is there anything I can do to help you, sweetheart?' She extended her hand to Sammy, but he was too distraught to listen. His focus was tunnelled, and his frantic state left no room for outside interference.

She persisted. 'Are you here on your own? Is there somebody I can call for you? Can I call your mummy?' Her concern was greater than her sense of personal safety. Sammy was a storm of emotion, and the offer didn't register. He couldn't comprehend the kind intentions of a stranger in his frantic state. Overstimulated, he hit out to keep her away and she had to jump back, stumbling into a ticket tout. She shook her head at Sammy, muttering about people causing chaos in the town.

Sammy was desperate. His shouts for Carthenage were louder, and his whistle cut through the sea mist like the sharp tang of lemon through the surrounding clamour.

Cathenage wasn't waiting for him. 'Bad dog.' He wasn't there. It hit Sammy with a wave of despair. Despite his trauma, he felt his disposition collapsing into his small Samuel May persona, and his voice was monotone as he called for his dog. This tower was Babel.

He didn't know what to do. So he did what he always did, and retreated into his mind, taking comfort in the way other people took shelter from the rain. He sat for hours after memorising the numbers and time sequence of passing trams. Curling into his coat, he sat on a bench across the road from the tower all night.

The wind came in from the Irish Sea and bit him. Sammy was miserable. He fixated on a point directly outside the entrance to the tower and was too scared to let his eyes close in case he missed his dog. The solid darkness enveloped him. When early morning partygoers from the nightclub scene passed by, he shrank further inside his coat and tried to melt into the structure of the concrete bench. They didn't look at him. The night was too long and by first light, he was so cold that he couldn't move.

He exercised his muscles and went back to the building at the base of the tower. Gazing at the brick and steel structure, he hoped Carthenage would appear out of the early morning fog.

He was the only one there. Samuel May might be the last person in the world. He stood for a long time. The clock chimed six, then seven, then eight. Now there were people. Carthenage didn't come, but somebody else got too close, a council worker. Sammy stood like a mime statue sprayed gold—but his gilded lacquer was painted in confliction. Concerned for his well-being, the worker suggested calling the police to help him. The mention of the police sent Sammy into a state of agitation.

With anxiety surging, his inability to convey his feelings rose with his stress. Grabbing the whistle, he blew it as thoughts overwhelmed him.

The road sweeper understood. 'You must be cold, mate. Come on, let's get you somewhere warm.' He guided Sammy to an amusement arcade with a cafe inside further down the road. He encouraged him to have a cup of tea and something to eat, offering a semblance of Sammy's homeland routine. It was past breakfast time, and knowing it made him moan.

When it bombarded him, he focused on an arcade game. He watched the machine to shut everything else out, and drinking tea gave him a respite from the overwhelming world outside. The man told him to go home to his mum. 'That's the best course of action, son,' he said. 'I've got to get back to work, now. Will you be all right?'

'Samuel May likes tea, and needs another bacon sandwich.'

He stared at the machine. The world was too much. The man ordered a second bacon sandwich for Sammy and paid for the boy's breakfast before he left.

Sammy settled into the cafe, the warmth easing his discomfort. It was a long way to Buckingham Palace.

Chapter 31

Shelly sat in front of the TV. The lead story focused on the Morecambe area, but it wasn't about Sammy. The woman who reported Sammy's story the day before cut to an outside broadcast with a team in the field, and a male reporter in a rainproof jacket zipped up to his throat.

Shelly was biting her nails again, a habit she'd kicked as a teenager. Only finding out her son was dead could be worse than this. She'd seen mothers on the TV after losing their children—this was worse because Sammy had so many special needs. Not knowing if he was suffering was akin to finding out he was dead. Her pain was physical and the ache was permanent until Sammy came home.

The evening news continued, the screen transitioning to the main story about an incident unfolding behind the Ventura Caravan Park.

'In a troubling development, a teenage girl was brutally attacked earlier today in a lane behind a local holiday park. She was airlifted to Lancaster Royal Infirmary where she is in a coma and is said to be in a critical condition. Her parents are by her bedside, hoping for a full recovery, and the spokesperson from the hospital stated that Lindsey Morris is "poorly but stable." Authorities are calling for witnesses to come forward to assist with their investigation.'

The TV screen showed the caravan park, with rows of colourful vans nestled among lush greenery. But the tranquillity was shattered by the intrusion of people in white PPE suits and cordoned-off areas. To the best of anybody's knowledge, her Sammy was in the same town as the girl who had been raped and left for dead.

The anchor's voice held the relevant level of uncondescending sympathy and gravitas as he continued, 'The victim, Lindsey, sixteen, was reportedly assaulted in broad daylight while walking in the beauty spot favoured by joggers and dog walkers. Police are urging anyone who may have seen or heard anything suspicious to contact them on this number.'

The news report cut to the studio, where Sabrina Green, the six o'clock newsreader, delivered a story about Syria, and a brief update on Sammy's disappearance.

'In an ongoing investigation, a young boy with autism, has been missing for two days. Search efforts in the Morecambe area are intensifying, with police, helicopters, and lifeboats combing the region for any sign of the missing child.'

So that was it, then. Sammy had been relegated to the 'in other news' segment, the last slot of the programme. Until they found his body. Then it would be worth talking about, wouldn't it? Shelly bit her nails until they bled.

Maura and Paul were in their living room, and Paul squeezed Maura's hand. The news of the boy's disappearance touched them. They knew the anguish that came with losing a child.

'Despite the extensive search, no witnesses have come forward with information about Samuel May's whereabouts. The authorities are urging anyone who may have seen anything unusual, or has any knowledge about the young boy's disappearance to contact the police immediately.'

Every minute was important in these cases, and their thoughts were with the kid's family as they endured the agonizing wait for his return. Maura was sympathetic, but her thoughts were selfish. She tried everything she could think of to get Paul out of the room before a dog was mentioned. She was grateful that the media concern focused on the boy and the fact that he'd run away to look for his dog had sunk into the annuls of recent times.

The broadcast moved on to traffic and weather. Maura hoped the rape victim would get better and the lost boy would be found and reunited with his family.

She stroked the dog's head—her dog.

It was five nights since that awful Sunday when Carthenage disappeared. Shelly and John were being tested. Their lives were changed by Sammy's disappearance and the terror of not knowing if he was okay was hell.

John scoured the Morecambe area. He told her that every day, he talked to people and searched for signs of Sammy. Combing the streets, parks, and lanes, he called his boy's name until his voice was hoarse. Worry drew sad faces on the empty canvas of his white face, a reflection of the torment gripping his heart. He missed Carthenage, too, and Shelly saw him clinging to the hope that if he found the dog, Sammy wouldn't be far behind. But one night led to two, and his faith was as shattered as his body. He told Shelly that Carthenage was looking after Sammy to keep her hopes up—but he didn't believe it. When she heard about the girl who'd been attacked she went into full meltdown and was inconsolable.

Shelly was trapped in the suffocating confines of their home, her world reduced to anxious waiting by the phone and liaising with the police. She ached with an acuteness that only her son could fix. Her thoughts were consumed by his absence. She longed to hear his voice and experience the aloofness of his presence. She craved the joy that his safety would bring.

Despite their isolation during the crisis, the community rallied with unending support. Their gifts ranged from casseroles, left on the doorstep so as not to intrude on their anguish, to help from a local minibus company. They laid on buses to take parties of people searching around Morecambe and surrounding areas where Shelly said he'd be. Neighbours, and friends they didn't know they had, were there for them. Their empathy united everybody in the possibility of tragedy and it was a lifeline for the grieving parents. It could happen to any of their children.

Even with the outpouring of kindness, the emptiness didn't lift. The spare bedroom, now John's temporary space, was filled with his walking gear and although having him there made her uncomfortable—it brought a special kind of closeness. He was physically exhausted, as well as emotionally. Her emotional trauma was mental. She acted like Sammy and tortured herself with all the things that might have happened. They clung to memories of his quirks and unique view of the world.

John came back late that night and Shelly took his lasagne from the oven when his car pulled up. His eyes, reflecting the anguish that consumed him for the past five nights, blinked in the kitchen light. Sammy's disappearance aged them.

'That young girl died. She never woke up.'

Shelly covered her mouth in shock and started crying.

'Those poor parents. We should send flowers.'

'We don't know them.'

'We've both lost children in that town this week. Maybe the two things are linked.' She screamed, 'You need to speak to the police about it.'

'Sammy was looking for his dog and got lost. It's completely different.'

'So why is he still lost?'

She looked at him as he tucked into his food. He didn't have an answer and gave small grunts as he ate. He looked like Sammy and his noises didn't disgust her the way they used to. But her cervix didn't recognise the man who'd been the love of her life since they were teenagers. Until her son was found, he was just a house guest. She'd even put towels out, rather than letting him get them himself.

'No chocolate on the pillow?' John had said the first night.

Shelly heard him keeping the bitterness out of his voice. He'd added a laugh to full-stop it without criticising.

John was cold, tired, and famished. The simple act of sharing a meal might ease their suffering for as long as it took to eat it.

They talked over coffee at the kitchen table.

'I'm dying for a cigarette,' Shelly said.

'We haven't smoked for twenty years.'

'It never leaves you, does it? Like Sammy. He'll always live in the fabric of the house.'

'And he'll be back to make it untidy again any time now. We've got to be positive.'

'It's Wednesday. It's been six days, John. You ask any police officer what happens to the incident board after a kid's been missing longer than five days.' He didn't respond, but she told him the answer as though he had. 'They treat it as a homicide. They aren't looking for Sammy anymore. They're searching for a body.'

John's mobile rang, and he covered her hand to comfort her as he answered. His expression shifted from exhaustion to dread.

Marian's voice echoed through the phone. It began with a throwaway, 'Hi John, I hope you've found your son.' She didn't give him time to answer before her tone turned sharp and accusatory. Shelly overheard the conversation as she tactfully got up to clear their plates. Marian demanded that John drop everything to take her some baby formula. He moaned to Shelly that Marian had changed Daisy over to bottle feeding without discussing it with him.

Shelly had grinned, 'Hashtag my body, my choice.'

Marian was still shouting at him. She accused him of being neglectful to their daughter and an absent father. 'In case you've forgotten, you have two children, you know. And while I've managed to catch you for once, I need you to have Daisy tomorrow.'

'I can't. You know that.'

Shelly understood how torn John was. Sammy's disappearance stretched them to the limit, and the strain between John and Marian was added pressure. Her hand rested on his shoulder and she motioned for him to go.

John explained the relentless search for Sammy, and the depth of their despair, but Marian's anger was unyielding. Her accusations were a cruel judgment and reminder of Shelly and John's inadequacies as parents. Shelly had let John get lost to her, and now Sammy was gone too. They all suffered in their own way, even Marian. The guilt and helplessness stung.

Shelly saw John's exhaustion showing as sorrow overwhelmed him. The search and added strain of Marian's call pushed him to breaking point. Tears welled in his eyes, and he cried as he slumped in his chair.

Shelly moved closer, aching as she saw the depth of his pain. After the call, she put her arm around him and drew him to her, offering the little comfort she had to give.

'I can't bear this. We're only good when we're together. Please, give me another chance,' he said.

Had she given him the wrong idea as they clung together? She loved John as Sammy's father, and the thought of losing him was unbearable. Their grief brought them close again, and she longed for the comfort of the old days. It would be so easy.

She wrestled with painful memories of his infidelity. Betrayal tore their relationship apart, but it was frayed long before that. The affair was just the wound that breached her trust. She couldn't mend it and time couldn't move backwards to before the rot set in.

She thought about what she wanted to say and made sure the words came out without blame. 'I've forgiven you, and I see now that Marian wasn't all your fault. I'd pushed you away for years. I love you. You're the only man I've ever been with. But I can't forget what happened. I'm so sorry, but I don't see a way back for us.'

Sammy connected them, but the scars of their relationship were significant. In a tender moment, they clung to each other, looking for comfort in their sorrow. Facing the painful reality again, sometimes, things were just done.

Chapter 32

Gareth Holmes was forty-six and washed up. He sat alone in the corner of the gaudy cafe, his gaze fixed on the strange boy at the next table. Gareth fussed with his creased dark suit, but his briefcase was forgotten at his feet. He was in a maelstrom of despair as he thought about suicide and watched the boy.

Gareth had crumbled into broken shards of misery. The noise of the arcade spilling money into troughs for lucky winners irritated him. Yeah, enjoy your pile of two pence pieces, loser, he thought. But he was the loser, not the thrill-seekers with their holiday faces in place. The last of his money—ten thousand pounds—and the laptop in his briefcase, were the remnants of his fortune. Last week, he was a millionaire. Today he was a man on the run. He'd lost everything due to the second deadly sin. His dubious deals and shady business strategy led him into financial ruin. The luxury home, his thriving businesses, and the respect he'd commanded from his peers were gone.

He reflected on the reckless choices that brought him to this point. He'd chased wealth without heed of the consequences. And he'd betrayed his shareholder's trust and his ethics along the way.

Replaying the events leading to his fugitive status, and his desperate escape from London to avoid the clutches of the law depressed him. His suit was a symbol of his fallen stature, a relic from the life he could never return to. He'd taken a grotty flat in the backstreets of Blackpool until the heat died down.

Gareth couldn't stay in one place with the authorities on his tail. But for now, he was distracted by the strange innocence of the boy. His intense absorption of the mundane happenings around him was intriguing.

He'd contemplated his uncertain future, and Gareth wondered if there was any redemption. Ten thousand pounds was scant compared to his past riches, but it might be a starting point, the knife to cut through the rope around his neck. He wanted to make amends for his past and rebuild his life with humility. But, at heart, he was still a bad bastard.

He cottoned on to what the kid was doing, and for the time it took to drink that one cup of coffee, he was distracted from his troubles. Something stirred inside him. That second deadly sin was still with him. A new path solidified as a germinating idea. It was as risky as hell, but he wouldn't harm the boy. It was a chance for his phoenix to rise against the wreckage of his past.

The kid watched, staring blankly at the rows of bandits from the café section of the arcade. He had an intensity that manifested as an obsession. His repeated shout of 'Crash' made Gareth jump. He paid attention to what the kid was doing from behind the cover of his newspaper.

After the third shout, it dawned on Gareth that he was predicting when the machines would drop their jackpots. Fascination rose in him as he watched the ability.

A tram rumbled into view and pulled into the stop by the tower. Its number was 713. It hadn't reached the kid's line of vision yet, but lost in his own world, and sight unseen, he mumbled the number with uncanny precision. When the next one came along with the same result, Gareth blinked in disbelief, realising that the boy reeled off the sequence of trams as well.

The tram's balloon cars were numbered in the 700s and were a mundane aspect of the city's infrastructure. But in the boy's presence, Gareth saw them as a hidden code.

The strange kid muttered the numbers of every tram, just before they passed. His ability left Gareth perplexed. A gift shared is a profit made.

Gareth's troubles faded and he contemplated the extraordinary skills and how he could utilise them to his advantage. He didn't want to die. There were wonders yet to be discovered, even in unexpected places. 'Right time, right place, my boy,' he whispered.

Going to the kid's table a waitress frowned at the kid. She was irritated. 'You've been sitting here since we opened. Either buy something or move along.'

Gareth had been watching him for over an hour. He figured it was time to move out too.

The boy seemed unfazed and stood up to move away. His dishevelled appearance gave him the look of one of the many homeless people begging on the streets of Blackpool and as he looked around, he expressed agitation in his body language. But it didn't seem to be from being told to move on. What was this kid's gig? He was searching for something. Gareth wondered what his story was.

He followed him, maintaining a distance, and not wanting to draw attention. Wandering into a dark corner of the arcade, hidden from the bustling main area where the machines beckoned patrons with their flashing lights and chiming calls, the boy settled again.

His focus shifted from predicting the outcomes of the games to looking at the machines themselves. It was as though he had an intimate understanding of how they worked. He memorised the wheels and options. How else could he predict the outcome? Gareth sat away from him and the staff. He saw the boy predicting the outcome of every game in the arcade. When he said 'Crash,' one of them paid out big time. His corner was a theatre, and Gareth was the curious spectator. How did a young soul gain such insight into the mathematics of chance and probability?

He felt a dawning connection to the boy, two nobodies on the fringes of society, looking for something elusive. The arcade transformed from a distraction to a place of worship. His prayers had been answered.

Moving closer, he stood at the nearest bandit to the boy and fed a precious five-pound note in the slot. The greedy machine boomed to life with a performance of lights and sounds. The second deadly sin.

The kid was focused on his hands and sounded contemptuous when he muttered under his breath, 'No good.'

Gareth tried striking up a conversation as he played. He leaned towards him and said in his special friendly voice, 'That's a great trick, predicting the outcome of these machines. My name's Gareth. What's yours?'

The boy's response wasn't what he expected.

'Stranger danger. Stranger danger.' He kept saying the words on repeat and his voice was rising. Gareth looked around and was glad the man in the change booth was busy with a customer. Nobody was paying them any attention.

'Pack it in, kid. Are you trying to get me arrested?'

'Samuel May is not trying to get Gareth the Pervert arrested. Samuel May is trying to find his dog.'

'Woah, kid. I'm no pervert. Knock it off, yeah? I'm your friend.'

'Gareth the Pervert is not Samuel May's friend.'

'Sure I am. Just the other day I was saying to your dad what a great guy you are. In fact, I'm going to call you Sam.'

'Samuel May is not called Sam. Shelly May calls Samuel May Sammy.'

'I knew that. Sammy, it is, then.'

The boy didn't reply but seemed to be taking it in. Instead of engaging in a natural conversation, the boy fixated on a topic of his own. He kept going on about a dog not being at the tower. His words were disjointed and difficult to follow. Yeah, whatever.

Gareth couldn't make sense of it. This kid had some serious issues, and striking up a conversation wasn't as straightforward as he thought. But he felt empathy with the young boy, lost in his own world, surrounded by the flashing lights of the arcade machines.

Gareth changed tactics and promised to help him look for his missing dog. Whatever it took. He tried getting around to what he wanted in return, but the kid couldn't be swayed and had to search for his dog immediately.

'We can't go now. Heck, even dogs know the tower is closed for lunch between twelve and two. That part of town is shut,' he lied. 'The dog won't get near yet.'

'Samuel May can see the tower up the street and many people are walking around outside on the pavement.'

'That's the clearance process. Don't you worry about it, son. We'll find your dog, but you have to be patient. These things are done at the proper time for them to work.' The kid was pissing him off now and he wondered if the plan was too much trouble. He passed Sammy the *Financial Times*. 'It just so happens that I've got a little problem you can help me with. If I'm going to find your dog, one good turn deserves another, doesn't it? I've been trying to understand all these stupid figures all morning, but they beat me. Can you make sense of them?'

Without looking up from the newspaper, Sammy evaluated the stock tables and the last week's data. In less than a minute, he advised Gareth which company was likely to make a return that week. Gareth's hunch was paying off, this could mean big bucks. Sammy understood the financial markets.

Gareth had already done his research, and he'd come to the same conclusion. But he was intrigued by the boy's insights and wanted to know more.

Sammy was still talking. Once he started, Gareth couldn't shut the bastard up. 'There are no differentials taken into consideration for crop viability due to the weather conditions, or for any disturbance to delivery times due to the lorry driver's strike or the border controls.'

Gareth was eager to take from Sammy's unique perspective. The boy's words held an understanding that Gareth hadn't expected, and he wanted to hear more about the intricacies of his approach to the financial world.

'And you must not underestimate market volatility.' Sammy talked up a storm, his eyes never leaving the financial page.

Gareth nodded. 'You're absolutely right,' he agreed. 'Market volatility is a game-changer. But speaking of games, have you heard of a company called SkyTech Enterprises?'

'SkyTech Enterprises Limited.' He adopted the voice of a news broadcaster. 'The financial world is sitting up and taking notice today. A brand new company called SkyTech Enterprises is ready to take the world by storm. They're gaining some serious momentum. Their stocks are rising, and they've secured a government contract for cutting-edge satellite technology. It's set to boost their revenue and produce an estimated ten thousand jobs in the UK alone.'

What the hell? Gareth was freaked out by the weird voice and mannerisms, but he was blown away by Sammy's knowledge. 'Exactly. Their stock has been on the rise for a few months, and I've been keeping an eye on it. Looks like we're on the same page.'

Sammy highlighted the finer details of market trends and investment strategies, going into television voices and reciting from memory what he'd seen in the media.

The noise of the machines faded into the background, and

they found solace in the world of numbers and speculation. But even though Gareth thought he had Sammy's attention he was still amazed every time he broke into the middle of a word to shout, 'Crash,' before a machine dropped.

The boy sounded as though he was reading from a textbook, but Gareth had stumbled on a gold mine of financial wisdom.

With the need for secrecy paramount, Gareth scanned the arcade and cafe to be sure nobody was watching them. He noted the positions of the security cameras. They were probably on camera right now, and there would be very few blind spots. But from their murky corner, they wouldn't be seen clearly, making them less conspicuous.

Gareth leaned closer, lowering his voice. 'We should go and find your dog, now. And can we agree on just Gareth? Adding that nasty word every time you say my name isn't good for my street cred, kid.'

Sammy's gaze rose but didn't meet his. He continued the story of Carthenage, every long word of it. Gareth was pragmatic about most things, and he could live with Just Gareth. It was an improvement. He listened until he could get a word in, but Sammy wouldn't be halted. The tale unfolded like a puzzle, with the boy's voice making him want to sleep.

Sammy explained how some boys had told him to go to Blackpool or London to search for Carthenage, and how he'd spent a cold night waiting by the tower, hoping for a sign of his pet. The desperation in Sammy's words was raw, even if he couldn't vocalise his torment the way other people did, and it tugged at Gareth's sympathy. They'd help each other, there was no harm in that. He'd be doing the kid a favour. And Gareth would do whatever he could to get the kid back home with his family. After he'd got what he wanted.

'We'll find him. I'm very good at finding lost dogs. I'll tell you what, you go to the tower now and I'll meet you outside in a few minutes. Make sure you wait for me because I know where Carthenage will be.' He excused himself on the pretext of needing to pee. They couldn't be seen leaving the arcade together. When he came out of the men's room, he checked to see that Sammy had left and then inserted a coin into one of the machines. Just an average Joe, doing his thing. In case they'd been linked, he needed to put distance between himself and the kid leaving the arcade.

When he met up with him, he was careful not to draw attention to their connection. He motioned for Sammy to keep walking, and tried not to look as though they were together. Gareth couldn't ignore the urgency of Sammy's quest, and if he found his damned dog it was a bonus and might keep him on side for what he needed. If he thought it was going to be a quick look around and then getting the kid out of sight, he was in for a shock. Sammy wouldn't let up and they were still there waiting for a non-existent dog two hours later. The boy was going to be difficult. Gareth wanted to get on with his business, but Sammy had to be handled with patience. He couldn't believe he was searching for a dog called Carthenage. What a stupid name.

CHAPTER 33

In areas where he was sure there was no CCTV, Gareth made a show of scanning the street. Calling the dog's name in a hopeful voice, they'd seem like any man and his son looking for their dog. Passersby had their own agenda—tourists mainly. They had no interest in him but he had to be careful. Silly errors got you caught.

The search was fruitless, and Gareth stopped Sammy with a thoughtful expression. He'd learned fast that putting his hand on him was a very bad move. 'I have an idea that might help us. I suggest we go to my place and use the internet to put an ad out. Maybe someone who has seen your dog will get in touch. Blackpool has a lost and found pets group.' He saw Sammy's doubtful look and watched his hand come up to do that weird thing in front of his face. 'We can put some out for London, too, if you like. Kill two birds with one stone.'

'Samuel May will not kill birds.'

'No, kid. It's an expression. It means—never mind.'

Sammy made the oddest damned noise that sounded like a harpooned seal. 'Samuel May knows. Samuel May was making a joke.'

The kid was laughing. Hell, he was super creepy. Sammy had obviously been through some stuff, and trusting a stranger couldn't be an easy decision.

'I bet you like cheeseburgers.' He heard the wheedling note in his voice and dialled down the desperation a notch. He backed off, giving him time. You didn't run multi-million-pound companies successfully without being able to read a situation. Engaging Sammy in conversation, and assuring him of his intent to find the dog helped. They stopped for burgers on the way back. Every step brought them closer to Gareth's flat and further away from curious eyes.

Building trust and offering comfort was the way forward. He explained a fabricated version of his experience with some loss and regret thrown into the mix. Emphasising the importance of hope, and relating it to finding the dog, stopped the boy in his diatribe, which was a result in itself. Sammy gave him a headache. He promised to keep him safe and do everything they could to find Carthenage.

'Okay,' Sammy said. 'Let's go to Just Gareth's house and find Carthenage by using the internet.'

At his unkempt flat, Gareth hoped the kid wouldn't freak out and start screaming. They'd had enough of that malarkey when Gareth had made the mistake of touching his arm to guide him across the road. The bloody kid damn near got them both run over.

The place brought home the turmoil in his life. He was used to private beaches and villas with pools. This shithole had frayed curtains that covered grimy windows. Faded wallpaper peeled away in the corners and was a throwback to the 1980s. The furniture was mismatched and worn.

Going to the cramped kitchenette, Gareth made them a cup of tea. He handed Sammy his cheeseburger in a polystyrene container. That was wrong. But the idiot didn't say so, he just wailed like a bloody police siren. Gareth had to work out his weirdness because he sure as hell wasn't talking. He put the burger on a plate and emptied a packet of crisps onto the side.

Wrong again.

Sammy's eyes were wide. The state of his distress was written all over his face. The crisps touching his burger and a tiny chip on the rim of the cup sent him into a meltdown.

'Come on, Samuel. Work with me here, lad.'

Sammy punched himself in the face, startling Gareth and making him take a step away. His nose burst like a frigging dam and he ran to get him a tea towel. That wasn't right either. He had some kind of sensory sensitivity, or an aversion to textures, or was used to living in luxury like Gareth. Whatever. He liked things done to his standards, and Gareth had to guess what those were. He separated the crisps from the food and replaced the cup with an unchipped one.

'Shut up, Sammy. You'll have the neighbours banging the door down, and then the police will come, and we'll never find your dog.'

Sammy shut up as if a switch had been flicked.

'I'm sorry, Sammy.' Gareth tried calming him. 'It's all right. We can fix this. Let's make sure it's just the way you like it.'

Sammy picked around in his food but didn't eat much, and Gareth felt a twinge of concern. The boy was famished, and Gareth suspected he hadn't eaten much for days.

Sammy finished eating, and Gareth turned on his laptop, loading the latest stock figures for them to study. He was eager to delve into their financial discussion and discover what Sammy was really capable of.

Sammy had other priorities. Pushing his chair back, he insisted they put the ad online.

'We'll do that next, but come and look at this. It's fascinating. You'll get a buzz out of it.'

'Just Gareth needs to post the ad for Missing Carthenage right now.' He charged up his wailing, but quietly—a threat.

'Okay, you win. I'll help you with that, but then we get back to studying the market. Yes?' Gareth got the message and gave in and they put an advert online.

Interacting with him took more patience than Gareth had. Sammy's ability to analyse and process information was remarkable, but the method of conveying his thoughts took time.

As Sammy shared his ideas, Gareth chipped in with his. Sammy's approach to the world of finance was different to other people's because, where they saw profit and loss, he manipulated numbers and variables. Gareth was fascinated by the depth of his talent.

Collaborating, they isolated five companies that looked promising for fast-return investment. Gareth was pleased with their progress in identifying potential opportunities, but he had another idea that had been brewing in his mind. Before leaving

London, he'd bought some insider information. And it didn't come cheap. He'd received a tip from a contact in the Exchange about a company ready to float a consignment of shares. The name of the company was GroGen Innovations.

Gareth explained the situation to Sammy, detailing the pros and cons of investing in them. He spoke with confidence, drawing on his experience in business.

'GroGen Innovations is in the biotech sector. They've just gone public, and there's a buzz surrounding their groundbreaking research in genetic growth. It's a blossoming industry, and early investors can see substantial returns. However, it's a new company with no track record, so they're a gamble,' Gareth said.

Absorbing the information, Sammy shook his head. 'Gambling is very bad. The bookmaker wins every time.'

Gareth ignored him and continued, 'I have a contact who can get us more insider trading for GroGen Innovations. We can invest ten grand, but we need to consider fees and the potential timeline for returns. What do you think?'

'Just Gareth could expect a return, after fees, of 53.6 per cent over three months.'

Too little, too long. He had to invest, get in, watch them sky-rocket and get out again, fast. Three months didn't work. Insider trading was a sensitive area legally—in that it wasn't legal. He'd have to be discreet. Withdrawing funds was okay, he could take a smaller return to get out fast and reinvest, but following the right channels and avoiding red flags was a minefield. He couldn't wait for small or slow dividends. He needed a lot of money. Now. When an evil thought crossed his mind, he pushed it away in disgust. It came back, spitting venom. How much would the kid's family pay to get him back? He poured accelerant on the idea—and burned it.

The allure of potential return was tempting, but he needed a faster close. Proceeding with caution, and keeping in mind the risks, against the rewards of investing in GroGen Innovations, meant that it was still on the stove and heating up. He leaned back in his chair, considering other options.

Sammy went into a new voice. This one was female, but Gareth had stopped freaking out by them. 'For faster and potentially higher returns, there are a few things you can explore. However, investors beware, because they come with increased risks. The higher the reward, the greater the risk.'

'Hit me with it, Samuel. I'm all ears.'

His voice changed. He was a young go-getter, fast and frenetic, as though he was operating on the stock exchange floor. 'Day Trading's the way to go, folks. Prices are good. Time is limited. Forty-five, Seventy-nine. Eighty-Seven. We buy and sell stocks within the same trading day. I offer fast returns, but it's frenetic and volatile. Be well-informed and prepared for potential losses, traders. Make your deposit and I'll open my bag of tricks. Let's go.'

'I've always been wary of day trading. But you could be right. I think that's the one.' His palms were sweaty as he made the decision. 'We'll do it.'

Sammy was still talking. New voice. 'Leverage is another form of trading. It involves borrowing funds to increase the size of your investment. While it can amplify gains, it can also magnify losses.'

'That's a little tricky in my present predicament, young man.'

'Go for options trading. We've got the best deals for you. Speculate on the price movements of a stock without owning it. It provides a quick return, but it's complex and comes with a steep learning curve.'

'Too risky.' Gareth emphasised the need for consideration. 'Any strategy is a gamble. There's no surefire way to achieve high returns fast without taking risks. But you are our ace in the hole, Sammy.'

His money could take different paths depending on the choices he made. 'Let's do it. Day trading is the way to go. I'll open an account, deposit my money and in the morning, after sleeping on it to be sure, I'm putting the full ten grand on GroGen. In at opening, and out by the close of play. What am I looking at, Samuel?'

'Just Gareth is looking at Samuel May.'

'Jesus, Christ, save me from imbeciles. I mean, what comeback can I expect on a day trading return?'

'It's a high-risk variable. If trading flies and stocks spike, it may make an increase of three hundred per cent. If they crash, Just Gareth will be very sad and lose his ten thousand pounds.'

'Tomorrow is going to be a good day, Samuel May.'

'And we will find Carthenage.'

'We will, indeed.'

Sammy put his coat on.

'Hang on there, Samuel. Where are you going?'

'Samuel May is going to Blackpool Tower to look for

Carthenage. And then Samuel May is going to London.'

CHAPTER 34

Maura walked through town and the morning drizzle threw a coppery tarnish on the old and weather-worn shops that had seen better days. Button was at her side, her mystery saviour from the streets. He was a beloved reminder of her daughter. They belonged together.

The town was active, as shopkeepers served customers, and the aroma of pastries invaded the street from a nearby bakery. Maura wandered around the shops, her morning unfolding in a two-hour escape from grief.

She couldn't go into the enclosed shops because she had the dog with her, something she hadn't considered, so she went to the open-air market to browse the stalls. She explored the boutique and speciality stands and stopped to buy an adorable pink baby-grow. *Mummy's Little Angel.* She told the stallholder that the little one was at home with Daddy and this was her first time out on her own since Nuala was born. Button trotted beside her, taking stranger-stroking as his right when it came. His presence was a comfort and he plugged part of the gaping hole in Maura's wellbeing. Passersby smiled at the dog and his owner, enjoying their time together. When she talked to the pet stall holder, she created a story about getting Button when he was a puppy.

She was steeped in depression, but the dog was a responsibility, taking her from the agony, and her life was better for him being with her. She cherished her morning, knowing that the bond between them was permanent and special.

But she forgot about Button, and her heart broke as she neared a pram and saw the distressed baby inside. The child couldn't have been more than a couple of months old, and its cries were heart-wrenching. The mother was agitated and snapped at the baby to be quiet.

Concerned for its wellbeing, Maura couldn't believe her eyes as the mother parked the pram outside the large delicatessen and disappeared into the shop, leaving the baby alone.

Maura didn't think. She had to do something. She went to the pram and tried to comfort the crying baby. She cooed soothing words and offered a gentle touch. The child needed its mother and its distress was increasing. She looked in the shop and saw the woman had her back to the baby. She had sausage rolls in her hand and was joining the queue. Maura couldn't believe she'd ignored her baby. The woman was low-grade, too young for motherhood, and plain heartless.

As she waited for her to come out, Maura ached because of the infant's distress, and she wondered about the circumstances that led to this situation. She built a story in her head of a young woman alone and at the end of her endurance. She imagined what the baby might have been born into, a cheap town flat, filthy and stinking. The mother shouldn't have left her child, but

Maura wanted to help.

She focused on keeping the baby safe. She couldn't bear seeing the child in distress. Her breasts ached and filled with milk in an emotional response to a baby in need of its mother. Two weeks after her child's birth, she was still distraught. The pain sometimes eased for a while, but it never went away. She'd refused a course of treatment to dry up her milk. Her baby was gone and the doctors wanted to take her milk, too. It was the last link she had to being a mother. Her freezer was full of expressed breast milk. She was a mum. It wasn't a figment of her imagination. Too briefly, she'd known the joy of motherhood.

Without thinking, she released the brake, to rock the pram. She talked to the baby in hushed, soothing tones, her voice gentle.

Maura intended to stay until the woman returned. She rocked it a few inches to lull the baby to sleep. But, as she talked to her little girl, she unconsciously took a few more steps forward, and then a few more.

The baby's cries stopped as the soothing rhythm of movement and Maura's soft words brought a sense of calm. The mother was nowhere in sight, and Maura was going to fix this.

She couldn't leave her baby unattended, so she walked with the pram. A mother and her sleeping child, the most natural thing in the world. She had the gift. The baby gave a couple of hitching sobs that tore into Maura's soul, and then she quieted. A few more steps and her eyes had closed and she fell asleep. Just as Maura intended.

As the shop disappeared, and she walked around the first corner—and then another and a third to lose herself in the backstreets of Morecambe. She was so forgetful, and couldn't believe she'd left the house without her privacy blanket to use for feeding her baby.

And Nuala's changing bag—she'd forgotten that, too.

She was a new mum, so it was understandable that she'd forget things.

Button started barking. He'd wake the baby. It was as though the dog sensed something was wrong—maybe he was jealous of the baby after being her only child for two years. He was barking and jumping around, drawing the attention of other pedestrians. Maura realised the situation was too dangerous and chaotic. She struggled to control the large dog and the pram. Button was causing a scene and when he pulled, the pram leaned onto two wheels and almost tipped over. She shouted at him to behave and felt her anxiety rising. They had to get home, Nuala was overdue a feed.

She steadied her nerves, and with a calm thought process, she bent down and released Carthenage from his lead. The dog was free and bounded away. He sprang forward and ran into the road, where a car screeched to a stop, its brakes squealing.

Maura didn't think about what she was doing. If she'd tried to analyse her mindset, she might have said that she thought Button would trot beside the pram. Or maybe she just didn't care. The dog had ceased to exist and was a nuisance. She was talking to her sleeping baby in the pram, trying to maintain some serenity in the commotion. She was scared and anxious, but she was also euphoric and filled with joy.

But the attention they'd drawn couldn't be dismissed. The

unexpected outing made her day extraordinary, and she was determined to see it through with care and responsibility.

As Button ran off, his barks faded into the distance, Maura should have found him, but she couldn't leave Nuala unattended. No mother would do that. She made the difficult decision to just get home and hopefully, he would turn up of his own accord. A minute later, she'd forgotten about the dog, as though he was never there.

She pushed the pram through the streets. She needed to feed and change her baby. She hummed as she walked and looked forward to bath time.

She noticed a dirty smear on Nuala's cheek. 'Who's my dirty baby?' She reached into the bag that swung on the pram's handle for a packet of wipes. As she groped around for them, she pulled out a bunch of keys. She must have picked them up by mistake. No matter. She put them on a garden wall and wiped Nuala's cheek. Somebody would find them.

The trek back seemed longer, and Maura couldn't shake a silly feeling of unease. There was nothing to worry about. She'd see to everything that needed to be done and would still have the house in order and a meal on the table when Paul came home.

CHAPTER 35

She was relieved when she wheeled the pram into the hall and closed the door on the world. How on earth had it got so dirty? This wouldn't do. She had so many tasks to complete that afternoon and now she had to clean the pram until it was gleaming again. She looked at the lead still wrapped around her hand and she hung it on a hook by the door.

'Button, we're home,' she called.

She'd stayed out too long that morning and it had caused her blood pressure to rise. Everything had to be perfect for Paul coming home. Maybe she'd take just one of the anti-depressants in the bathroom cabinet. She'd been prescribed them, but couldn't remember what for.

With the hungry and filthy baby to see to, she set to work. She didn't understand how Nuala had got so grimy. She took her from the pram and the baby grizzled at being woken. She needed to be fed and broke into wails, but Maura couldn't stand seeing her in that state. She stripped Nuala of her clothes and was horrified to see the angry nappy rash. She breathed, telling herself she was a good mother and all babies got it. She'd sort it out after the bath. With the child in her arms, she ran to the nursery and grabbed a sheet from the bassinet to wrap her in so she wouldn't get cold. She was charging around to make things right. The baby was screaming. She had to slow down, this wasn't good for Nuala, but she needed to clean up the mess before she put her baby on her breast. She ran to the kitchen for a bin liner. It was awkward with only one free hand. She put the sodden nappy and all the baby's clothes and pram linen into it. Then she took the bag out and hid it behind the shed. 'There, precious. We're better now. Let's get you sorted out.'

In her beautiful, well-appointed nursery, every detail had been thought out to create a serene and inviting space. The soft, pastel-coloured walls of the nursery gave a feeling of love and tranquillity. Billowing curtains cooled the room and she turned on the projector to cast gentle pictures. They danced across the ceiling. The room was brought to life with charming stuffed animals, a crib with delicate quilts and buffers, and a comfortable rocking chair where Maura could sit and cradle her baby. She hoped she had enough milk, and then admonished herself. Of course, she had. Why wouldn't she?

Maura put Nuala on her breast. The baby pulled at her, and although it was painful, she had never felt such peace or contentment. The sound of her child feeding was the sweetest thing she'd heard and she complemented it by telling Alexa to play Nuala's playlist. Maura relaxed into the moment she'd spent the last nine months dreaming about. After feeding, the baby slept on her chest and all the urgency to get things done left. She had nothing to do except look after her beautiful daughter.

She let the baby sleep for an hour and then woke her gently. She unwrapped Nuala from the brushed cotton sheet, taking care to make the process as gentle as possible. She prepared a warm bath in the baby tub and tested the water with her elbow to check it was the right temperature. As she bathed the baby, she whispered sweet words and hummed a lullaby, and like every bath time before this one, she created a joyful memory. Nuala's eyes were as wide as saucers and she stared at Mummy, taking everything in and studying her.

Wrapping Nuala in a soft towel, she held the child close, letting the baby feel the security of her love. She put cream on Nuala's rash and took her time deciding which of the beautiful dresses she would put her in ready to see Daddy. The baby's cries turned into contented coos as she was dressed, warm and cuddled. She took photos on her phone and made a video which she was proud to post on TikTok.

Maura marvelled at the simplicity and beauty of the moment. The nursery was a haven of peace, a place where the cares of the world faded away. She would die for her child.

As the baby drifted off to sleep, Maura rocked her, cherishing the afternoon. In the nursery's tranquil ambience, surrounded by the innocence of her baby's presence, Maura remembered hearing stories about all the women who had lost their children and she couldn't bear it. She couldn't imagine the pain of ever losing Nuala.

When Paul was due home from work, she put the sleeping infant into her cot and turned on the baby monitor.

She moved the pram out of the hall so Paul wouldn't trip over it and wheeled it into the dining room. 'Let's not look at that. Nuala needs a better one.' She shut the door and felt nervous waiting for her husband. She was anxious because she hadn't cleaned the pram and never got around to putting a wash on or his dinner. She hoped he wouldn't be annoyed.

Maura couldn't understand why she was apprehensive. Paul was the most understanding man in the world. He wouldn't mind that she hadn't finished her chores. She took another tablet, just to calm her nerves as she waited. Everything should be perfect, nothing less was acceptable.

Maura waited for him by the front door, her heart filled with a mix of joy and relief. She kissed him on the cheek and walked ahead to the kitchen. 'I'll get started on dinner,' she said.

'Are you okay? Do you need a hand?'

There was a crackle from the baby monitor and Paul looked confused. 'What's that? Is somebody upstairs?' he said.

The baby murmured in her sleep and Maura smiled at her husband. 'Shush,' she said with her finger to her lips. 'Don't wake the baby.'

She saw the pain on Paul's face as he ran out of the room. He flung the nursery door open and saw the child in the cot.

'Maura. My God, what have you done?' he said.

'Isn't she gorgeous?'

Their perfect moment was interrupted by knocking. The police were there and they burst through the door as Paul opened it. The first one flashed his warrant card and two others moved around Paul and barged through the rooms until they found the baby.

Maura was arrested. Confusion and disbelief washed over her as she was taken into custody. 'What are you doing?'

She was back in the nightmare again—but it was different this time. The weight of the situation wouldn't sink in and she couldn't make sense of anything.

'Don't hurt her,' Paul said.

He looked stunned. He said the emotional rollercoaster of his wife's mental health had left him utterly bewildered. He was talking about a dog. Maura told the officer they didn't have any pets. And then the police were talking about a stolen baby. It was too confusing. Maura laughed. This was ridiculous, and she'd wake up when Nuala needed to be fed again.

'This is a silly mistake, Paul. Look after Nuala until I get home.'

As the police put Maura in handcuffs, the beautiful nursery that had been filled with hope was a place of horror. Paul was emotional. He listened to the police officer's words and told them about his concern for Maura. 'I knew she wasn't coping, but I never expected this.'

'I know.' Maura was laughing. She looked younger and happy. 'Tell them to go away and I'll get our tea on while the baby's asleep.'

The police were understanding and kind. They led her away before the baby was taken out of the nursery to return to her mother.

They said Maura would be admitted to a mental health unit. She was lapsing into lucidity and then back to her fantasy. Under the unusual circumstances, Maura was deemed as no immediate threat and they understood that her crime wasn't intentional. She was taken straight to Dale View for assessment, and Paul was allowed to travel with her to keep her calm.

'The baby?' she asked.

'It's okay, darling. The baby's fine.'

'But she's due her feed. I need to feed her.'

'It's okay. She's being taken care of.'

CHAPTER 36

After crushing a couple of sleeping pills into Sammy's tea, Gareth watched the boy drink. He urged him to take it all and waited for the effects of the medication to take hold. He had to act quickly. Persuading him that staying in his spare room was preferable to sleeping on the pavement in front of the tower took time. He played on the sub-zero temperatures and succeeded. But it was hard work. He had to tell increasingly elaborate lies to keep Sammy settled. Gareth had asked about his home life, and it was obvious the kid wasn't used to being lied to. He was amazed that Sammy took onboard anything he said—as long as it was grounded in logic.

He thought about tying him to the bed and forcing him to stay, but the kid would have screamed the place down. Gareth opted for cunning and guile to persuade him. 'Sammy, Social Services are looking for you. It's crazy out there. You've been on the news and everything.' The lies came easily. 'They're on the streets in force.' Sammy panicked and tried to put his coat on. The drugs were doing their stuff and he missed the armhole.

'They want to put you in a home for people like you.' The kid was horrified, and that did the trick for a while. Gareth's voice was soothing. 'I know how much you want to find Carthenage, and I promise we'll look for him first thing in the morning. But for now, why don't you get some rest? You'll be better equipped to help your dog if you're well-rested and ready.'

With Sammy falling asleep, Gareth led him to the second bedroom and showed him the single bed. Now, it was easier than he expected. He assured Sammy they'd start their search early, and that gave the boy a sense of comfort as unconsciousness took him.

As Sammy drifted into sleep, Gareth felt guilty for resorting to low measures. He'd had a hell of a job calming the boy and had no choice but to drug him to make him stay the night. Time was running out, and he was driven by ambition and the belief that Sammy could lead him to something massive.

Gareth was aware that the decisions he'd made would have far-reaching consequences. The word kidnap insinuated itself into his brain and he pushed it away. He was helping a kid in trouble, and Sammy had gone to his flat willingly. Nobody could take him down for any wrongdoing.

He was impatient to get the investment in GroGen Innovations done and excited at the prospect of day trading. He had one day to rise valiant and make a fortune—or sink and drown. He felt lucky. The intel he'd gained through insider trading made it a healthy gamble. It held the promise of good returns, but it was just the beginning of what he could achieve with Sammy's financial insight. Keeping the boy with him long enough to make the withdrawal and reinvest was crucial. But the kid was a damn nightmare.

Sammy had him up at five the next morning. He wanted to go and look for his sodding dog. Gareth had to come up with something. 'While you were asleep, I spoke to the police about Carthenage. Don't worry I didn't mention you. Relax. The thing is, hundreds of people are looking for him and hundreds more looking for you. We have to stay in to keep you safe, and we need to be by the phone for when somebody rings with news about Carthenage.'

Sammy was too tech-savvy to fall for that, and he'd motioned to Gareth's mobile. 'Just Gareth will take his mobile phone with us to find Carthenage. Samuel May will wear a disguise of dark glasses and a hat.'

'No kid, you've been watching too many movies. You don't understand. The police said we have to stay here now. Don't forget all those social workers and do-gooders who are looking for you.'

Sammy screwed his face up and his hands made shapes in the air.

'And the police themselves. Don't forget them. You're a wanted man, Samuel May. They'll arrest you and throw you in jail for running away if they see you. Best to stay here today until the heat dies down. It's too dangerous out there. Somebody's going to find him, I can feel it. They'll ring and then we can get you back home.'

Sammy's gullibility tugged at Gareth's conscience, but he had to keep him in the flat. He'd tell him anything he had to. He'd give the kid a few quid to take home with him when the dealing was done.

Gareth persuaded Sammy to sit with him while he created a bank account in a fake name. The boy was still groggy from the effects of the sleeping pills and more compliant than the day before. It was a double-edged sword. He was easier to handle in the dopey state, but Gareth needed him razor-sharp.

Sammy sat by Gareth's side in front of the laptop. His trust in Gareth was growing, and it would be instrumental in carrying out their plan.

Gareth created the bank account with stolen information that he'd paid a fortune for. He was using the details of somebody who'd died in a car accident fifteen years earlier. His conscience bothered him again, but only until he looked around. He couldn't live in this hovel forever. Sometimes good people do bad things. Gareth tried to convince himself he was that good person backed into a corner, and failed. He knew the process. He'd been involved in various financial grey areas in the past—when his back was against other corners, or more often, when he'd been greedy. Creating the account with the ID he bought from the dark web came naturally. Feeling guilty about it, not so much.

Sammy watched him with curiosity and questioned him about the false name and driving licence. Gareth fobbed him off with a story about changing his name after working for MI6 for ten years. 'But I'm forbidden from talking about that.'

Sammy put his finger to his lips to show that he'd keep the secret agent's secret. His trust meant that he didn't question it, and that's how Gareth wanted him. The kid had more peculiarities than your average dingbat, but his intuition for the financial world was remarkable.

With the bank account set up, Gareth was ready for the next step. It would be tricky. 'I need to go to the bank to deposit the money we're going to invest. Listen to me, Sammy. This is important.'

Sammy didn't look at him.

'I'll be back before you know it. I need you to be very quiet and look after the place. There's some biscuits in the cupboard if you get peckish, and I'll bring something nice in for lunch.'

'Okay.'

'Keep the phone by you in case anybody rings about your dog.' Gareth didn't want to leave his phone with Sammy but checked it was locked before giving it to him. There was no way that even a savant could decode his password. That was something that only he and his god knew.

Sammy was still drowsy, but he nodded, and Gareth figured he understood. He left the flat and locked the door as quietly as he could so Sammy wouldn't realise he was a prisoner.

Gareth ran to the bank. It was a huge risk leaving the kid in the flat on his own. He'd chosen the place for its privacy, a two-bed above a boarded-up shop, but it wasn't soundproof. He was terrified the kid would play up and make a fuss while he was out. It felt like leaving a ticking bomb in a firework factory, but Sammy was all over the morning news—he'd seen the reports on his phone that morning. He couldn't let him out of the house. It was enough of a risk bringing him home the day before.

Gareth was anxious and sweating. Bloody kid. The teller in the bank looked at him—with suspicion? He was paranoid and jumping at shadows. A nervous sweat felt sticky on his back, and he made his deposit with a head full of Sammy and the possibility of being stopped. If his plan went well, he could ditch the kid after today and the future was bright.

When Gareth got back he expected carnage. The grotty flat he'd left behind had undergone a transformation that wasn't entirely good. The haphazard and unkempt space he'd left had been arranged to suit Sammy's needs. Sammy was doing Sudoku on Gareth's phone. How the hell?

Despite being asked not to move, he told Gareth what happened in his broken speech pattern. 'Samuel May needed to use the bathroom, but Samuel May couldn't use the bathroom because it was dirty filthy. Samuel May had to wipe the disgusting toilet seat.'

With his OCD in overdrive, he'd cleaned up to a degree. Everything was arranged to his liking, with things moved into two categories—the things Sammy used, and in a separate heaped pile, Gareth's. Kitchen utensils and bathroom products were heaped together and Sammy's pile contained all the soap and other essentials. Gareth was expected to buy more for his use.

The changes were odd, and the clutter was redirected to other places more agreeable to Sammy. The flat had a sense of Sammy's order. Gareth tried not to see the huge heap of items belonging to the flat mixed with rubbish and takeaway boxes that Sammy found offensive. Rather than moving things, and throwing the rubbish away, he'd piled everything into a heap in the corner. But it was better than before, he guessed, so he'd take it.

'This is different.' Gareth surveyed the changes. 'You've done a good job.'

Gareth understood that Sammy's actions were driven by a need for order and control, a symptom of the way his mind worked.

He wondered how Sammy's precise nature would factor into their decisions. Their temporary co-dependency needed Gareth's patience to work out the idiosyncrasies and how they complemented each other. One was a crook and the other was weird, the perfect combo. Gareth smiled at the way fate had gifted him.

It wasn't long before Sammy was back on the treadmill of agitation. He expressed his concern about his dog, but Gareth was busy working on their financial tasks. He focused on the urgency, and the need to act quickly, but he had to have Sammy's ability for their plan to work. Dealing with his meltdowns took patience that Gareth didn't have.

With his decision to make a day trader deal that morning, Gareth had to keep the momentum going. To be ready to trade again the next day, he needed Sammy's input for making decisions. And then there were the days to come. It was the first time he'd considered that maybe he could keep him longer. It was a mess, but it worked. Time was limited, and he had to make the most of every day that he could carry this off.

'Find Carthenage, now. Just Gareth.'

'Quit bitching. We'll find your dog later. But right now, we have an opportunity to make some significant gains in the stock market. It's important.'

'Carthenage is important.'

'I agree, but your ability to analyse financial data and provide

259

solutions is way beyond my experience. We can achieve remarkable things today.'

'We can find Carthenage. That is a remarkable thing.'

Gareth tried to make Sammy see the importance and the potential for substantial returns. He needed to get the most out of their trading, and he had to keep Sammy engaged. He didn't like it, but if that meant getting rough, he would.

He gave Sammy a snack to keep him quiet. Ideally, he should have been online for the Exchange opening. He went over the figures with Sammy to see if there had been any fluctuation overnight. The figures were improved. These babies were flying high. Gareth was nervous and the kid's noise, because his breakfast was late, made it worse. He had to stop himself from yelling and frightening him.

The deal went through like a dream, and when it was done, Gareth sat back and basked in his satisfaction. Now they watched—and waited. The stock market was a fast-paced world, and timing was everything. With Sammy's view and Gareth's financial acumen, the trade was well executed.

The hours passed and Gareth pacified Sammy by making internet posts about the dog. His anticipation and excitement grew as the afternoon stock increased in value. The performance fluctuated, and he monitored the numbers on the screen. The minutes felt like hours as they waited to see the outcome of their trade.

The kid had meltdowns all day and Gareth had to jump through hoops to keep him from going crazy in the flat. The door was locked on the inside.

At the close of play, the deal was complete, and the results were in. Gareth and Sammy watched the screen. The stock's performance moved in their favour. Christ, the gods loved Gareth and his gamble had paid off. He was overjoyed waiting for the final figures to be released. As he watched Sammy, a surge of irritation got to him and he wanted to hurt him to get a reaction. The boy just sat there, like a big lump of concrete. Didn't anything excite him?

With the success of their first deal, the sense of accomplishment was huge, and Gareth knew Sammy had the potential to lead him to massive success. But this one was only half down to them. They'd had help from the insider information. Tomorrow they were flying solo and he hoped the kid knew what he was doing, and this wasn't a fluke.

Gareth had to keep Sammy invested. He'd do whatever he had to. The promise of finding his dog was an important part of that. With reluctance, he agreed to go to the dog pound to see if Carthenage had been handed in. It was a downer he intended to swerve. He persuaded Sammy to stay at the flat, using a technique of bribes and lies. It had worked for him last time. He didn't offer his phone this time, and couldn't work out how Sammy had got in. Gareth left in the guise of going to the kennels after pandering to Sammy's peace of mind. He intended to bypass the pound and recover from Sammy with a few pints in a backstreet pub, but Sammy's insistence that he call ahead and make an appointment to see their three stray Alsatians left him with no choice but to follow through.

Still concerned about his dog, Sammy had driven Gareth to

distraction. 'Samuel May will come to the dog kennels to get Carthenage.'

Gareth played on the kid's hygiene phobia and told him how dirty it would be and that some of the kennels might have faeces on the floor. 'Sammy, I don't even want to go there myself, it's an awful place. Some of those animals will have diseases.'

'Just Gareth will bathe when he comes back with Carthenage.'

'You bet I will.'

'Just Gareth will bath Carthenage.'

That was enough for him to accept Gareth's proposal. Sammy trusted him to do his best to find Carthenage and bring him back, and Gareth knew he was a terrible person.

His late visit to the kennels was fruitless and as much of a waste of time as he'd expected. They'd told him they had three German shepherds and some other mixed breeds of similar appearance.

Carthenage wasn't there, or at least, Gareth didn't think it was. Who knew? He dreaded the repercussions of going back empty-handed. He listened at the door when he got back and it was quiet. What if the kid had one of his fits and died?

When Gareth went in, Sammy didn't acknowledge him. He didn't even turn around to see if he had the dog and waited for Gareth to stand in front of him. Sammy's reaction to the news was strange. He didn't show any emotion on the surface, but Gareth sensed the sadness in him.

'We will find Carthenage,' Sammy said.

'Yes, we will.'

Gareth wanted to keep Sammy with him as long as possible to maximize their trading but, that night, the boy was fractious.

The need to find his dog was paramount, and Gareth was frustrated by the urgency behind it. He considered using force to make Sammy comply again, but it was too risky.

Gareth and Sammy had a day far surpassing Gareth's expectations. They earned a profit of £20,546.00 on their initial investment after fees. The gains exceeded what Gareth anticipated, and he was delighted with the outcome.

With the substantial earnings in his online account and the necessary fees subtracted, he'd made a deposit of £30,500.00. The financial gamble they'd taken was showing real promise with the potential for more success the next day.

As the funds were deposited, Gareth stared at the balance on the screen. Over twenty grand in one day, it was phenomenal. But he couldn't let it go to his head, as fast as he'd come out on top today, he could lose everything tomorrow.

CHAPTER 37

Balancing his financial goals with Sammy's emotional needs was more challenging by the hour. Keeping Sammy committed to what Gareth needed from him while distracting the boy from his obsession with the dog had Gareth tearing his hair out. It was a pain in the arse that he could do without. Why couldn't the kid just be normal? But if he was, he wouldn't have the ability to understand the market the way he did.

Gareth paced his living room while the naked lightbulb cast shadows of monsters on the walls. His mind raced to come up with something to persuade Sammy to stay another night. Making a lot of money fast was his only goal and if there had to be sacrifices along the way, who was he to argue?

Sammy was getting worse. He had some weird tics and kept jerking his head around. When Gareth asked him about it, Sammy answered in a deadpan voice, 'Samuel May had a fit while Just Gareth was at the bank. Samuel May might have a fit now. Samuel May will lapse into a seizure on Just Gareth's floor and Samuel May will need Shelly May to stroke his forehead and say, "It's all right, Sammy. Relax." It's coming.'

Gareth freaked out.

He got within a second of shoving twenty quid into the boy's hand and telling him to go home. He wasn't this kid's carer, but he'd come too far to give up now.

Gareth calmed down. He went to Sammy, who was sitting on the sofa. 'Sammy, I know how much you want to find your dog, and I promise we'll search for him, but the stock market won't wait for us.'

Sammy moaned in his throat. It was louder.

'It's money, kid. Lots of money for you to take home and spend on women and booze. You'd like that wouldn't you?'

'No.'

'Money can buy anything you want. Even a new dog.'

Sammy lashed out with his fist and gave him a scathing look. Gareth felt like a five-year-old in front of the headmaster. 'Samuel May does not need a new dog. Samuel May needs Carthenage.'

'Keep your hands to yourself. Shut up and help me with this shit.'

Sammy's expression wavered, torn between finding his dog and being wary of Gareth's flare of temper.

'Samuel May must help people.'

'I'm people. Samuel May needs to help Gareth. Gareth's success needs you and me, buddy.'

'Just Gareth sounds stupid when he speaks in the third person. Just Gareth wants money. Samuel May wants Carthenage.'

'Okay. I've got a plan. You work well on logic and plans, right? We need to focus on trading, and then we can think about finding your stupid dog. It's a compromise that benefits us both.'

'Carthenage is not stupid. Just Gareth is—' Sammy lost the confidence to say more and tailed off into a mumble.

'What was that, Sammy?'

'Nothing. Carthenage will be very hungry. We need food for Carthenage.'

'And you'll have it. As much food as you like. But first, you have to look at these charts for me.'

Sammy looked doubtful and Gareth put the laptop on Sammy's knee, without giving him time to argue. He showed him the charts and numbers representing their financial portfolio. 'Look at this,' he said. 'This is the path to being rich again. With your insight, we can make a fortune.' That set Sammy off on another diatribe about the value of his dog over money. He started shaking and Gareth had to rescue the laptop before it hit the ground. Sammy lashed out trying to headbutt Gareth and was flailing his arms around with his teeth gnashing to bite him like a demented dog. Sammy stood up and Gareth grabbed him by his arms and forced him back into his seat. 'Do as I damn well tell you.'

It was a minor episode that never developed into a fit. Gareth got him to concentrate and outline a schedule that balanced their goals and gave them a structure to work to. Every time Sammy veered off on a tangent, Gareth had to drag him back. He was learning how to deal with him. 'We'll trade in the mornings. It's a plan that keeps us on track.'

'Samuel May is not here every day forever and a long time.'

'Every day until we catch your dog, then.' Gareth wrapped up his plea, 'You'll stay for another night, for both our sakes. It's going to be colder out there tonight. You don't want to be sleeping rough, kid.' Gareth made a show of picking his keys up from the mantelpiece and putting them in his jeans pocket. Sammy glared at him.

After making their final preparations online, the atmosphere in the flat changed. Sammy had been composed for a while but acted out again with growing signs of distress.

It seemed as though his mental health was crumbling. The boy's face contorted with anxiety and frustration, and he was trembling. The fit that he'd prophesied terrified Gareth. What if he died? It was bad enough worrying about kidnapping without adding manslaughter to his rap sheet—or murder. Sammy's hands were shaking violently, and his eyes darted around the room as if he was searching for something to hold onto.

Gareth panicked as Sammy's distress intensified. The boy's breathing was rapid and shallow, and he was muttering to himself in a fast, incomprehensible stream of words. His mind spiralled into chaos, and he was losing his grip on reality.

Gareth rushed to his side, putting a hand on his shoulder to provide some comfort. But the kid screamed like an air-raid siren. It sounded as if he was being murdered. In his panic, Gareth had forgotten about not touching him. He spoke in a soothing voice, trying to reach the boy and fighting his own overwhelming storm of emotions. He was ready to Top-Trump Sammy's fit with a full-on coronary.

'Take deep breaths, and don't piss yourself on my carpet.'

But Sammy's meltdown continued with his agitation growing. Gareth didn't know what to do. He considered calling an ambulance. Or a priest to exorcise the bastard. 'Jesus.'

He stayed with him, trying to give Sammy the reassurance he got from his mother. Their creepy partnership came with challenges, and Gareth was out of his depth. Only a desperate man would have the tenacity to see this through. It was this or a noose on the stairs, and for the time being, this was winning. Sammy had two fits that day and Gareth was hanging on by a thread. He asked about medication—did Sammy take any? But he drew a blank.

He'd seen that Sammy liked his food. He tried a new tack to pull him away from his anxiety and tics. Distraction had worked before. 'Sammy, You must be hungry by now.'

The change was instant, the boy stopped shaking to listen to him.

'You can choose anything you want but keep it under a fiver.'

Sammy was calm, and Gareth noticed that unless he was using his mind as a tool, such as working out the trams and bandits, he only focused on one thing at a time. He could go freaking ballistic, or he could think about what he wanted to eat, but he didn't seem able to do both. It was a valuable piece of information that Gareth could use.

Sammy considered his options. 'A quarter-pound cheeseburger, and chicken nuggets and fries, and chicken gravy, and garlic bread, and nachos—no jalapenos—and Ben & Jerry's Cookie Dough ice-cream, and a Mars bar and a bag of candy floss, and a tub of toffee popcorn.'

Gareth grinned. This kid was something else. 'Would your mother let you eat all that?'

'No.'

'What makes you think I will?'

'Just Gareth is a pushover.'

'Not this time, kid.'

Sammy sulked.

Gareth nodded. 'Chicken nuggets and fries it is. Do you want a drink?'

Sammy opened his mouth to speak and Gareth jumped in. 'A-ha. Just one. Don't go getting all smart-arse on me again.'

Sammy made his choice. 'Do you need anything else?'

Then his expression brightened when he had an idea. 'A jigsaw puzzle,' he said. 'Samuel May needs a thousand-piece jigsaw puzzle.'

Asda would be open and Gareth saw the wisdom in Sammy's choice. The method and structured nature of a jigsaw might keep him focused, and therefore calm. Unless he functioned like a toddler and had a two-minute attention span. It was a gamble Gareth was willing to take. Anything was worth a try. 'A thousand pieces. You don't mess around. I'll buy one while I'm out.'

He was disgruntled at the boy's lack of manners as Sammy stared at him.

'What do you say, Sammy?'

'Get ketchup.'

Gareth needed to get the hell out of the flat, it was suffocating him and he was on the point of losing it with the kid. With the plan in place, he hoped the gestures would buy him some peace to get them through to bedtime.

The decisions Gareth made by bringing the boy home were more complex than he planned for, but he was determined to get what he wanted. He locked the door on Sammy to keep him in.

He ran his errands and dreaded having to go back.

The puzzle was a stroke of genius, and Gareth patted himself on the back, even though it wasn't his idea. It was a distraction and the boy was keen to get stuck in. As Sammy delved into the intricacies of the thousand-piece jigsaw puzzle, the transformation in his demeanour was striking. It was a captivating collage of colours, shapes, and patterns, and its complexity required a methodical approach. He'd opted for the most difficult one on the shelf, and Gareth wouldn't have tried it. He figured Sammy would like the steam locomotive surrounded by a vibrant station—it had been that or a million baked beans.

The chipped Formica dining table was only just big enough and Sammy had it spread with puzzle pieces. His face showed no sign of concentration. His brow wasn't furrowed as he sorted through the pieces, examining them for corners and edges. He was deadpan.

Gareth turned the electric fire on to warm them as night crept in with her chill. Sammy didn't seem to notice either way. He immersed himself in the puzzle. The detonation of anxieties that troubled him earlier was replaced with purpose and control. Every time he fixed a piece, he gave a grunt of accomplishment and satisfaction, until Gareth wanted to smash his face in. Christ, the kid had some annoying habits. But it was a tiny victory for Sammy every time, and a shot of endorphins to the brain. Gareth had treated himself to a bottle of whiskey, and a couple of tots of that had the same effect.

Sammy's mind was channelled away from harping on about

his lost dog. The puzzle made him focus on a task of repetition. The room was filled with the rhythmic clicking of puzzle pieces coming together. Gareth was amazed that he seemed to have forgotten about the dog. For the rest of the evening, it was as though it had never been an issue.

Convincing him to leave the puzzle and go to bed was a delicate task and he had to avoid another meltdown. One more like before and he swore he'd knock seven kinds of shit out of the kid. As Gareth stood next to the table, he noticed that more than half of the jigsaw was complete, a testament to Sammy's focus and dexterity.

'Sammy,' Gareth broached the subject, 'It's time you got your head down. I need some sleep.'

Sammy looked up, his expression calm. He had adapted to a new routine, like turning the page in a book. It explained why the fifteen-year-old had shown no signs of being homesick or missing his parents, only the dog. One thing replaced the other. Parents to dog to the jigsaw. He adapted to structured activities as they were introduced. Gareth would buy every jigsaw in the shop if that's what it took.

'Just Gareth. Samuel May will go to bed now.'

Gareth was relieved by the sudden compliance. The kid was a full-time interactive experience.

With the decision made, Sammy's evening routine, built in just two nights, continued. Gareth prepared a cup of tea and added the sleeping pills, as he had the night before. The boy's acceptance was reassuring, and the pills served a purpose beyond their intended use. They were helping Sammy adapt to his new normal, giving him cushioning and routine in a world that was unpredictable.

In the quiet that evening, they'd found peace as they sat in silence. Gareth hoped they'd turned a corner, and his greed consumed him, flashing green— just as long as there were enough jigsaws in the world, he thought.

CHAPTER 38

The man ran along the deserted beach path. There were traces of dried blood staining his clothes and the sweat patches under his arms felt cold against his skin. If he didn't get away fast, somebody would see what he'd done.

As he sprinted around a bend in the path, he heard a noise. Somebody might have seen him. He panicked. But apart from a dog that looked terrified, he was standing alone on the bleak headland. The German shepherd was shivering with the cold and it was traumatised. Everything about it transmitted fear. Owen knew how it felt.

With his fight-or-flight instincts in overdrive, time was against him. The dog looked as lonely and scared as he felt. Owen didn't like people much—especially the ones at home. They were an alien species, but he loved animals. He hunkered down to make himself small and kept his voice soft. Offering a steady hand for the dog to sniff he bridged the physical and emotional gap between them to establish a level of trust.

The dog was wary but seemed to want human contact. The cold and cruel rainfall of earlier had taken its toll, and the dog's instinct for companionship outweighed its apprehension. He whimpered but didn't run. Owen managed to stroke him and the dog allowed it but was ready to flee. He kept petting him until he could get his arm around the dog to cuddle him. With his tail tucked between his legs, it dropped to the ground and rolled over, a sign of submission and a plea for kindness.

Owen got closer and knelt on the muddy path beside the dog. He understood the vulnerable creature's misery and kept talking to him. It had happened when he needed it to, and they'd met on the desolate headland for a reason. He'd done a terrible thing but could atone for it in part by helping the dog and currying some favour at home.

Their fates converged.

Owen Proctor led a double life. The weight of his secret dragged him down and it was straining the relationship with his wife. He thought he loved her before this, but maybe it was hatred all along. His mind was jumbled and it was difficult to tell them apart. Rachel was suspicious and had taken to nagging, asking probing questions, and putting herself in a bad position. Their love had fractured and it was pressure he could do without.

The thrill of his other life was intoxicating and he didn't want to resist it, even when he said he wouldn't do it again. He couldn't break free of it—or his family—and didn't know which mattered to him more. He knew he'd never stop.

He wasn't far from his car, and decided to take the dog home, thinking it might work as a goodwill gesture to appease Rachel. He had no qualms about taking somebody else's pet. They should have looked after it better. Letting it get in this state was neglectful. The way the dog looked at him told Owen how desperate it was, and he needed something to love that didn't ask questions. The kids were his, but they were hard work. Some said feral, which Owen thought was a stretch, but they weren't easy kids. Little bastards that he could live without if it came to it. He thought about striking out on his own. He could leave, just him and the dog. A new life on the road. He wouldn't do it. He had a job and responsibilities at home. It was a fantasy, but the dream kept him warm until he got to the car.

He held the dog by its collar and noticed that it looked new, a contrast in care to the bedraggled state of the animal. The dog belonged to somebody, but there was no identification tag, so they couldn't care that much about losing it.

Without a tag, the dog was fair game, and maybe a way to ease the rift in his marriage. If he saw anything advertising a missing dog in the area, he'd deal with it when it happened. He looked around to make sure nobody was in view. The last thing he needed was confrontation.

Owen got home by nine that night, and his timing couldn't have been worse. The family would still be awake, and there was no chance of slipping in unnoticed. He left the dog in the car for now—this needed the right approach—and he covered his stained hoodie with an overcoat he kept in the car. It was raining, so Rachel wouldn't make a thing about it.

He went in and was met with her attitude. 'Where the hell have you been?'

'Nowhere. And before you start your nagging, I'm going for a shower.'

She poked her finger at him in temper and should have known better. Owen fought the urge to bite it off. Another bitter argument for his welcome home. Same old story, same old song.

'Why didn't you come straight home from work?'

They were supposed to go to a friend's birthday party that night. And he'd wanted to. He was looking forward to it. With a few drinks and a smoochy dance with the missus, it would be a good night. Just what they needed. But it happened again, and he couldn't fight it. When it came, it took over him and even good stuff that he wanted to do went out of the window. Rachel moaned that she'd been calling him and had been ready since half past six.

'Right. Lay off, will you? Give me five minutes to get ready and we'll go.'

'It's too late now. The babysitter's already come, been paid and gone home.' He was in trouble and the argument would last all night. She looked pretty with her hair curly like that. But she wasn't letting this one go. He doubted make-up sex was on the cards.

It was now or never. 'I've got a surprise for you in the car,' he said.

'To hell with your surprises, and to hell with you. What is it? A bit of honesty for once?'

Owen sighed and went to get the dog. As he brought it into the house, their three children went wild. Their faces were crazed with joy and they fought each other to get in there first. Every ADHD tendency floating around in their precious bloodstreams came to the fore. At least Owen still knew how to make the rest of his family happy.

'A dog? Are you insane?' Rachel screamed.

He held his hands up to calm her. To his ears, he thought he was the voice of reason. It was that stroppy cow who was out of order and he fantasised about shutting her up. 'I found him on The Tops and thought we'd call him Cliff. Get it?'

The room was filled with a blaze of reactions. The children were overjoyed. Dad said they could keep the dog, but Rachel was stunned into disbelief. Her face said otherwise.

Their voices rose in anger and frustration and the dog cowered. The kids went into hyperdrive and the noise could split the eardrums of neighbours half a street away— and maybe the atom, too. They surrounded Cliff and mauled him with affection.

They all shouted at once, vying for the dog's attention, and overwhelmed it. Henry, the four-year-old, tried to climb on his back for a ride. Cliff was cornered and agitated, but the adults were too busy screaming at each other to notice. Surrounded and frightened, he growled at the boy and bared his teeth in a warning.

Rachel, already furious from the argument, reached her limit. She turned on Owen and her face was a grotesque mask of anger that the pretty curls couldn't soften. Even when she was prettied up, she was ugly. He didn't know why he'd married her.

'Get that dog out of my house.'

If this carried on, the police would be on the doorstep again. The nosy neighbours would have called them by now. He pulled the boy off Cliff's back. 'Pack it in, you lot. Give the dog some space. You're scaring him.' He looked at Rachel. 'I'll take him for a walk. Let's talk about this when I get back.'

'We'll talk about it now. That dog is dangerous. I want it out.'

'It's too late to take him anywhere now. Don't make hasty decisions, okay? He's soft. The kids were pulling him about. You'll see. Can we discuss this tomorrow when we've calmed down?'

'Fine, but it's sleeping in the shed and I want it gone as soon as the kids have gone to school. You can stay out there with it if you want, but I don't want to see either of you in the house.'

The kids went mad in protest. Two of them started crying and the oldest boy kicked his mother. 'I hate you. You won't let us have anything good. Tell her, Dad.'

'See what you've done?' Rachel said. She went into the living room and slammed the door.

'That's right. Walk away, bitch.' Owen shouted after her.

He took Cliff to the shed. He was seething after the argument and at the thought of settling the dog. He felt the badness welling up and swallowed it down. He found a musty old blanket and spread it on the floor for Cliff. 'It's just for one night, buddy. We'll figure this out tomorrow.'

He sat down and stroked the dog to settle him. The nocturnal creepy crawlies came out, and the shed's darkness was impenetrable. He played on his phone until it died, and then swore. He hadn't even had his supper and wondered how the party was going down. He heard his kids whining and bawling inside and was glad to be out of it. Maybe he could leave the dog here and go

278

out again without being noticed. He fought the urge. Too risky.

He had to come up with a plan to address Rachel's concerns about Cliff's behaviour. But the dog was scratching at the door. He couldn't leave him yet in case he started barking and set Rachel off again. He sat in the cold shed, frustrated, and worried about the future.

Chapter 39

The next morning, Owen was determined to convince Rachel to let Cliff stay. He approached her in the kitchen and put his arms around her as she was doing the washing up. She tutted and shrugged him off without saying good morning.

'I know you're worried about Cliff's behaviour, but we can work on training him. He's not a lost cause. The kids already love him, and I want him to stay.'

'And that's you decided, is it? The big man of the house, making all the decisions?'

The kids had heard their dad talking and were yelling around their parents about keeping the dog.

'Get ready for school,' Rachel shouted at them before turning on Owen. 'See, how you turn them against me? You're never here, and guess what? I'm the bad guy again.' She pushed him out of her way as she gathered up the kids' lunchboxes. 'I can't take the risk. He's been aggressive, and I can't have the children put in danger. You need to take him to the dog pound.'

'All right, I'll take him, but you know he's going to be put down, right? That's on you.'

Maisy, their seven-year-old reacted to the argument and wailed at the thought of the dog being put to sleep. Rachel bent over the child, cuddling and trying to calm her. She glared at Owen. 'God, I hate you right now. I want it gone by the time I get back from the school run. Unless you want to deal with this?' She pointed at the three kids, two of them crying again and the oldest boy glaring at his mother.

The council-operated kennels for stray dogs were a hive of frenetic activity. As Owen arrived with Cliff, he was greeted by a cacophony of noise. The barking was off the scale. No wonder the kennels were at the end of a long lane with no neighbours. It was a sprawling, utilitarian facility with rows of chain-link enclosures, housing dogs in various states of distress.

It bustled with staff that tended to the dogs. The atmosphere was charged with sadness as the animals faced an uncertain future.

The mingling scents of desperation, Jeyes Fluid, urine, and sorrow were an assault on the nose. It saddened Owen to see that the enclosures were overcrowded, with too many dogs sharing a limited space. Some wagged their tails, but others cowered in corners, terrified.

He saw volunteers scrubbing enclosures, feeding the dogs, and giving what affection they could when they had time. The sound of barking and howling echoed along the pens, creating a miserable opera of canine harmonies. Dogs pressed their noses through the fences, their eyes begging for attention.

Owen went to the reception desk, where a busy attendant tried to keep up with paperwork and enquiries. The pound was overwhelmed with animals in need of new homes, and the staff were doing their best to manage the overcrowded chaos.

He handed Cliff to the staff and filled out the paperwork. He hated Rachel for making him do this. His phone pinged and he looked at it. *Have you got rid of that bloody dog, yet? Don't come home until you have.*

He typed a reply, *You're going to pay for this, bitch.* The woman behind the counter was talking to him as he deleted it and rammed his phone back into his pocket. Cliff stood no chance of being rehomed among all the other abandoned dogs. He was one more stray in a hundred needy faces. The staff faced a losing battle to find the dogs a loving home. They were kept for one week. Seven days to show that they were the cutest, kindest, best dog.

A woman called Helen handed Owen a receipt for the dog, and she checked over the form Owen had filled in. 'Is there a problem?' Owen asked, hoping there was.

'No. Something's just struck me.' She smiled and he wondered if she was working all day. He could forget something and have to come back at closing time. He'd offer her a lift home, maybe take her for a drink.

Her eyes fell on the dog's description. She looked at it and then at Cliff. 'That's what was bugging me. There was something on Facebook yesterday about a lost dog like this.'

Helen picked up the phone as she checked her computer for that week's call logs about lost dogs. 'It might not be him, of course, but it's worth a try.' Owen's face fell as Helen dialled the number of the potential owner. Helen was betraying him. She didn't deserve a date, but he might still wait for her to come out. All women were bitches and this one was a dog murderer. He couldn't believe he'd fancied her. Bitches—the stinking lot of them.

The admin continued around them and Owen wanted to grab the dog and run. He could. He could take off with Cliff and never come back. The ringing on the other end stretched on, and he waited.

A voice answered, and Helen asked questions, describing the dog in their care. The possibility of reuniting Cliff with his owner hung in the balance, and the atmosphere was charged with emotion as the conversation unfolded.

Owen left the kennels on his own. Even with a noisy family, he was always alone. A storm of emotions raged in him. He was angry and fantasised about killing his wife as he drove. Helen had spoken down to him in a condescending tone, making him feel like a piece of shit. His rage was too big to contain, and he couldn't let this slide. He'd wanted to keep the dog. And his wife was worse. Rachel wouldn't get away with treating him like that. But she was his woman—she would get away with it because he couldn't hurt her—not her. The bitch.

Owen's anger towards his wife blazed in him. He drove around town, a hunter. The rejection of his efforts to please her and the kids enraged him. The anger intensified. He couldn't go home.

He drove through the streets, his thoughts a mass of resentment. His expression was inscrutable, but anyone who saw him would know not to confront him.

He was a predator seeking a release from his fury, but he kept his intentions internalised as he drove.

He had an outlet for his wrath.

Chapter 40

Shelly was having coffee in the kitchen with Pauline like every other morning before Sammy ran away. And now they continued as if everything was normal because they didn't know what else to do. Every lead the police had was cold. 'Cold? It's cryogenically frozen,' Pauline said. 'When are they going to find him?'

She patted Shelly's hand but didn't have anything more to say. Words were useless. To fill the silence she told Alexa to play The Bay radio station. They listened to the morning broadcaster until the news came on.

'There has been another attack in Morecambe in the early hours of this morning. We're going live to our local correspondent, Sally Blair, who has news of this latest development.' A newscast on the morning show delivered the unsettling report that a fifth young girl had been attacked in the area. The reporter's voice was sombre as she relayed the details.

'This morning, a fifth teenager has fallen victim to the perpetrator of a series of heinous sexual attacks in the area, leaving two of the victims dead. Authorities have now officially confirmed that these incidents are linked. The latest victim, who has not yet been named, is in critical condition in hospital. We'll keep you updated throughout the day.'

The reporter continued, 'Police are urging young people in the region to exercise caution. They recommend staying indoors whenever possible or, if venturing outside, moving in groups.'

The announcement sent a shiver through Shelly, and she knew the residents of Morecambe would be left in fear. The need for vigilance was vital as the unsettling incidents unfolded.

She jumped up from her chair as the phone rang. Her hopes soared as they did every time. And then she battled with the rising dread of expected bad news. Living in limbo, her anxiety coloured every action black. She clutched the phone with a tight fist, praying it was the police with good news.

When she didn't recognise the voice on the other end, her spirits plummeted. It wasn't the police. 'Hello. It's just Helen, from the County Kennels at Lancaster.' Her voice was kind. 'We believe we may have found your dog.'

'Is Sammy with him?'

'Who?'

He wasn't there. Finding Carthenage would bring joy to her despair. But it wasn't Sammy who was found and safe in one of their cages, it was just a dog. She wished with all her heart that it was Sammy. She expressed her gratitude. The description of the dog sounded like Carthenage, but she was used to disappointment and wouldn't get her hopes up. All German shepherds looked the same.

As Helen described the circumstances of his being brought in, a cloud of depression cast its gloom over Shelley. If Carthenage was at the kennels, he wasn't with Sammy, keeping him safe. Her son was still out there somewhere, and it was agony since he went missing. The poignant mix of emotions left her relieved and heartbroken, as the reality of Sammy's situation hit her. If he wasn't with his dog, where was he?

She was in a state of frantic disarray as she hung up the phone, telling the woman from the kennels that she'd leave immediately to see if it was their dog. Her voice was breaking with worry as she ran around the room picking up her purse, car keys and handbag. She conveyed the urgency of her mercy dash to Pauline. 'Are you okay to watch Sammy while I'm gone, please?' she blurted.

Reality hit her like a tidal wave. Sammy wasn't there. He was missing. On her way out, she went to the coat hooks by the front door for Carthenage's lead, but Sammy had taken it with him. She'd be judged. Shelly would look like an owner who'd been careless enough to lose her dog and didn't even have him chipped or have a lead for him.

Tears welled up in her eyes as she hurried to the car. The drive to the kennels felt like an eternity, with her mind adrift in chaotic thoughts. Her son was out there, in the same area where those terrifying murders had occurred. She imagined the worst scenarios, and they evolved in her head until she couldn't cope with the images assaulting her. Despite all the attacks being on girls, she imagined Sammy dead with his trousers around his ankles and a bleeding rectum.

Her anxiety was overpowering and she lost control of the car. She had to oversteer to bring it back from the grass verge onto the road. She pulled to a stop, flung the door open and vomited into the line of oncoming traffic. She wasn't even embarrassed. But she was no good to Sammy if she was dead. Tightening her hands on the wheel, and sitting up straighter, she regained her composure and paid attention to her driving. Her face was streaked with tears when she got to the pound, and her heart ached with the uncertainty of what had happened to Sammy. The hope of being reunited with Carthenage made her impatient, but she smiled politely as Helen met her at reception. She felt mixed emotions, a glimmer of hope in a storm of despair.

They knew who she was. She caught the side eyes of the staff. She's the mother of that missing boy—the disabled one. They were all very kind, but their pity was unbearable.

Helen led Shelley down the rows of barking and cowering dogs. The noise deafened her and she put her hands over her ears. The barking reflected every canine emotion from excitement to anxiety. Many of the animals poking their noses through the wire yearned for affection. They all deserved the chance to go home. But Shelly didn't give a damn. She only cared about Sammy's dog.

She followed Helen through the kennels and tried not to get her hopes up. Helen had said it might not be him. The rows of dogs were endless but none of them was Carthenage. Her anxiety grew.

And there he was.

It was an electrifying moment. Lying in his basket, Shelly had never seen her dog looking so depressed. His head rested on his paws, utterly miserable. When he heard Shelley's voice, he sprang to his feet with unbridled excitement, barking and wagging his tail. His eyes sparkled with joy, and his body quivered, twisting in delight. The world had burst into colour for him, and he couldn't contain his happiness. He jumped up at the cage door, trying to reach her, his tongue lolling out, and his devotion unmistakable.

Then he looked past her for Sammy.

After a lecture about having her dog microchipped, Shelly and Carthenage went home, and she understood his sadness. She was delighted to have their beloved dog back, but she blamed him. Part of her held the dog accountable for Sammy running away. She pushed the thought out of her mind—today was a good day. But her elation was overshadowed by worry for Sammy. Carthenage charged into the house as soon as the door was opened, looking for Sammy. He sensed the sombre atmosphere. He searched every room, sniffing and investigating to find any trace of him. His ears were perked, but his tail was low. He was sad and that mirrored the unease in the household.

After a thorough search, Carthenage settled in Sammy's place on the sofa. The bond between them was strong, and he understood her sorrow. Shelly stroked him, her fingers getting lost in his fur, but not as lost as Sammy was. They shared their misery in silence.

As they watched the TV, Shelley felt many emotions—relief, joy, and overwhelming love for their dog. The dramatic reunion intensified the bond between them, and the world was better now that Carthenage was home.

'Breaking news. A man has been arrested on suspicion of sexual attacks on several teenage girls, resulting in the murder of two, in the Morecambe area. The man, identified as Owen Proctor, thirty-four, of Westgate Drive is being held for questioning.'

The house felt heavy as she sat on the sofa, waiting for Jo, the family liaison officer, to arrive. It was days since Sammy went missing, and every moment had stretched like an eternity. As the doorbell rang, Shelly went to answer it, her hopes raised at the prospect of receiving news about Sammy. Jo came in and sat down. Her expression was guarded, her eyes filled with empathy. It was assumed that Sammy had run away to find Carthenage, but they didn't know that. He could have been taken. Nothing was certain, and Shelly ran the same tired questions on repeat.

'I wish I had better news, but we still don't have any new information about Sammy's whereabouts. I'm sorry,' Jo said.

Shelly's shoulders slumped as disappointment dissolved her into a molten heap in her seat, as it did every time they came to her without good news.

They had their dog home, and she'd hoped that today would bring a breakthrough. Carthenage had to be a turning point in their luck. They were unrelated events. But like John wearing his lucky pants when they were on date night, superstitious rituals were easy to adopt. Especially when your kid was missing. If she stirred her tea anti-clockwise, Sammy might walk through the door. If she walked up the stairs backwards—she'd probably break her neck. Any tiny thing that she could do, no matter how ridiculous, gave her new hope that her son would be found. Like the sprig of heather in her hair. It was artificial, but she doubted fate would hold it against her.

Jo described the efforts the police had made to find Sammy.

She detailed the operations, the air searches, the use of K9 units, and the review of hours spent watching surveillance footage. The community involvement, social media, and the specialised approach to dealing with Sammy's needs all played their part in the ongoing efforts.

Shelly listened, grateful for the dedication of the police force. But, she couldn't shake the despair. Sammy was somewhere, exposed to danger.

Jo wrapped up her explanation and assured Shelly that the police were doing everything they could to find him and bring him home safely. Jo's words were comforting, but they couldn't get rid of her anxiety. She'd developed restless leg syndrome which annoyed her, never mind anybody else.

She looked around the room. Sammy was everywhere. His things, photographs, and a random jumper that Shelly had left over his seat ready for him. And memories they shared cluttered the room as if they were a thousand treasured ornaments. But still, the emptiness was unbearable.

Something had been playing on her mind and as much as she dreaded the answer, she had to ask. 'I heard that they've caught the attacker. Do you think Owen Proctor could have Sammy?'

Jo, replied gently, 'We can't say for certain at this point, but it's very unlikely. Proctor preyed on young girls in the area. His motivation was sexual. We've no reason to suspect that he'd have any interest in Sammy. Try not to think like that because you'll drive yourself mad. The investigation will continue, and we'll do everything we can to find him.'

It was the same tired platitudes, and Jo always had a look

of pity on her face, that made her professionalism slip. Shelly nodded. The surge of emotions took over her voice. The man had been arrested, and it gave her a glimmer of hope that had been absent for days. She clung to it, desperate to reunite with her son. But what if he did have him somewhere? Sammy could be locked in a cellar, or chained up in an old barn. There were plenty around. If Proctor didn't have Sammy, why the hell hadn't he been found wandering around?

Shelly's living room was quiet after Jo's visit. Her eyes drifted to the television set. The news was still filled with Proctor's arrest. There was no room for Sammy.

The news anchor's voice was solemn. 'In a significant development, a man was arrested today on suspicion of the violent attacks on young females in the Morecambe area. After his brutal rampage over the last week, two girls are dead and three more gravely injured in Lancaster Royal Infirmary. Owen Proctor, thirty-four, of Westgate Drive, Morecambe, was taken into custody on an unrelated charge when police were called to a domestic incident.'

Shelly felt dizzy as the report continued. Owen Proctor's name was unfamiliar. The anchor went on, 'Proctor's wife was badly beaten and sustained several injuries in the attack. It is feared that she may not survive. A knife, which police believe may be related to other crimes, was found at the scene. Officers noticed on questioning that Proctor was acting suspiciously, resulting in his car being searched. Items belonging to three of the five victims were found in the boot of his car.'

The room spun as the implications of the report sank in.

Maybe something of Sammy's was in that boot, or hidden in his house somewhere. Shelly was convinced that Proctor knew about her son's disappearance.

CHAPTER 41

Gareth was watching Sammy with fascination and concern. On the third morning, he went out and bought every thousand-piece jigsaw they had in the town's toy shop, thinking it would occupy Sammy and ease his anxiety.

Gareth didn't have to coax him to do the puzzles. He was biddable and worked on them without joy or sadness. When he finished one, he moved on to the next without self-congratulation. Working to piece them together with unwavering focus, he never got frustrated or bored. It had the same effect as locking Sammy in a cage or taking the batteries out of a toy. It was instant magic, and he stopped being a pain in the arse. They got up, traded, and then Sammy did his jigsaws until bedtime. It didn't matter what the picture on the puzzle was. It could have been a scenic landscape or an abstract design—Sammy worked on the same puzzle if Gareth didn't intervene. He'd make it, break it, and build it again. When Gareth realised that the design was immaterial, he didn't even bother swapping them. To hell with him.

Gareth wondered about the peculiar shift in Sammy's priorities. He expected him to ask about the dog the second he woke up, but he never mentioned Carthenage or expressed any desire to look for him. His singular goal was completing the same jigsaw puzzle on a loop.

It had a hypnotic power over him, drawing him in and controlling his attention. But Gareth was glad that Sammy didn't have a problem puzzling while he traded. Sammy never argued, he'd wait for Gareth to put the laptop between them. His change in focus was like flipping a switch. He'd tune into the numbers with an intensity that took all his attention. Flip. Jigsaws to stocks. No problem. Flip.

Gareth wondered if the trauma of leaving home had affected Sammy. He had never known him before, so had no comparison for his behaviour. He was freaked out by the singular fixation on the puzzles, but the peace was heaven-sent.

The next four days of trading brought extraordinary wealth. They couldn't put a foot wrong. The stock did drop, but every time it dipped and Gareth expected losses, the tide always turned and it rose higher than before the fall. Every morning, Sammy huddled over the laptop, scanning the financial markets for the best investment opportunities. He explored companies, searching for deals in the flow of stock prices throughout the trading day in case they needed to switch.

After the success with GroGen Innovations on Monday, they invested ten thousand pounds in them again on Tuesday. They put the other twenty on Quantum Tech Solutions, a solid-growth technology company. The stock showed promise as it fluctuated, but as the closing bell rang, their diligence paid off, resulting in another satisfying profit. On Wednesday, they capitalised on the current trend and invested in five companies, securing smaller, but still substantial gains by day's end.

Thursday presented an opportunity in the medical sector, and they chose a pharmaceutical giant, as their investment target. The stock experienced movement in both directions, but Sammy's market-analysis skills netted them another positive return.

By Friday, with the help of calming drugs, their routine was established. They had their moments when Sammy went out of his gargantuan mind with spectacular meltdowns that left Gareth with bruises and broken crockery. But there was no denying that the boy was a walking talking trading doll and the money rolled in. There was no reason why Gareth couldn't keep him. The kid didn't give a shit where he was.

For their first option that morning, they chose the retail sector and opted for a company called Cosmo Mart, a chain of confectionary stores that were soaring. They split the stocks again and put the other half of their stake on a strategic endeavour involving Skylark Airways, a company that had replaced one of the giants in customer ranking. Watching the growing interest in travel and transportation stocks in the media, they gambled on its continued success as the stock ascended and flew high over eight trading hours.

The closing bell rang on Friday afternoon, and Gareth's total income after fees had reached £203,868.34. Their trading had proven lucrative.

When he reached the remarkable total of £50,000 profit from their initial investment of £10,000, Gareth was greedy to reinvest every penny, seeking to maximise their gains. Sammy reminded him it was an unstable platform and warned him the stock could crash in an instant and to be careful. Gareth agreed to split the stake over multiple companies. But he was stubborn and refused to only gamble with half of their balance, leaving the other half safe in his account. Sammy started twitching. 'Just Gareth is going to lose all of Just Gareth and Samuel May's money.'

'Let's get one thing straight here, little man. No part of that money is ours. Who brought in the big bucks, to begin with?'

'Just Gareth is going to lose. Just Gareth will be angry. And Just Gareth will shout at Samuel May.' He'd had a few terrifying seizures over the week and every time Gareth worried he was going to die.

'All right. You win. Stop with the Shakin' Steven's routine, already.' He left half of their balance and agreed to a system where they'd only reinvest half of their money to build the pot. It reduced Gareth's risk and cushioned any losses.

Their run of luck was excellent, thanks to Sammy's guidance about when and where to buy shares. He had a golden touch and wisdom beyond his years. Gareth tuned out when he explained that it was a matter of mathematical inevitability. However, he calculated that within five trading days, they had a 90% chance of hitting a market crash, potentially losing that day's gains. It was all about probability.

'Yeah, yeah, Grandma. Let's just get on with it. You run the figures and let me do the worrying. Okay?'

'Just Gareth needs to worry more. Just Gareth is a worrying void.'

Gareth wasn't fazed by the specific numerical prediction. But decided to take Sammy's advice. From Wednesday, they'd gone with the half-stake strategy. The thought of losing everything in a single day was more of an incentive to change his system than the boy going into another fit.

It was another great day, and Gareth stared at his bank balance on the screen. The week had been lucrative, and the wealth they'd accumulated in a short time was inspirational.

Sammy didn't share Gareth's elation and that pissed him off. The kid looked like a robot. His eyes were locked on the jigsaw, his fingers clicking the pieces together—and that grunt every time one fit.

'You make food, Just Gareth.'

'What am I, your goddammed servant?'

'You make food, now, Just Gareth.'

Gareth prepared a meal with only dry foods that didn't touch each other on the plate. They settled into their evening routine. An unexpected thunderstorm rolled in. The dark skies were illuminated by bursts of lightning and punctuated by the rumble of thunder. The power flickered and then went out, leaving the house in darkness except for the glow of the laptop screen.

He fumbled for his phone's flashlight and talked to Sammy to keep him calm. Sammy didn't react to the blackout at first. He continued fingering jigsaw pieces, illuminated by the flashes of lightning.

As the storm intensified, Gareth noticed Sammy getting annoyed. Three days had passed since his fixation began, and he hadn't mentioned the dog once. He realised it was a way for

Sammy to cope with new situations.

The sudden change in weather sparked a shift in him. Sammy broke the silence. 'We must go and find Carthenage now.'

The transformation of his focus came out of nowhere, and Gareth tried to dissuade him. 'It's pissing down out there, Sammy. We can't go out in that. We'll catch our death.'

'Just Gareth can catch a train. Just Gareth can catch a fish. Just Gareth can catch a cold. But just Gareth cannot catch his death.' Sammy had picked up his coat and the hat with the ridiculous bobble on top that made him look like a toddler, especially if he nodded his head and the bobble wobbled.

'We must go now, Just Gareth.'

Gareth searched for the right words. It was a formula. Put x, y and z together in the right order, and he could make Sammy do what he wanted him to. He explained the complexities of the situation. 'We've talked about this before. We need to wait for the right time and let the authorities handle it.'

'We must go now, Just Gareth.'

It was like passive-aggressive warfare. The kid spouted words at him in a monotone. There was no damn emotion at all, and it boiled Gareth's piss.

'Sammy, wait. You need to do your jigsaw now.'

'Okay.'

CHAPTER 42

The morning news was on, and the serious tone of Sabrina Green gripped the nation. She wore a blue blouse, and a sympathetic voice with just the right note of compassion. Her eyes had the same expression as Jennie Bond's when she'd announced Jill Dando's murder. Sabrina had a great rack. What Gareth wouldn't do with two hours alone with her. Sammy's story had passed the five-day missing boy stage and was a national headline.

'Barrow-in-Furness schoolboy, Samuel May, aged Fifteen, has been missing for seven nights. The desperate search for his whereabouts continues. Samuel, who is known as Sammy, was last seen at his home in Barrow but was believed to be in the Morecambe Bay area. Despite extensive efforts, the search has yielded no results.'

Sabrina's voice deepened a semitone with concern as she continued. The media loved this shit. 'Police and local authorities initially focused their search in Morecambe, but as each day passes without any leads, the operation has been upscaled. A nationwide hunt is underway for the missing boy who has autism.'

The camera shifted to a map of the United Kingdom, with

a marked area encompassing Morecambe in red and extending with a softer, rose-blush colour to cover the whole country. It signalled a dramatic shift in the search, and the urgency was palpable. The nation was glued to news of Sammy and you couldn't move without seeing his face. Every resource was expended to find the boy's body so that his family could lay him to rest. They didn't say that—but it's what they meant.

Gareth comforted himself with a chocolate digestive. Sammy was okay here. He was looking after him. Gareth was doing a good thing, ensuring the boy's safety rather than letting him roam the streets looking for his dog. With him the way he was, it meant he'd be vulnerable to harm out there. Gareth blotted out the faces of his distraught parents.

He took his role seriously. He made sure Sammy was fed and created a decent space for him to sleep. In the confines of the flat, Sammy was protected from the danger of the outside world. Blackpool had an underbelly filled with all sorts of lowlife.

But Sammy wasn't where he belonged. He was living in a tarnished cage, and it was only a matter of time until Gareth got caught. But sometimes kids went missing for years, and at least Gareth wasn't touching him the way a kidnapper would. He could dump him at any point if it got too hot around here. But the days of hiding were taking a toll, and the tension was a constant presence in Gareth's life. The weekend was a nightmare of broken routines and endless hours. Gareth didn't even get a lie in—but they got through it.

On Monday morning, he opened the laptop. The joy of his ongoing success obliterated any worry about keeping Sammy—just a little longer. Their routine was unchanged as they entered the cyber world of the stock exchange. With a neat stake of £100,000 at their disposal today, they were ready to invest. Gareth couldn't get enough of looking at the balance of £203,8 68.34 and he tried to persuade Sammy to let him invest it all, but Sammy held fast. The boy was good for him.

Following Sammy's advice, Gareth put his faith in another technology firm poised for significant growth and a company that had an app that had gone viral. They made their investment, putting fifty thousand on each, and watched the numbers on the screen shift as they waited for results.

Sammy's predictions were accurate, and Gareth's anticipation was high. They aimed to double their investment, leaving them with a profit of £97,500,00 after the commission and spread fees were accounted for. It was ambitious, but their history of successful investments had given Gareth confidence. And he wasn't disappointed. By lunchtime, they were less than ten grand from their goal, and it was exceeding Sammy's prediction.

Gareth spent the day glued to the screen while Sammy did his favourite puzzle. He opted for the visually bland jigsaw of baked beans. The rest had been discarded and were stacked beside Gareth's pile of belongings. Sammy had no use for them.

The tides of fortune shifted soon after three P.M. Gareth's run of luck was disrupted by a crisis with the tech company.

The first signs of trouble came with an unexpected press release from the CEO. It said they were facing a shortage of essential microchips, a critical component of their products. The shortfall was due to a global supply chain disruption, which had been exacerbated by unforeseen events, including political tensions in Syria. This had a knock-on effect with the trading agreements with South Korea where the chips were manufactured. Trucks were halted at the border and couldn't get through. Production in England was stopped that morning, causing a chain reaction that negatively impacted the company's quarterly projection.

Soon after, news broke of a legal dispute involving the app company. They were embroiled in a lawsuit over alleged patent infringement with a major competitor. The uncertainty surrounding the outcome of the legal battle weighed on investors' confidence, leading to a massive sell-off of the company's stock.

'Sammy.' Gareth screamed his name across the room, making Sammy jump—but other than that he didn't react.

'Both companies are crashing at the same time. What the hell have you done?'

'Samuel May took one hundred thousand pounds of Just Gareth's investment and split it equally between the two companies. Both companies have gone bad.'

'Is that all you've got to say?'

'Oops.'

'It's going tits up.'

'Just Gareth said a bad word.'

'Never mind bad words, what's happening to my money?'

'It's going tits up.' Sammy made a laughing noise that sounded like a sea lion. 'It does not matter, Just Gareth has the other half safe in the bank.'

Gareth thought about hitting Sammy over the head with the

heaviest object he could find.

As a result of the interconnected crises, the share value of both investments plummeted. The market was flooded with panicked investors trying to cut their losses. A cascade of sell orders hit the boards, driving the stock price lower.

Gareth watched in disbelief as their investment lost value. The morning's financial success had reversed, crashing, and making Gareth face the harsh reality of the stock market's inherent volatility.

Gareth ordered Sammy over, as they watched the investment nosedive. Sometimes you had to hold your nerve, he thought. Every time they moved money, they incurred charges and he couldn't afford to just jump ship. 'Come on, baby,' he said to the computer screen. 'Come on. Pick up again for me.' the initial £100,000 dwindled to £13,000 in less than an hour.

'Oh, dear,' Sammy said, as though he'd dropped a puzzle piece on the floor.

Gareth's face contorted with rage. 'What have you done, you idiot? You were supposed to make it work. I've lost my money.'

'Tit's up,' Sammy said.

'I trusted you.'

Sammy's comprehension of their respective emotions challenged his ability to answer, and his vacant expression infuriated Gareth.

He slammed his fist down on the arm of the sofa as he yelled, 'You moron. You've just cost me a hundred grand. Have you any idea how much that is?'

Sammy watched in silence.

'Well?'

'A hundred grand is a hundred thousand pounds.'

He didn't justify his decisions. But he flinched when Gareth shouted in his face.

After the stock crashed, Gareth put their shares up for sale but there were no buyers in either commodity. And their investment was still dropping.

'Just Gareth has more money in the bank,' Sammy said.

Gareth's rage poured out, but Sammy was unnaturally devoid of any emotion. To him, the numbers on the screen were abstract figures that held no sway over feelings. His disinterest and lack of remorse enraged Gareth. He hit Sammy on the side of his head with an open hand and the boy screamed, holding his face.

'You were supposed to know what you were doing,' Gareth ranted.

Sammy glanced at the screen. 'It is okay, Just Gareth.'

'I trusted you. All that money's gone.'

Sammy stood up and went back to his jigsaw puzzle, and Gareth let him go. It would give him a chance to calm down. He wanted to jump on top of the boy and punch him until his face was pulp. He knew Sammy's loud moaning noise was to shut his voice out. Sammy's indifference took Gareth to a new pinnacle of rage that he hadn't experienced before. He didn't like it and struggled to keep his hands off the boy.

'Samuel May needs a cup of tea, Just Gareth.'

Gareth wanted to throw boiling tea over him. In a fit of rage, his temper reached a breaking point. He yanked the window open. A strong breeze blew into the room, and the sudden blast

305

of it made Sammy screech. Gareth grabbed a handful of Sammy's jigsaw pieces. 'Is this all you care about? Is it? Watch how much your shit means to me.' He flung them into the street. The fragments scattered like bridal confetti while Sammy screamed in horror.

The puzzle pieces hit the ground, and Gareth finally got a reaction as Sammy's world exploded with them. He watched in satisfaction as he went into a full-blown meltdown. He wanted to see it and revelled in Sammy's discomfort.

'There. It's not nice when it's your stuff, is it? You don't like that. Do you, moron?'

Sammy's meltdown was non-verbal screaming and Gareth laughed when he punched himself in the face. Sammy's features twisted in anguish as he unleashed a guttural scream of frustration.

'See what it feels like, boy?'

Sammy's body spasmed, and he writhed in his seat with his fists clenched. 'Go on, do it again. Punch yourself, idiot.'

Sammy lurched over to attack Gareth and the older man sidestepped out of the way. He was still laughing and Sammy was making indescribable noises. He blundered around the room and crashed into the overhead kitchen cupboard and hit his face. The sight of blood coming from Sammy's wound sobered Gareth. He stopped laughing and put his hands out to catch Sammy. But the boy reeled away, crashing into the wall.

His eyes were dancing in their sockets, and Gareth's temper left him. This had gone too far now. Sammy was going to have a fit and concern replaced his anger.

Terrified by the intensity of Sammy's meltdown, he tried to reach out and calm him, but it only escalated the situation as Sammy shrank away.

Gareth could see that he was overwhelmed by emotion and the loss of his puzzle. He lashed out in a frenzy. He hit Gareth, and the uncontrolled violence gave him more strength than his size warranted.

Gareth was torn between fear and guilt. He couldn't touch Sammy because it would only make things worse, but he made shushing noises to try and calm him. 'Hey, lad. I was only kidding with you. Come on. It's all right. You're going to be okay. Come and sit down and I'll make you that cup of tea.'

Sammy screamed in rage.

'Look, I'll even go and get all your missing pieces from the street. It's nothing that can't be fixed. For God's sake calm down, you're going to make yourself ill.' Gareth's temper with the kid had led to this, leaving them on the precipice of an outburst that neither of them understood.

Gareth tried to restrain Sammy in the throes of his violent meltdown. It was too much for Sammy to cope with, his over-loaded nervous system made him a volatile mass of seething rage.

With a violent jolt, he fell from Gareth's hold onto the dirty floor. His body convulsed, writhing in a grand mal seizure. He'd had several fits, but this one was on a different level. Gareth was frozen with terror and didn't know what to do. Sammy vomited, and foaming bile purged from his mouth as he convulsed.

Time stretched, and the seizure continued. The air was filled with the haunting sounds of Sammy's suffering, his body contorted and his noise was unintelligible.

Gareth had been governed by his frustration. This was the outcome of shouting at the boy and hitting him. He was paralysed with helplessness and watched as Sammy was seized by forces that looked like demonic possession. Gareth couldn't give him the care he needed. He should call for an ambulance—but his self-preservation stopped him.

CHAPTER 43

He reached for his phone. Fear clouded his vision and he wiped an oily film of sweat from his forehead. The mobile was dead, its screen dark. What the hell was he going to do? Panic surged through him as he plugged the charger in to revive it, but it was lifeless and unresponsive for too long. He couldn't ring emergency services, anyway.

He'd picked it up to ring Bianca, his ex. She was a nurse and would know what to do. Getting in touch with anybody from his old life was risky, but she was a good egg. Not bad in the sack, either. It was the best he could do, but he couldn't even manage that.

Sammy's seizure was horrific. He writhed on the floor, his body convulsing and he was sick again. Vomit splattered the carpet, making it stink and mingling with puzzle pieces, while Sammy contorted in his mess.

The dead phone was a cruel reminder that communication with the outside world was severed. It was for the best. Ringing anybody would be a mistake. He had to stop reacting and think clearly. Dread engulfed him—if he sent Sammy to the hospital, the danger was that the police could be at the flat in no time.

Fear, guilt, and desperation collided, crashing together to create an emotional chest bump that consumed him. The decision was impossible—whether to seek medical help or hide in the shadows, running from a past that was always going to catch up with him.

Gareth froze in horror. He couldn't move and didn't know what to do. His mind came up with nothing rational to help and he floundered in a vortex of hopelessness. He did nothing and watched as Sammy endured the torment of the seizure. The seconds stretched into what felt like hours, a reminder of his impotence to Sammy's suffering.

The fit subsided, Sammy's convulsions slowed and then stopped.

He was still.

The trembling ceased, and the boy was limp on the floor. Gareth's surge of remorse made tears prickle behind his eyes. He moved closer to Sammy's—dead body?—still form.

Kneeling beside him, Gareth put his head near Sammy's chest and felt for life. His relief was indescribable as he felt Sammy's breath against his ear. The youngster's pigeon chest rose in the shallow disturbance of struggling respiration. He was still unconscious, and there were no indications of him waking up.

Five minutes had gone by since he'd thrown the jigsaw pieces out of the window. They were an eternity in purgatory. The room had been filled with chaos and distress, but now the silence made him want to scream. He felt it rising and forced it down. The aftermath of Sammy's seizure left an eerie nothingness. It was as if even the air was gone. The remnants of the fit were scattered around them, an overturned chair, jigsaw parts, vomit and other bodily fluids. Gareth's emotions tangled, mixing with his fear and guilt. He sat on the floor far away from Sammy and his spewed stomach contents. He should try to bring him around, but he didn't do anything. He hadn't taken a first aid course for years and, when he had, it was only to tick boxes for insurance purposes. He'd spent that day responding to important emails on his phone. It's not as though he'd listened. Gareth felt good for nothing—accomplished at it.

He should pull himself together and attend to Sammy's immediate needs, though. The boy had come out of a traumatic grand mal seizure, and he'd pissed and shit himself. Gareth plucked up every ounce of his courage. The thought of touching Sammy, who looked like a corpse, disgusted him. He rolled him onto his side. Gareth expected the emotional scars of the fit would be obvious when he woke up. If he ever did. But he was here now and it had left a physical aftermath that needed addressing. Sammy had run the whole gauntlet of bodily functions. Gareth gagged as he saw the puke, shit, and piss stains. The waft of warm faeces over his nose, when he turned Sammy, was overpowering and even more forceful than the stench of vomit.

He eased open the soiled clothing. Sammy's shirt was stained with spew. He unbuttoned it, and his pale skin contrasted with the mess clinging to the fabric. Trying not to jostle him, Gareth wrestled the shirt off, folded it into itself, and threw it in the waste bin. He was a fantasist and lived on tall stories to get him through life. He imagined tending a wounded soldier on the battlefield. Gareth's head swerved as he avoided gunfire and hand grenades. He was in Cambodia, and he'd carry the wounded soldier through the field of landmines. He was a hero.

The next task daunted him, but Major Gareth Holmes—sir, yes sir—would do whatever his battalion needed from him. Sammy urinated in his jeans again, and the result, stark and offensive, assaulted his nostrils. But that was the lesser of two toileting evils. Gareth unfastened the trousers, exposing the wetness and soiling at the back, that touched his hands. Looser than an average stool, it seeped through the fabric. The smell was pungent.

He took the wet trousers off and battled his gorge. 'I'm all right. I've got this, men. Stand down,' he shouted into the killing fields. He would make the undignified moment better for the soldier. Gareth's anger rose as Sammy's vulnerability and exposure to his condition was laid bare. But the soldier was one of his troops so he played the part of respecting his dignity.

Going beyond the call of duty, there was a medal in this for him if he succeeded. He got some of his own clothing and everything he needed from the bathroom. Among all the dead and fallen heroes on the field, he knelt beside his comrade. He took a yellow car sponge and squirted it with tea tree shower gel. He had an almost scientific interest in the fact that even though he was unconscious, while Gareth had been gathering what he needed and preparing the washing-up bowl, Sammy had gone cold and was shivering. His naked body was infested with a million goose pimples. Starting at the top, Gareth moved him as gently as he could to wash his back and front. He lifted each arm, scrubbed the armpits and made sure his neck and chest were clean. As the sponge brushed over his front, Sammy's nipples rose, making Gareth feel like an abusive pervert. He gagged at the thought but still needed to keep washing the top half to avoid having to do the dirty parts. He steeled himself for it as he rinsed the sponge and re-soaped it. Front or back first? He didn't know. It was all disgusting. He started at mid-thigh level where the urine had soaked into his legs and worked up a lather. Sammy's lower legs were covered in adolescent hair, but towards his groin, it was smooth apart from his pubic region. He used the sponge so he didn't have to touch him and washed his legs, trying to be gentle, but feeling like a lover with each brush of the sponge. He hated every dirty, depraved second of how sexual it felt when it couldn't have been further removed. He just wanted it to be over. With the tips of his fingers, he raised Sammy's testicles to get below them. He averted his eyes, and pushed the sponge around between Sammy's legs, encompassing a front and back wash at the same time. The water was filthy as he rinsed and there was so much faeces that when it mixed with the soap on the sponge, lighter brown smears spread in a filthy rainbow arc on his skin. He had to get up to change the water, it wasn't clean enough to do any kind of job as it was, and there was soap everywhere. He hoped the boy didn't freeze to death in the time it took. Then he worried that he'd made the fresh water too hot and fretted about scalding him. He rinsed and towel-dried Sammy. Touching the teenager's penis was the most disgusting thing he'd ever had to do. Because of the perverted implications, it was worse even than washing the shit.

Gareth's actions, infused with responsibility, gave him purpose. He wouldn't think about this being his fault. He wished he hadn't taken the boy, and sank into his fantasy world to get him through the ordeal. Sammy's suffering wasn't important. Only Gareth's bravery scored points in this battle. He finished the clean-up operation and dressed him in Gareth's oversized clothes. All that was left was hoping the boy would wake up.

Putting his hands under Sammy's armpits, he tried lifting him from the floor. Unconscious, he couldn't be moved. Gareth cursed his inability to call for help. Trapped in a situation that was spiralling out of control, he thought about giving up and leaving. The room closed in around him, and a suffocating sense of helplessness pressed him down.

Sammy's unconsciousness was deeply rooted and he was a dead weight. Moving people looked easy on TV. A cloud of doom hung over him, and Gareth was miserable in his terror. The responsibility crushed him. What now?

Grabbing a quilt and pillow, he put them on the floor beside Sammy and rolled the unconscious boy onto the makeshift bed. He prayed, talking to God for the first time in twenty years, but he didn't respond. Giving up on Jesus, he spoke to Sammy. 'Please be okay, kid.' Murder was a terrifying word.

Powerless, he couldn't provide the help Sammy needed. He flung the window wider—the air abandoned him when he needed it most. Major Gareth Holmes was a hero.

There was nothing more he could do. He sat until his legs stiffened and felt as if he was going mad with worry. The battlefield faded and he needed another distraction. The kid was dying. His breathing worsened, rattling in his diaphragm. Gareth couldn't look at him.

He retreated to the sanctuary of his laptop. He knew he was in shock. It protected and detached him, and the room carried the echo of traumatic events. His dimly lit prison offered no way out of the mess. The stock exchange was an escape from the terrifying reality he'd brought in. His greed lay in the visible form of an unconscious child ten feet away from him, and he turned his back on Sammy, blocking the images out.

He scanned the fluctuating numbers on the screen, his lifeline to a semblance of control and predictability. The crashed stock hadn't sold, but they might have turned in the last hour. They could be rising again.

In the quiet after the madness, Gareth's face was pale, his eyes reflecting the terror that gripped him. And on the laptop's screen, he saw himself for what he was. His life and future decades in prison hung in the balance. His helplessness tightened a vice around his chest.

Checking the stock market fluctuations in a desperate attempt to regain stability helped. Sammy might not make it, and the uncertainty took him to a place of detachment. The kid taught him how to disappear into his own world and now he understood how that felt. The real world was overwhelming. But the numbers on the screen danced as they calculated and changed, distracting him from the fear.

He fixated on the changing numbers. The room's eerie silence punctuated by the hum of the computer, lulled him into a dopiness that he enjoyed. In a state of heightened agitation once removed, he sought hope in the familiar rhythm of the stock market's ebb and flow.

He watched the stock prices rise and fall, and separated himself from Sammy's evaporating life.

Every fluctuation brought a glimmer of hope or a harbinger of despair. Trapped between the digital world of his crashing stock and the real-world crisis, he didn't want to see, or feel, or think. He existed.

And he waited for Sammy to die.

CHAPTER 44

Gareth's eyes were fixed on the stock graphs when the screen flashed.

'What the hell?'

Staring at the screen, a warning notice appeared. He was terrified when he read the words. His stock exchange account had been frozen and the fraud department had been alerted. The reason cited was the presence of illicit and irregular trading patterns on his account.

He felt his blood pressure rising and his vision blurred. Reading the damning message again, the earth felt as though it was sliding from under him. The financial stability and control he'd clung to disintegrated. He was finished.

He searched for more information and a way to rectify the situation. With his future doomed, and the turn of events shattering any illusion of getting his life back, Gareth was trapped in a nightmare he couldn't escape. And it was all the retard's fault.

Shit, they were on to him. He shut out the trading site, slamming the lid down. Paranoia as profound as a belief structure battered him. They were coming. They were monitoring him through the computer. What if they could see him? hear him? He struggled to focus. He should transfer the rest of the money out of his bank account, just in case. He opened the laptop as though it might bite him and signed into his email. There could be further explanation or a resolution. False Alarm, Buddy. Click here to confirm that everything is okay, after all. Get a grip. You're panicking over nothing. It's probably a scam.

But it was as real as could be.

His heart sank as he read the email notification from the Exchange. It informed him that, due to his unrealistic success in recent day trading transactions, insider information was suspected. The investigation was thorough, and the authorities had been alerted. The damnedest thing about it was that, apart from his initial insider trading tip-off he'd received before leaving London, everything he'd done was above board. Okay, so he had his pet savant. Was that illegal? Surely the Supreme Court of Human Rights would say that, had he been old enough, Sammy was as entitled to trade as the next person.

The words on the screen struck him like a death knoll. Gareth was accused of illicit trading practices, and the consequences were dire. With his world collapsing, the threat of legal repercussions was a certainty.

Despair gripped him and panic held its hand as he tried to comprehend the enormity of it. There was no escape from the fallout.

He had to get rid of the boy.

But before he could move, his phone pinged.

It was an email from the bank. The account he'd opened using a dead man's details was also under investigation due to suspected fraudulent activity. His accounts had been frozen, and an investigation had been launched. The financial disaster Sammy warned him about was unfolding like a mosaic of falling dominoes.

His dreams of financial security and the fortune he'd amassed, were slipping through his fingers. He had no access to his money, apart from the couple of hundred quid in his wallet. Even the original ten grand stake was lost. A week ago, he'd had it in his hand in cold hard cash. It was the foundation of his trading, but it was gone.

The dread suffocated him. It wouldn't take much scrutiny for the police to get to the truth – that he'd opened a bank account using the details of a deceased man to facilitate his trading activities. The walls were closing in, and the threat of being exposed was imminent.

He had to get rid of the boy.

He looked at Sammy, unconscious on the floor. His respirations were worse and Gareth was trapped in a horrific scenario of his own making. Every choice he made came back to haunt him. With his world in tatters, the fear of losing everything was debilitating. His brain was cotton wool, and he couldn't move.

He had to get rid of the damn boy.

He couldn't carry him. If he didn't dump Sammy's body—alive or dead—away from the flat, his only option was to run.

But calm down. You need to think. Make a plan. They don't know who you are, and won't be here yet.

They had to trace and then find him. All they had was a dead man's details—and his IP address. Could they locate him through the computer? Think.

He needed to eat and prepare, he didn't know how far he'd have to go before he could risk stopping somewhere for food. Gareth filled the kettle to make a Pot Noodle. His hands trembled and water spilled onto the counter. Get a grip. He'd have tea and something to eat. That was sensible. And then he'd leave. Where? It didn't matter. He couldn't get out of the country. Once they found the kid, all exit routes out of England would be blocked. He had enough money to scrape by for a couple of days. Then what?

He was startled out of his thoughts by a pained groan coming from Sammy. He reached over to turn the tap off, but Sammy took it up a notch. Gareth put the kettle down, leaving the tap running, and ran to him to shut him up. The sound pierced the air like bagpipes cutting through a highland mist.

Scotland. How could he get there?

Gareth knelt by Sammy's side as the boy stirred, his disoriented movements sluggish.

His eyes opened and stared at Gareth—vacant. There was no recognition, just a moronic, bewildered gaze. He groaned again, struggling to sit up, unaware of his surroundings. His voice was the perfect contradiction. He was both monotone and panicked. He screeched, 'Shelly May,' on repeat. And Gareth ran to slam the window shut.

Sammy's confusion riled him. The last thing he needed was more drama.

Clamping his hand hard over Sammy's mouth, he shouted at him. 'Shut up. Do you hear me? Shut up.'

A siren wailed in the distance. He gripped the boy's mouth harder, twisting his neck—just a little, the bastard. The sirens—more than one—were closer. Christ, there was only one way out of this rattrap. He wanted to twist Sammy's neck some more—until it snapped. But the sirens were passing. The wailing faded into the distance.

Sammy struggled against his hand. His eyeballs danced. He'd fall into another fit if Gareth didn't let him go. 'If I move my hand are you going to be quiet?'

Sammy nodded and Gareth lifted his hand.

'Shelly May. Just Gareth has got Samuel May, Shelly May.'

Gareth punched him in the face. And Sammy was quiet. Blood poured from his nose and Gareth was pretty sure it was broken, he'd felt the cartilage give under his knuckles.

Sammy's screaming bounced off the walls and rattled the cups on the draining board. He struggled to stand, his movements unsteady and fragile. Gareth watched the bewilderment leave him. He let him get up.

Sammy's disoriented state evolved into a frenzy of confusion and fear. His eyes were filled with terror. In a frenetic state, he lashed out, trying to bite, his screams piercing the air. Letting him stand was a mistake. It was like releasing King Kong on the Empire State Building. Sammy was strong and wild. Gareth had to knock him out to make a clean escape. He had nothing left to lose.

Grappling with Sammy, meant that he couldn't get a clean

punch in. He was a lot stronger than he looked. Gareth tried to stop the violent outburst and get a decent shot to drop him, but the kid was like a black eel. They wrestled in the living room, Sammy's strength increasing in his agitated state, and Gareth had the thought that he may not come out of this on top.

Sammy took Gareth by surprise and pushed him with unexpected force. He taxied backwards, losing his balance, and tumbled to the floor with a thud as his skull struck the wooden table. Pain surged through him, and he was aware of blood gushing from the side of his head as he landed.

The room blurred as darkness blanketed his vision. Everything faded and he struggled to maintain his grip on consciousness. The last thing he heard was the sound of running water from the tap he'd left on when he filled the kettle. It was a melancholic echo of the gushing sounds of death.

The kidnapper lay on the floor with glassy eyes and a slick of blood pooling from his head.

He died poor.

For Samuel May time had no relevance or meaning. There was breakfast, lunch, dinner and bed. There was school and Carthenage—and now there was the flat and Just Gareth on the floor. He sat at the table fixated on a new jigsaw puzzle. The room was an anarchic landscape of confusion and distress.

Just Gareth was lying on the floor in a pool of blood.

'You get up now, Just Gareth.'

The baked beans jigsaw was ruined. Missing pieces offended him. He thought about Carthenage as he found the four corners of the London at Night design. He sat for hours until there was no light left and he'd built the jigsaw twice. He could put together two thousand pieces of cardboard in three hours but didn't have the common sense to get up and turn a light on, or a tap off.

Carthenage was somewhere. Sammy's determination to find his dog was a solid action in his fragmented reality. The bond between them was his security, something to hold onto in the new disorder. This was bad, finding Carthenage was good.

As he sloshed across the sodden carpet, his actions were instinctive rather than conscious decisions. He put his warm coat on and zipped it up to the throat. 'Goodbye, Just Gareth.'

He stood over Just Gareth and waved at him.

Samuel May left.

He walked out of the flat and left the door open behind him. His purpose was singular. Find Carthenage.

CHAPTER 45

Shelly's hands shook so much that she couldn't grip the phone. She sobbed and felt faint. John was there to get a daily update and groaned, 'Oh, God, no.'

She stared at her mobile with the thunder of her pulse pounding in her ears. Her strength gave way and she collapsed, dropping the phone. It clattered to the floor beside her.

She couldn't speak and saw John steeling himself to hear the bad news. He picked up the phone and put it to his ear. 'Hello?' The call had disconnected. He helped Shelly up and she saw him drawing conclusions from her reaction. His face caved like an unstable wall. 'They've found him,' he said. It wasn't a question, just the inevitable truth that their son's violated and murdered body had been found.

Overwhelmed by a tidal wave of emotions, Shelly slumped onto the sofa, her tears stopping her from speaking. Her body trembled from weeks of pent-up terror. The world faded into a blur and she tried to formulate words that wouldn't come.

John sat beside her, his face tight with concern. 'Shelly, tell me. Have they found him?'

'Yes.' A new wave of tears washed her face.

The simple but profound words hung in the air. The best ones ever spoken. She still had to get them out.

John clutched the arm of the sofa, his knuckles turning white as his nails dug into the upholstery.

'He's alive.'

John broke down in tears, as Shelly gulped back a surge of relief to get the story out. 'He's in Blackpool. In the hospital, suffering from hypothermia. But he's going to be okay.'

There were a multitude of unanswered questions surrounding Sammy's turning up in Blackpool. They had no idea how he got there, or what circumstance led to his hypothermia.

Shelly's sobs punctuated the quiet. 'What if he's been out in the cold for a whole week and a half?'

The initial shock passed. She had to get to him. Now. She stood up but her legs betrayed her, making her fall back onto the cushions. John tried to comfort her, but she pushed him away.

'Come on. Don't sit there looking gormless. Our son needs us,' she said.

As they left the house, Shelly raised her coat over her head and ran for the car. News that there had been developments in the case had travelled fast. But it seemed they didn't have any details. She'd only been told herself ten minutes before, but the vultures were descending. The reporters had been camped on her doorstep since Friday, and they flashed cameras in their faces and shouted questions at them. They were a firing squad, and the parents were in front of the snipers. Opening the door for her, John pushed them out of the way to get in the car.

A reporter knocked on Shelly's window and made her flinch. There were more flashes as they surrounded the car and took pictures through the windows.

The reporters' questions were a relentless assault, their voices a cacophony of inquiries, each more invasive than the last.

'Has Sammy been found?'

'Is your son alive, Mrs May?'

'Are you suspects in your son's murder?'

'What do you know about Sammy's disappearance?'

Words cut through the pandemonium. The media's insatiable thirst for information made their every move a public spectacle. Shelly's eyes glistened with tears as she wrestled with her scarf to put it across the window as a shield.

Burying her face in the seat, John screeched away. The reporters didn't give up and ran down the road behind the car still snapping their infernal pictures. Looking in the rearview mirror, John told her they were scrambling like pack rats for their cars and motorbikes. 'They're going to follow us.'

The relentless pursuit of the press hounded them as they left Barrow along the A590. Shelly's fear of the media was heightened by the dangerous chase. John tried to lose them, overtaking other cars and risking their lives. Her vulnerability, accentuated by the way they'd been treated, made her nervous. Sometimes the press was on their side, the next day they'd turn against them. They accused them of murdering Sammy and burying the body—because he was different. One headline called them *The Beasts of Barrow* and it had stuck.

In the car, Shelly asked all the questions that John couldn't answer. 'What's going on?' Her eyes filled with confusion. 'The lady said the police need to interview him.' She wanted to prepare them for it coming out that there'd been a suspicious death surrounding their son, but couldn't tell them any more over the phone. Shelly tried to grasp the gravity of the situation, but despite the press and the police, she couldn't get beyond the joy of knowing she was going to see her boy again.

'I don't know. I guess we'll find out when we get there,' John said.

'They wouldn't tell me anymore.'

As the miles stretched out, Blackpool had never seemed so far away. She tried to make sense of the jumbled fragments of information she'd been given. 'Who can be dead?' she voiced the numbing fear. 'We don't know anybody in Blackpool.'

John gripped the steering wheel hard. His attention was split between the road and the media on their tail. 'It doesn't matter who it is. The main thing is it's not our Sammy.' His voice filled the car. 'Right now, all that matters is that Sammy is alive and that he's safe. We'll face whatever comes as a family, and we'll get through it together. We can cope with anything as long as he's okay. I swear, I'll never let anything hurt either of you again.'

The unknown circumstances surrounding Sammy's disappearance and the police interview loomed over their reunion, casting a new layer of worry on their jagged nerves.

'I thought he was dead, but he's come back to us. I'll make a cottage pie for him coming home. It's his favourite.'

'No carrots, Shelly May,' John said, checking on the press in his mirror. And they laughed.

She dreaded waking up and finding that this was a nightmare. If it was, she'd wake to another endless day of Sammy being out there. And not knowing.

The nightmare continued when they got to the hospital. Their desperation to see their son was all-encompassing. Nothing else mattered.

But their hopes of an immediate reunion were dashed when they were told that the police wanted to speak with them first. The anxiety built as the minutes stretched on.

'Let me see my son and then I'll speak to anybody you want me to,' Shelly said to the lady at the reception desk.

'The detective will be here to see you in a minute. Please take a seat.'

'No. I need to see my son. Now.'

A security officer came over from his duty by the door. He recognised her from the TV and from what he'd overheard her say to the receptionist. He took Shelly by the elbow and motioned for John to follow them away from prying eyes. The first of the press stormed into the waiting room as John and Shelly were led away. The guard took them to a private room far from the A&E department. Shelly worried that they wouldn't be able to find them to go to Sammy.

A doctor tapped on the door and came in. He was a reassuring sight at the height of their distress. 'He was found walking around Blackpool Tower last night. He was wandering in a disoriented state and had traces of blood on him. But I assure you, it wasn't his. And he's going to be all right. You'll be able to see him very soon, but the police are with him at the moment.'

'I need to see him now.' Shelly was wailing. 'What are they saying to him? He'll be terrified.'

'Please be patient, Mrs May. I understand how distressing this is for you, and I'm sure they won't keep you away from him any longer than they need to. The good news is that I see no reason why he can't go home today.' Patting her hand, he nodded at John.

Knowing Sammy was okay made her weak with relief. And hearing it from the doctor made it real. Her son was coming home. Today, he'd said. She needed to buy mince for the pie. The prospect of what the police had to say hung over her like a dark cloud, but she pushed it away. She'd waited for nine days, she could manage a few more minutes if she had to, but she wasn't taking any shit from them. She clung to the hope that her family would emerge from this ordeal stronger. She had no idea how Sammy had been affected. But she couldn't wait to tell him that Carthenage was waiting for him at home.

Chapter 46

The family room was quiet and decorated in a style that begged for calm and peacefulness. They were left alone for another five minutes before the police came in without knocking.

'Mr and Mrs May, I'm sorry to keep you waiting.' The officer introduced them as Detectives Varney and Turner. They shook hands.

'I want to see my son,' John said.

'All in good time, sir. We just want to talk you through what we've uncovered so far.'

The atmosphere was tense, and no amount of pastel could help that. Shelly and John faced the officers. Intimidated by their serious expressions, Shelly refused to be cowed by them.

Varney said, 'Sammy is fine. He's sitting up in bed and leading the nurses a merry dance. Jelly has to be red, apparently.' He smiled and he had a kind face. Shelly realised he was trying to ease her tension. 'However, Sammy's been through quite an ordeal. We were alerted when we received a report of water coming from what was believed to be an unused building. It was in the North Shore area.' His words were calm but carried a tone that said to prepare themselves. Shelly didn't like it.

'When firemen entered the building, they traced it to an up-stairs flat, where we believe Sammy had been staying for at least some of the time he was away. The officers found a body in that flat.'

Shelly gasped and John clutched her hand. 'What has Sammy been through?' she said, but it was a rhetorical question. Bodies on flat floors weren't part of Sammy's world.

The detective's voice was steady as he continued. 'I'm afraid to say, the man in the flat was deceased and the circumstances of his death are still under investigation.'

'What's that got to do with Sammy?' John asked.

'We have strong reason to believe that Sammy was the last person to see Gareth Holmes alive.'

'We've never heard of him. Who is he?' Shelly said. 'Why was Sammy there?'

Shelly and John exchanged worried glances, the news hanging heavy in the air. The unknown details surrounding the man's death and the police's interest in Sammy's presence at the scene added another layer of complexity to an already emotional situation.

The second officer added, 'We'd like to ask your son some questions about what he may have witnessed or knows about the incident. It's a standard procedure in cases like this. Until you got here, all we were legally able to do was ascertain that he's going to be all right.'

Shelly and Paul nodded, the gravity of the situation settling in. They were relieved to know that Sammy was safe, but the questions about the circumstances worried them.

'Why was Sammy with this man?' Shelly asked.

The detective's voice was steady. 'The man in that upstairs flat was found bleeding from a head wound. His blood was found on your son's clothing. The circumstances of his death are why we need to speak to Sammy.'

'You can't be suggesting that Sammy had anything to do with this. It's preposterous. Sammy would never hurt anybody.' Despite her jumper and coat covering it, Shelly instinctively put her hand over the scar on her arm where Sammy had pulled a boiling pan onto her during a meltdown two years ago.

'That's what we intend to find out, Mrs May. Clothing, including a hat and scarf set, were found in the flat. We believe they belong to Sammy.'

'Sunday. Blue ones,' Shelly said in a faraway voice as she disconnected from reality.

'That's correct.'

'He wears blue clothes on a Sunday—but it's Wednesday.' The thought that he had the wrong hat devastated her. But it hadn't bothered Sammy. Had John been right about her overprotectiveness all along? Had Shelly spent fifteen years perpetuating her son's compulsive obsessions? The thought made her feel sick.

'Did the man hurt him?' John asked.

'He was beaten. However, at this stage, we don't think it was extreme. Certainly not to a life-threatening level physically. He's been thoroughly examined. He has a broken nose, and some bruising to his body, but nothing serious.'

Shelly burst into tears again. 'I can't stand the thought of that man's hands on him.'

Varney saw the look on John's face and knew what he was thinking. 'It's okay, Mr May. He wasn't hurt in that way.'

'Thank God,' John said. 'He's so vulnerable.'

'We won't know more until we speak to your son, but we wanted to prepare you before we take you to him.'

'We appreciate that,' John said.

The police interest in Sammy's presence at the scene added to the stress, but they didn't know much more than Shelly and John.

Turner smiled at them. 'We'll try to make the questioning as painless as possible for him, and if you want us to stop at any point, you just have to say. We'll take this at Sammy's pace. He's quite a character.'

'Can we see him now?' Shelly asked.

Varney explained that they'd be in the room with them until after the formal taped interview had taken place. He said he'd give them a few minutes with him beforehand, and confirmed that John and Shelly could be with Sammy throughout.

'Good, because I can't bear the thought of him being taken away from me again—not even for a second,' Shelly said.

'I have a fifteen-year-old myself,' Varney said. No other words were needed.

She was going to see her son, but as Shelly walked down the corridor to his private room, her steps slowed. What was wrong with her? She was going to Sammy. She should have been sprinting to get to him before another second passed without him. But she hung back. A horrible fear came over her that she couldn't understand, or even try to explain. She was scared of how Sammy would look, and frightened to hear what he had to say. This was everything she'd dreamed of every waking moment of the last week, but now that it was here, she wanted to turn around and run away. She wanted to go home and back to waiting for news. She was terrified because she was worried that Sammy would have changed.

Her feet kept moving one step in front of the other. They passed the nurses' station where a sister in a dark blue uniform looked at her with pity. Detective Varney had this hand on the door. She wanted to scream at him to stop, but then she was over the threshold. And there was Sammy.

Her Sammy.

The police officers stood against the wall, and Shelly and John walked to his bedside. The sight of him broke their hearts. Sammy was sitting up in the hospital bed. He looked frail and vulnerable. Shelly couldn't even see his eyes but his expression was distant.

He had two black eyes as a result of the broken nose. He could only see with partial vision due to the terrible swelling. The padding in his nostrils and dressing over his nose gave him an epicanthic look as he peered at them through tiny slits.

Shelly cried, but she couldn't contain her joy at seeing her son again. She rushed to his side, flinging herself over him and sobbing with joy. And then she cried some more in pain and guilt that this had happened to him.

Overwhelmed with emotion, she put her needs above his. She had to touch him. She wasn't thinking. Her gesture was too much and triggered Sammy's sensory aversions. He flinched and pulled away.

'Sammy, we've missed you so much.'

'Missed you so much,' he repeated. But he said it in her voice. It meant nothing.

John greeted him with tears in his eyes, but less gushing emotion, understanding that Sammy needed space. His expression was full of love. 'We're here for you, son,' he said.

Sammy didn't show any emotion at Shelly's effusive words as she overshared the news about Carthenage being safe and happy at home. She knew he was tuning her out, but couldn't stop herself. John put his hand on her shoulder and tried to pull her back, but Shelly needed to be within touching distance of Sammy, even if she couldn't. 'Shush, give him time.' John hugged his wife. Sammy had to process. They all did.

Sammy didn't speak for a long time. When he did, he responded in his typical way. 'Carthenage ran away from Samuel May at Heysham Cliffs. Shelly May should not have let that happen,' he said.

Great. The first words he'd said to her in over a week, after he'd been through God knows what, and he had to play the blame game.

'I'm sorry,' she said.

'Use a tissue, Shelly May.'

John squeezed her shoulder. 'It's okay. He doesn't mean it.'

'Samuel May does mean it. Shelly May has mucus coming out of her nose.'

Sammy had come back to her different. Shelly saw it in the

muscle of his upper arms and the way his hair had grown a millimetre or two, but he'd changed in other ways, too. They waited for a textbook reading about mucus causing diseases, and for Sammy to relate pages of information, and a multitude of television voices, but he didn't. He stopped talking. His hands didn't butterfly. He sat in bed staring at nothing, eyes top right—some things hadn't changed.

'Carthenage can't wait to see you,' John said.

'Get me a jigsaw puzzle, Shelly May. One thousand pieces.'

Chapter 47

The police wore their masks of kind faces as they stood by Sammy's bed. They introduced themselves in soothing voices to put him at ease.

Detective Varney put a goofy smile on his face. 'Now that your folks are here, we want to ask you some important questions. But we need you to know there's no wrong answer.'

'There are absolutely, definitely and conclusively some wrong answers. The earth is six thousand years old. That is a wrong answer. It is actually 4.5 billion years old.'

Varney laughed.

'It is not an amusing fact. It is a fact. No joke.'

Turner said, 'We'll be conducting a brief interview to find out what you know about the situation at Mr Holmes' flat. Your parents will be here, so you won't be alone. Do you understand, Sammy?'

Sammy didn't reply, and John gave a nod of permission for him to start the tape. They all stated their names—except Sammy.

Their kind approach created a buffer for Sammy so that he

wouldn't be overwhelmed by the situation.

'Sammy,' Varney said, 'we're glad that you and Carthenage are safe. That's really good to know. Can you tell us how you've been feeling? Were you comfortable last week?'

Sammy's response was literal and detached. 'Samuel May is not cold today. And Carthenage is not cold at home in his blue bed.'

The officers acknowledged his response with soft smiles, maintaining their approach of patience. 'That's right. We're here to make sure you were safe this week, too,' Varney said.

'Samuel May was not safe. Samuel May was punched on the nose.'

Turner said, 'We understand you know a man called Gareth Holmes. Can you tell us about him?'

'Just Gareth punched Samuel May on the nose.'

Shelly and John had been told not to interrupt, but Varney saw John's fist clench, and Shelly's hands tightened on her son's making him pull away.

'That must have been very scary. What else happened, Sammy?'

Sammy's eyes regained a hint of focus. 'Just Gareth is Samuel May's friend. Samuel May and Just Gareth made a lot of money.'

The police officers exchanged a glance. Sammy's statement about making money with Gareth raised questions, but Varney's look warned Turner to tread carefully. With a head tilt, Varney indicated that Turner should step back. Varney led the questioning.

'We'd like to understand how you ended up in Blackpool. Can

you tell us how you got there?'

'Samuel May got on a train.'

'And when you got there, what did you do?'

They explained to Shelly and John that they needed to create a timeline so they could piece together the events leading to Sammy's discovery. Starting at the beginning gave Sammy's logical mind a chance to process his week in chronological order. Varney eased him into meeting Holmes before broaching the subject of their trading activities. They'd been sent encrypted emails of the official reports regarding the allegations. The information was sent in liaison with the fraud squad. And they had a grip on the vague outline of the story. However, there were still details to be filled in. The question at the forefront of the investigation was, how did Gareth Holmes die? Varney wanted to know if Sammy killed Holmes. The circumstances surrounding his death were still cloudy.

Varney took Sammy through his first night alone in Blackpool and sympathised with him, gaining his trust.

'Samuel May got tea and two bacon sandwiches from the street sweeper.'

'Holmes?'

'Not at homes. At a café.'

Varney guided him back on topic and Sammy told them about meeting Holmes. He talked them through the exchange fraud. It was clear from Sammy's simple view that he had no understanding of having done anything wrong. He spouted textbook passages about it being illegal, but he was an innocent clownfish in a shark-infested sea.

'Let me interrupt you there, Sammy. You just told me a whole lot of stuff about the legalities of trading stock. Did you do anything illegal while you were trading?'

He didn't understand the question so he didn't answer. His hands rose from the sheet as if somebody had pulled them on a string and he let them make weird shapes in front of his eyes. Any fool could see that he was clueless. Varney probed some more about the trading, but they got nothing that said he was anything other than a victim.

'Now, Sammy, can you tell us what happened to your friend Gareth?'

Sammy's gaze fixed on the ceiling. His words were staccato. 'Samuel May was doing trading. Samuel May picked names on the computer.'

'Can you tell us more about what happened?'

'Just Gareth said he needs lots of money. We did day trading every day, and we got lots of money.'

Varney needed full disclosure to wrap this up. 'Were you and Gareth staying together while you were trading?'

'Samuel May was in Just Gareth's flat.'

He stopped talking, blinked, and then mimicked the dead man's voice and even though she'd never heard it, Shelly recognised it for what it was. She shuddered.

'Pack it in, kid. We'll look for your stupid dog. Shut up. Stop that. Knock it off. Which company? Focus dammit. Which one? Oh shit. He's having a fit. Chicken Nuggets and chips, it is. Go to bed kid. I need sleep.'

The officers realised they were getting into the heart of the investigation.

'What happened next?' Varney asked.

Sammy's fingers danced and it didn't look as though he was going to answer. 'What happened, Sammy?'

'Give him time, detective. He's thinking,' Shelly said.

'Yesterday, Just Gareth was asleep. He didn't wake up.'

'What happened to him, Sammy?'

'Samuel May pushed Just Gareth over.'

'Wow. You must be really strong. Why did you do that, Sammy?'

'Samuel May had a fit. Samuel May pushed Gareth over.'

'There was a lot of blood. You must have seen that. Why was he bleeding?'

'Just Gareth banged his head on the table.'

'I want you to think about this next question very hard, Sammy, because it's important. Did you mean to hurt Gareth Holmes when you pushed him?' Varney asked.

'Did you mean to hurt Gareth Holmes when you pushed him?' Sammy repeated.

'Sammy I need you to concentrate. Did you hurt Gareth Holmes on purpose?'

'Gareth Holmes is Samuel May's friend. "Do you like Billie Eilish? Sure you like Billie. Wow, you dance real good, kid." Gareth Holmes does not dance to Billie Eilish on Google. "Hey, Google, play *What Was I Made For?*" Gareth Holmes is Samuel May's friend. Samuel May and Gareth Holmes made lots of money. Samuel May thinks Samuel May killed Just Gareth Holmes. Samuel May is bad.'

'Did you intentionally kill Gareth Holmes?'

'Samuel May would not hurt Just Gareth Holmes on purpose.'

'It's okay, son. You're doing well,' John said. Shelly started crying again and Turner discretely put a box of tissues beside her. She smiled her thanks.

'And then what did you do, Sammy?' Varney asked.

'Sammy went to find Carthenage. Sammy was walking.'

Detective Varney smiled at him. 'You're answering your questions very well, Sammy. But can you tell us why you didn't tell anybody that Gareth was in trouble?'

'Just Gareth was angry. Just Gareth was shouting. Sammy was scared.'

'Haven't you got enough, Detective? Please. We just want to take him home,' Shelly said. Her nerves were in tatters, and she didn't know how much more of this she could listen to without screaming.

'We're almost done, Mrs May. Go on, Sammy.'

'Samuel May had a fit. Samuel May woke up. Just Gareth was angry. Samuel May was hitting Just Gareth. Samuel May didn't mean to, but Samuel May pushed.' His words came out in the same tone that he'd used when talking about getting on a train.

This was pivotal to the question of premeditation and Sammy's mental capacity and understanding during the tragedy.

'I'm sorry to hear about what happened to Gareth. Can you tell us what you did after you got out of the flat? Did you tell a policeman?'

'Samuel May looked for Carthenage.'

The officers paused, giving Sammy time to collect his thoughts. It was a challenging task with his limited emotional expression.

Turner said, 'We appreciate you telling us all this, Sammy. It's helping us understand what happened.'

Detective Varney steered the conversation to the final questions. 'Why didn't you tell anybody about Gareth when you were walking around Blackpool?'

'Some people found Samuel May and called a policeman.'

'Why didn't you tell the police officers about Gareth when they found you?'

'The police officers took Samuel May to the hospital.'

Detective Varney said, 'That'll do for now, Sammy. Thank you for sharing that with us. We're here to help you, and we'll make sure you get home with your parents safely. You're with your family now, and they're going to take good care of you.'

There were still questions to be answered about Gareth's death. But Varney said they might never get to the finer details. He was satisfied that Sammy didn't have the capacity to stand trial on any of the charges. 'I'm confident that your boy didn't intentionally do anything wrong. There's still some red tape to clear up, but we'll be closing the fraud and murder investigations,' he told them. He explained that their next steps involved uncovering as many details as they could to close the case and ensure Sammy's well-being.

John had his arm around Shelly and she was hiding her face in his chest as they spoke about Sammy being hurt.

Varney looked solemn before he spoke to them. 'This has been an unimaginable ordeal for you both—and for Sammy. Before we wrap it up, I want to try and give you some comfort, if there's any to take from this. It's true that Sammy was coerced by Holmes, kidnapped even—but it could have been far worse.'

Shelly raised her head. 'Worse? What are you saying? I should be grateful that the monster didn't kill my son?'

'You misunderstand me. I can't imagine what you've all suffered, but what I'm trying to say is that I don't think Holmes intended to hurt Sammy. From what we've gathered—in his own way—he looked after him quite well for most of the time. I know he hurt Sammy, but I don't think his time there was all bad.'

'Great. I'm so grateful that he only beat him up a couple of times.'

'I'm making a mess of this. I don't think Sammy was suffering all the time, and I'm sure it'll play back in your heads as far worse than it was for him—and if I can take a small part of those nightmares away for you, I'd like to.'

'With respect, Detective, that's bullshit. I'll always remember every detail of the last week and nothing can soften that. We want to take him home, now,' Shelly said.

'The doctors have given him the all-clear and I think that would be a great idea,' Varney said, smiling at Sammy. 'You've been a big help, Sammy.' He addressed John and Shelly. 'It all seems straightforward and a horrible accident. Somebody will probably need to speak to Sammy again, but I think we can pass this over to Barrow station from here.'

Shelly was so relieved that she burst into tears again. Not that she'd ever really stopped.

CHAPTER 48

Sammy was going home. Shelly's range of emotions had to be put aside because his needs came first. She hated that she couldn't hold him. Her body cried out to gather her son the way a protective mother should after an ordeal. But this was Sammy, and she smiled at the thought. Since Friday she'd been living life as the grieving mother of a murdered child and now it was all changed. Her happiness engulfed her and was too much, she was delirious with joy but still had to adapt and face what Sammy had been through. It haunted her. They left the hospital and drove home as a complete family.

John was gripping the steering wheel tight, and she knew he was dealing with his horror images on replay. They'd prayed for this day, but now that it was here, it was surreal.

When they pulled into their drive, Shelly let out all the frustration and fear. She let it go and imagined it soaring into the sky like a helium balloon. She waved it goodbye, and when she explained it to John, he laughed. Their home welcomed Sammy back as if the bricks knew the trauma was over, all bar the media hounding them.

Sammy was quiet in the back seat, and when he got out, his gaze fixed on the house. In little over a week, Shelly had forgotten how to read him. She had no idea what was going on in his mind, and that broke her heart. Sammy had come back to her a different boy. Maybe she had to be a different mum. Shelly had to learn him again. John said she was being silly. He was the same old Sammy he'd always been, but Shelly felt it.

The moment they stepped inside, a swell of emotion carried her on a cushion of haziness. The familiar scents of home—the fresh smell of the living room carpet, and the lingering aroma of the biscuits she'd made for something to do that morning—embraced her like an old friend.

This was where they belonged—but not John. Not anymore. It was something else she had to face. He'd got himself comfortable in the spare room, and Shelly noticed his books on the bookcase. It was going to hurt him, and she didn't know how Sammy would take him leaving again—but then, how would he take to John being back? Who knew anything where Sammy was concerned?

Carthenage bounded into the hallway. His eyes lit up with joy as he saw Sammy. He barked with delight and danced around them, his tail wagging like a metronome set on the fastest speed. The dog bent double in ecstasy until his nose nearly met his backside because he was so filled with joy. He stopped barking and was so happy to see Sammy that he cried. She'd never heard this sound of unparalleled joy before. The dog's grief was replaced with ecstasy. Shelly had tears in her eyes as she watched the reunion and heard Carthenage's whimpers. Sammy patted the dog's head, but barely touched him, fingertips only. Shelly had wipes at the ready.

'Carthenage, do not run away,' Sammy said. And then he adopted the man's voice they'd heard in the hospital—Holmes. 'You little shit,' he added. And he'd outgrown the 'oops' of apology, it seemed.

Shelly's blood turned to ice when she heard that awful voice. It tainted her house and had no right to be there. It was as though Sammy had been possessed by the dead man. But John laughed. 'It looks like some changes are going to have to be made. Give him time, Shell,' he said, squeezing her arm.

Shelly laughed too, and Sammy joined in with his broken sea-lion laugh. This was a happy home. Things were different. But they were okay—even John.

In the living room, Carthenage revelled in the company of his family. He nosed Sammy's hand and pressed his face against his master. His tail created a blur of movement, and although it was hell for the dog, he remembered not to jump up. But his front paws kept leaving the floor until he checked himself. Sammy accepted the affection, and Shelly saw the bond between her son and his four-legged friend in every gentle touch and calm response. He'd never let Carthenage touch his face before.

Dinner was a special affair—they turned it into an event with a bottle of red wine, a glass of Ribena, and Sammy's favourite dessert. Shelly and John reestablished the rhythms of family life. Sammy being with them at the table was a joy that Shelly thought she'd never see again. She'd resigned herself to the empty chair, and the fact that Sammy was on it made her cry. Everything made her cry. John told Sammy it was her hormones and, mishearing, Sammy went into a long explanation of what homophones were, highlighting *to*, *too*, and *two* as his first of many examples. It was a delight to hear. The chasm between his world and theirs was wide, but being family was a bridge they could rebuild.

As they finished the meal, Sammy put down his fork and spoke to Carthenage. 'Carthenage, you must not run away. It is not safe.' It was a running theme. Shelly and John exchanged amused glances as they listened to Sammy telling him off.

The days that followed were filled with a return to normalcy. John packed his holdall and left like a whipped puppy. But Shelly knew he'd be okay. Sammy wanted jigsaw puzzles. That was new. He hadn't done one for years. The repetition of fitting the pieces seemed to soothe his soul. And if it helped him to forget sleeping rough and being with that awful man, then Shelly was all for it. She'd buy every jigsaw in town if it made him happy.

They trawled online toyshops and Shelly showed him all the beautiful options, but he had some strange ideas. Sammy chose the most boring jigsaw in the world. She laughed when she said to Pauline, 'It was just a picture of baked beans.'

Carthenage lay at his feet, his steadfast shadow. Sammy was more independent and insisted on taking his walks with Carthenage alone. Shelly worried, but John put his hand on her arm. 'He's growing up, Shell. You have to let him.'

One morning Sammy looked perturbed. 'Carthenage, must not run away. It is not safe.' We're on that loop again, Shelly thought, but Sammy wasn't finished. 'Carthenage ran away and missed Shelly May.' Shelly watched him talking to his dog, and a lump formed in her throat. 'Samuel May had to look for Carthenage.' He touched the dog's head. 'Samuel May missed Shelly May.'

She had waited for this moment—for Sammy to find his voice and tell them how he felt. 'I love you, Sammy,' she said.

'Love is a meaningless word that is an ineffectual way of describing deep affection.' He stopped. He stared out of the window. His expression was vacant. But he said it. For the first time in his life, Sammy said, 'Samuel May loves Shelly May.'

His words were a simple and profound expression of the emotions he felt. Shelly felt the familiar tears and was surprised she had any left. Sammy had connected with the heartache of their time apart, even if he couldn't express it in the way others might.

That week, Shelly received two pieces of mail. The first was her decree Nisi. She read it with bittersweet regret. The second was a congratulations card. It congratulated her on Sammy's safe return. The card with the picture of a goofy dog on the front contained a gift voucher. The voucher was for free pet microchipping. The card was signed by Graham, with two kisses. She held it to her chest and gave a girly giggle. Could there be something there? Maybe?

In the weeks that followed, Shelly and John watched their son for any permanent emotional scars. The beauty of his condition meant that he didn't hold onto things. He didn't talk about his time away after the first couple of weeks and even telling Carthenage off for running away stopped. His world was a kingdom governed by routine. His emotions were wrapped in lagging and hidden beneath layers of logic and practicality.

Yet there were moments, fleeting and subtle when Shelly caught a glimpse of a deeper connection than before. It was in the way he touched Carthenage's fur, and in the rare smiles that were that bit wider and more natural. These moments were the treasures of Shelly's life and she collected them in photographs and memories.

On a frosty December evening, the sun was setting, painting the sky with gold and pink undertones. Shelly and Graham watched through the kitchen window as Sammy and Carthenage played in the garden. His strange laughter and the sound of their ball bouncing on the grass were a symphony of the love that would always bind them together.

John wasn't there that night, but they'd faced unimaginable challenges and emerged on the other side with a deeper appreciation for the blessings in their lives.

They weren't together, but they were content. In the heart of her home, Sammy was the constant, the true north that guided them through rough waters.

'Shelly May, Samuel May needs a cup of tea.'

'What do you say, Sammy?' Shelly asked.

'Please.' He paused and his fingers came up to make butterflies. 'Mum.'

Printed in Great Britain
by Amazon

42482796R00202